Benedictus

Benedictus

THE STORY OF SISTER ANNE

A NOVEL BASED ON A TRUE STORY

Anne E. O'Neill

Copyright © 2011 by Anne E. O'Neill.
Cover design by Raymond Chin

Library of Congress Control Number:		2011916392
ISBN:	Hardcover	978-1-4653-6409-8
	Softcover	978-1-4653-6408-1
	Ebook	978-1-4653-6410-4

All rights reserved. No part of this book may be reproduced or transmitted in any form or by any means, electronic or mechanical, including photocopying, recording, or by any information storage and retrieval system, without permission in writing from the copyright owner.

This is a work of fiction. Names, characters, places and incidents either are the product of the author's imagination or are used fictitiously, and any resemblance to any actual persons, living or dead, events, or locales is entirely coincidental.

This book was printed in the United States of America.

To order additional copies of this book, contact:
Xlibris Corporation
1-888-795-4274
www.Xlibris.com
Orders@Xlibris.com

Contents

Foreword 9

Introduction 11

Prologue
    The Dark Night of Dreams 13

Part One
    The Nun 15

Part Two
    The Psychologist 109

Epilogue
    The Lovers 235

A Word From The Author
    Perspective of Time 237

Joseph Has the Last Word 239

Acknowledgments 241

Reference Notes 243

In memory of my husband,
Laban,
known to many as Joseph.
Without him, there would be
no such story as this.
Love forever.

Foreword

It seems providential that Anne's ship would take her to the shores of Casa Colina Rehabilitation Hospital, where I served as medical director and physiatrist, a specialist in sports medicine and rehabilitation. The wave that brought her was a giant one. It was the wave of the sixties that had led us to question everything—including our ability to control all our "involuntary" functions, such as blood pressure. At the time I was doing special studies on the phenomena of postural hypotension—low blood pressure with partial or total loss of consciousness on standing—and while training at Letterman Hospital, I had coauthored a paper, "Blood Volume Following Spinal Cord Injury." I was seeing this condition frequently in nerve-damaged paraplegics and quadriplegics. Also, I had the opportunity to observe jet pilots walk away in their G suits after performing unbelievable aerial acrobatics that normally would have caused "blackouts."

This medical focus prepared me to be favorably disposed to considering Anne's admittance to Casa Colina when her physician inquired if we could help this nun with a "chronic, severely debilitating case of postural hypotension." I believed we could, based on my experience, and planned to procure a G suit, a total-body-compression suit, from nearby March Air Force Base. Physical measures alone, however, would never have been sufficient in Anne's case—or even acceptable in an existential sense. The extent of her physical, mental, and spiritual perplexities required all the resources at our individual and collective command and strained our beliefs to the limit.

I admire Anne's courage in making the life changes required of her in her quest for truth. The honest telling of her story in *Benedictus* required no less courage. I feel indebted for the opportunity to relive one of the more exciting and challenging chapters of my career. Very rarely does a patient undergo a *real* transformation, showing that true healing can occur. In so doing, the patient becomes our teacher. It is just such a teacher that Anne has become for me.

Herbert E. Johnson, MD

Introduction

I see a long, narrow hallway lined with doors, one upon the other like frames of a kaleidoscope: the first, opening, and then the next and the next until my vision rests upon the last door, which is but a dot upon the horizon. The opening . . . opening . . . reverberates in my soul and lifts me to increasing levels of awareness from which I can see the transitions from one internal place to the next—not as reincarnations, but as many lives within this one.

I sit at my typewriter, staring out to sea, the sea of the Pacific Northwest. It is a remote area distancing me from all that I've known. I call it the wilderness. As one enters our small town bearing a Pomo Indian name, a sign declares the population to be 526. The move here from the sprawling city of Los Angeles was one opening of a door that shook my roots and left me on unsteady ground of change, loneliness, and adaptation. All this has passed in the course of years. My roots have found new, solid ground, and here I sit at a bay window framing ocean blue, quite at home and intent on telling my story.

Remembering means turning around and looking back, back through the lens of the kaleidoscope, the opening of all those doors. Do I have the courage? Is it of interest to me—or to anyone else? I raise my eyes upward until my vantage point is that of the gulls soaring outside my window: a bird's-eye view from birth to the grave—and back again as I do write from the land of the living. For years I had walked in a veritable valley of death, caught in a web of a belief system and conditioning that told me I had a vocation to be a nun. My search for the truth demanded no door be left unopened. I came to realize I had been deaf to the only voice that mattered—my own. Listening to that voice launched a healing process guided, I believe, by Spirit. The touch of Joseph, my psychologist and lover, was part of this miracle and fills more than one frame of the revealing kaleidoscope.

Each frame of this journey is complete unto itself, yet somehow, all are threaded together so that one message comes into focus. What is that message? What is the common thread? What are the lessons learned and worthy of passing on? To find out, I must take the risk of *standing naked* and invite the reader to walk down that narrow hallway with me and look deeply through each frame of the kaleidoscope and allow the far-reaching light of time to illuminate the story of Sister Anne. It is a love story of both human and divine dimensions and worthy of being told.

Prologue

THE DARK NIGHT OF DREAMS

The eerie reflection was a phenomenon of light cast by a full moon on a dark night of dreams. The waters of the lake shimmered at my feet, red fading to pink, speaking of wounds I could not see. I dipped my hand into its murky depth to find out, to know. Is this the blood of sacrifice? And then I realized, as I stood and my full red skirt swirled about my legs, the nature of the mirrored image. The reflection was nothing more than my own—Anne dressed in "worldly clothes," as nuns would say.

I looked to the distant shore on the other side of the lake, my eye following the slippery narrow path that crossed the waters—a mirage of moonlight. Its depths of silvery grays and black, undulating in constant rhythmic motion, were mesmerizing, the rise and fall beckoning me to go, to walk that perilous path. I strained my eyes to see exactly where it would lead, and slowly, an imposing building came into focus on the far shore, which I recognized as a convent from the large cross at its apex, which cast an ominous shadow over me from afar. Ghostly figures standing on the shoreline came slowly into focus as well—nuns clothed in ethereal moonlight, silent sentinels, looking at me as though waiting. Watching. And then I knew. It was my last chance. My last chance to go back! To stand among them once again! Torn between love and fear, I cried out, "No! No! I can't walk that treacherous path! I want to live!"

I quickly turned away and started running, my speed impeded by the rocky ground strewn with unearthed, gnarled roots. I was panting, out of breath, beginning to wonder if I would make it or fall into an abyss. Now and then,

I would glance back to see if the silent ones were still watching, aware of my vulnerability born of wounds. Then, from out of nowhere, materializing, a hand reached down to me from above; and I grabbed it frantically and raised my head, looking up into penetrating dark eyes that looked right through me in a knowing way—uncomfortably so. I did not resist; however, the stranger's firm warm grasp as he pulled me upward to higher ground with a strength far beyond mine. I stood there for a moment, studying the unfamiliar face and wondered, Is he the one?

I looked back to the bridge of light just in time to see it dissolve into the mists. Without question, there would not be another chance. I would be no more Sister Francis. I would be Anne.

PART ONE

The Nun

If any man will come after Me,
let him deny himself and
take up his cross, and follow Me.

—Matthew 16:24

Chapter I

THE PREMONITION

1958

I would be Anne. The woman of my dream was a haunting, disturbing presence. She seemed like a friend of some long-distant past, rather ephemeral and unreal. A former self. "Anne," I whispered, and the name echoed in some nameless depth within. It had seemed more than a dream, clinging to my consciousness. I had retrieved it upon awakening when its images were still vivid and potent. Those eyes had hovered about me throughout the day, threatening the unveiling of some hidden thing. I wasn't so sure I wanted to *see* what lay behind that veil. Even now, as I sat at my teacher's desk in the empty classroom, I couldn't keep my mind on the task at hand—signing monthly report cards. It kept roaming the lakefront in the moonlight, seeing the undulating waters.

Needing an anchor to the present, I focused on my signature: Sister Mary Francis. That was my identity now, a member of a Catholic order of nuns whose mission was primarily teaching. I had chosen the name Francis, however, as a very young child.

> *F-R-A-N-C-I-S . . . Francis. It was cool in the shade of the rose arbor as I practiced writing my name. The name I wanted to be mine, my other name. I observed my signature and knew it didn't look quite like it should. Big. Scrawly. But then I was only six years old. I kept*

practicing. F-R-A-N-C-I-S . . . F-R-A-N-C-I-S. Just looking at the name made me feel better—like I could be someone else. When I am twelve, I will be confirmed as a soldier of Christ and take the name Francis . . . F-R-A-N-C-I-S . . . And when I become a nun . . . F-R-A-N-C-I-S.

My penmanship is *Palmer* perfect, I thought, just as the nuns had taught me all those years ago. *Perfect.* A sigh of weariness escaped me as I laid the pen down, folded the last of the report cards, and slipped it into the envelope.

This was the end of a long teaching day, and the shadows forming on the walls of my third-grade classroom I perceived as spectral long fingers pointing to some future I could not see. I felt a chill and pulled my black woolen shawl more closely about my shoulders. The radiators echoed a sound of emptiness and settling for the nonuse of the winter night. *It must be getting near prayer time!* I pulled on my black rubber boots, gathered my books, and descended the stairs to the playground.

It was a short distance to the convent, but each step was an effort as though I were pulling a great weight. I paused at the one tree that somehow had survived the school construction, an elm of many years that had shaded many children, many nuns. Today it had no shelter to give, its stark structure of bare branches etched black against the snow-reflecting sky. I felt a shiver go through me and drew a deep breath. *Something is wrong! What is it?* I didn't know. But I did know with a flash of nonordinary consciousness that I would be changed by it. The feeling of numbing cold took on the shape of dread. Of foreboding. I reached out, leaned on the trunk of the elm for support, and looked down at its roots, gnarled roots that seemed strangely familiar. *Jesus, help me!* Prayer was as natural to me as the air I breathed. There was nothing for me to do but go on—*one foot in front of the other,* as my mother would say. I walked slowly to the convent door and entered, uttering a deep sigh of relief. Instantly, a peace descended upon me. This was the *House of the Lord,* his presence palpable in the pervasive silence. I closed the door quietly behind me, shutting out any intrusions of the world.

St. Joseph's Convent, originally a private residence, was located in the heart of Milwaukee and dated back some one hundred years. This was 1958, but little had changed with the passage of time. Its high-ceilinged rooms were filled with rare antiques, which were not perceived by the nuns as anything beyond the utilitarian. An exception, perhaps, were the gaslight fixtures, which were inoperable and merely decorative. The nuns sat on the needlepoint chairs and washed in the porcelain basins. The furnishings also spoke of another time: heavy mahogany, cherry—pieces rarely seen in an ordinary home simply made the convent livable. Sliding pocket doors separated the two parlors with their lace curtains and marble-top tables. Here the nuns entertained family and friends, which was a rare occurrence. There were twelve small bedrooms with single beds, desks, and armoires. Each room had its own washbasin and medicine chest, but no mirror lest we be tempted to vanity. The hardwood floors were bare, the windows high and narrow with pull-down blinds and white lace curtains.

The stained glass of the entry splashed little color on the yellow-aged walls this late wintry afternoon. The parquet hardwood floors gleamed with their own polished brilliance. As I made my way down the dark hallway, I passed Sister Ambrose, the eldest member of the community, a golden jubilarian. There was no acknowledgment; we did not speak. I felt glad for the rule of silence when, as now, I was too tired to talk. Slowly, I climbed the stairs to the room that was mine, at least for now. Nuns are always ready to move, if not to another location of great distance, at least to another room down the hall. It kept one "detached." It made one more ready for the final transition to the next life. It kept one "in practice" was my way of thinking about it, though I didn't like to think about it and found this custom one of the more difficult among many. I knew myself to be what I called a rooted person, and my roots were embedded deeply in the fertile ground of this old home. Quite simply, I loved it. Strange for a California girl, I thought, one who was city bred and used to modern comforts and even luxuries. I dropped my books on the small desk and sat down on the edge of the narrow bed with the thin mattress.

The bed was hard to resist. *What is wrong with me! I feel so ill . . . my head.* All I wanted to do was rest for a while, a long while. The ringing of the bell, a voice of the holy rule, made that impossible. It was calling the nuns to community prayer. *I had better hurry!* Quickly, I changed my habit of black wool serge for heavy poplin and washed my hands in the porcelain basin.

On my way to the chapel, I passed Sister Therese, a diminutive nun with sparkling Irish eyes. Only in her thirties, she was young for the position of superior but not lacking in wisdom and competence. A very personable and sensitive woman, I found her approachable and understanding. She did acknowledge me—she always had that privilege as superior in caring for her nuns. "How are you feeling, Sister Francis?" There was a genuine concern in her eyes and a solicitous tone in her voice.

What am I to say? I never feel well anymore . . . How does a nun complain? I smiled my perpetual smile and answered my superior with few words, "Better, thank you, Sister."

"Well, go to bed right after supper, Francis. I really think you should." She reached out and patted my hand before hurrying down the hall.

Reluctantly, I had to agree. "Thank you, Sister Therese, I'll do that."

For all my superior's compassion, the encounter gave me no comfort. I felt such a need to communicate what I was feeling and could not. Even with doctors, somehow, words were always inadequate. I felt so alone in a world of many people, an island unto myself. There was only one comfort, one solace, and I was drawn to it as a thirsting, dying person. The chapel.

The only light illuminating the chapel was coming from the tall beeswax candles on the altar that had been lit for community prayer—six of them, three on either side of the tabernacle. There were also vigil lights of cut red glass, and their reflections danced brightly on the white linen altar cloth. It was a small chapel, seating about twenty-four nuns, and had been the main parlor of the original house in the days of the Civil War. The diminutive antique organ fit into what had been the fireplace. I had been assigned to the front pew, just below the statue of the Virgin Mary, because at twenty-five I was the youngest member of the small community.

Struggling for breath, I slowly made my way up the narrow aisle, genuflected, and knelt down on the bare wooden kneeler. Strange what came over me, always. A great stillness. It was as though I were the only one there, alone. I buried my head in my hands. The boxlike headdress of my religious habit supported my illusion of *invisibility*. It not only blocked my peripheral vision but also shielded my face from being seen by others. I breathed deeply and let the spirit of this sacred place enter my being. *My Lord and my God! I believe thou art here present.* I was understood. I could communicate. I was not alone, after all. I could go on. I would.

Tears were felt somewhere deep inside me, but they were not allowed life. That would be self-indulgent. The consolation of the moment was quickly disturbed by my pain and fatigue. Suddenly, I was simply hanging on, moment by the next challenging moment. There was no relief, and prayer was beyond me. *If I could only sit down!* But then everyone would know I'm not feeling well. I had to support the mirage of the smile. The half hour of prayer became an exercise in endurance and nothing more.

"Hail Mary, full of grace . . ." The soft voices of the nuns were rhythmic, soothing. Occasionally, the clicking of rosary beads could be heard. And then it was over. I gripped the railing and raised myself from the wooden kneeler. I had been so intensely focused on getting through what had become an ordeal that I had forgotten the premonition and the haunting dream was but a phantom memory, slipping back into the night.

Chapter 2

THE CONFLICT

That night I did retire early, glad to remove from my aching head the stiffly starched headdress. My room was on the second floor, above the community room, where the nuns gathered for an hour of recreation after supper. I could hear the grandfather clock chiming seven and the muted voices of the nuns saying the clock prayer, which marked each passing hour of the day. "Blessed be the hour in which the Son of God became man . . ." The rule of silence was suspended and the muted voices of prayer became a buzz of feminine chatter and laughter. I could hear the scraping of straight-back chairs on the hardwood floor, the scraping of sewing boxes on the oak table. I could see it all in my mind's eye as the nuns began their hour of relaxation—and productivity. Our hands were always weaving the needle in mending old garments or making the new. The rule required this of us. There was no room in our lives for idleness, just doing *nothing*.

As I lay there in the darkness, a crushing loneliness descended on me, a feeling of not belonging. I thought of how far I had removed myself from community living, the essence of religious life. *Why?* I was ill, of course, but I felt no loss. I didn't miss it. I did miss the freedom of directing my own life, of simply choosing to be or not to be at a certain place at a certain time. I missed my solitude. I'd rather be alone even if it was with my pain. My body shook with the chills of fever. My head throbbed with pain. My joints ached. A great, indefinable pressure weighed on my chest, making it difficult to breathe. I closed my eyes and longed for sleep. Lately, my nights had not been much better than my days. Even in sleep there were those dreams that would not give me rest.

Solitude. There had always been that dimension to my life when I was at home. Still, I craved for more and certainly thought I would find it in the convent; I did not. Living in community allowed for rare moments alone. In my family home, there always had been that place of refuge for me, a place to be alone. I called it the Blue Room, the upstairs bedroom—the bedroom that was exclusively mine. The decor was all in blue and white and the dark-stained pine floor was buffed to a high polish. A rose vine climbed a trellis from the patio below, and its high branches, laden with white blossoms, hugged the small-paned windows. I could reach out and pick a bouquet to place in front of Our Lady's statue on my dresser. This room was off-limits to my three sisters and one brother. Here I could be alone with my thoughts and, sitting at the small table by my bed, record them in my journal. This familiar room, the room that was mine up until the day I left for the convent, was the setting of one of those dreams that had so disturbed me.

All was just as I had left it years ago. Even my life-size doll, Elizabeth, was propped up on the blue ruffled pillows. I set my suitcase down and walked over to the rose-framed windows. Pulling back the white eyelet curtains, I reached out and picked a bouquet of white buds and placed them in front of Our Lady's statue. "I'm home, Blessed Mother, home. I have left the convent. I am no longer a bride of Christ. I'm afraid I've made a terrible mistake!" Feelings of great sadness and remorse overwhelmed me. I ran down the stairs to my mother's bedroom below. She was sitting on the rocker by the window as though expecting me. I threw myself at her knees and cried, "Mother, I've made a terrible mistake! I should never have left the convent!" And I sobbed and sobbed and would not be comforted.

The sobbing had awakened me. The intensity of the dream was such that it drifted on the edges of my mind, asking the unsettling question, *Is it a premonition of the future? Of course not! Dreams are just dreams. But it was so real!* I had many dreams like this. At times it was not my mother but the novice mistress before whom my dream form knelt and poured out my fears. I cannot say the precise moment when subtle fears began to crystallize, taking shape within my soul that took on the name of *conflict*. I do know they showed themselves as early as the novitiate, no longer consigned to the realm of dreams.

It was a summer evening, and the day's heat had not abated to the point of comfort as it probably would not, I had learned. Adjusting to the climate of the Midwest was not easy for a native Californian. The lightweight summer habit of poplin material was a welcome change from the heavy wool serge. The starched, fluted headdress, however, still hugged my face and I could feel the perspiration on my brow as I strolled down the tree-lined walk of the novitiate grounds. It was not the heat alone but the humidity that made the season so intolerable, especially here on the banks of the Mississippi River. The moisture formed rivulets on the novitiate walls and curled the pages of our prayer books. It was oppressive and made even slight exertion feel like an overwhelming task at times. One tried to sleep, tossing and turning, and praying for a cool breeze, "offering it up," thereby turning the oppression into a benefactor of grace. One awakened to the same unpleasantness and bore it as a cross.

The heat and humidity were not the only scourges of summer; there were the mosquitoes. They came in swarms from the spawning waters below, undeterred by their victims' many layers of clothing. To refrain from scratching was a form of asceticism! But I could not blame entirely the climatic trials for my persistent insomnia, loss of appetite, and ennui. Night after night and day after day.

It was the hour of recreation after supper, and I tried to enter into the casual conversation of my fellow novices as we made our way up the sloping path to the fir-crested hilltop. Somehow I could not, and my silence was noticeable as it was uncharacteristic of me. I felt myself an observer, removed from my companions internally, absorbed in my own thoughts. The dialogue within was taking on an entity that seemed to have some life of its own, independent of me. As the *voices* grew in intensity, the chatter about me dimmed and I no longer heard the external reality.

You're not like them, Sister Francis. You never will be! You feel it, don't you? What are you doing here anyway? You know you don't belong! You never did have a vocation. You're not sleeping . . . not eating . . . certain signs . . . God? What God?

I could feel the entity that I recognized as evil. It was a tangible presence trying to suck me into itself, into its darkness. *It is the hour of darkness.* I reached down to the rosary that hung from the cincture at my waist, gripping the crucifix. It was a soldier's response to danger, reaching for the sword at her side. The crucifix was my weapon, my defense, and grasping it was an automatic response whenever these feelings came upon me, which they did quite frequently of late.

No, that's not true! I do have a vocation. You lie! I do belong. Everyone tells me that! Leave me alone! Get behind me.

I raised the crucifix to my breast, believing in its power to dispel the evil that oppressed my soul. My gait slowed until I was standing still. I hadn't noticed that the novices were now at the hilltop and I was alone on the tree-lined path. Alone . . . *not one of them.* The *voices* would not be silenced. I turned and stepped off the path onto the grassy slope leading to the river's edge. Dusk was settling, and the dark foliage, tall reeds, and grasses were etched against the river banks, the evening light soft and vaporous. The muddy brown waters of daylight were now black, brackish, beckoning me. *Yes, "the hour of darkness."* Down the grassy slope, my steps were taking me, slowly . . . slowly . . . and the *voices* were following, pursuing without mercy, unrelenting. *No vocation . . . don't belong . . . What God.* "Satan," I whispered into the darkness. *He wants to destroy my vocation.*

The conflict had *materialized* and become a viable entity outside myself, overwhelming me. I could fight it no longer. Slowly . . . with heavy steps, I moved closer . . . closer . . . to the river. I let the crucifix fall to my side as I approached the edge of the steep bluff. The *voices* were all around me now, taunting. *You never did have a vocation, Sister Francis . . . never . . . never.* I looked down into the murky waters moving sluggishly, heavily, growing blacker, darker like the night. A live mass of motion embodying the evil that I could now sense physically as well as spiritually.

Yes, there is a way out, Sister Francis . . . a way out . . . It would be so easy . . . so easy to end your conflict . . . Here, come to me . . . See, I will carry you along peacefully, peace . . . peace . . . no more struggle . . . no more.

Mesmerized by the moving waters and the *voices*, I took a step closer to the edge . . . closer. *I will end this torment . . .* and another step.

I will never know what gentle hand had drawn me back from the bluff's edge. Something had surfaced from within, from a deep, lost place of light. As a sleepwalker, I had slowly moved away from the blackness of the river, realizing for the first time how dark was the night. *The edge* had given me a new perspective and one that secured my deliverance. A threshold had been crossed, and I had survived. Never would I approach that mythical *bluff's edge* again. I was in for the heat of the battle, and I intended to win. The foe had been named.

Chapter 3

THE CHOSEN

The conflict was taking on layers of fear. I knew I had to tell someone of my struggle even at the risk of being sent home, which was a real possibility. I feared the decision would be taken out of my hands. Sister Janine was the superior in charge of the young novices, functioning as their teacher and spiritual director. She was tall, painfully thin, and her large dark eyes penetrated the soul. The starched white linen framing her face only made this attribute of *seeing* more pronounced. Her bearing was one of dignity and grace, even patrician as though she had come from another time.

My given name, the name by which I was known in the world, was Anne. Sister Janine often called me Annie, an endearment that made me feel special. Now as I approached her, she smiled warmly. She always enjoyed my sense of humor, and her eyes twinkled in expectation, as though she would have a moment of relief from the ever-present, ever-heavy issues the novices usually presented to her. I regretted my inability to play that role with what was weighing on my heart and knew she would be quick to see this in my eyes.

"Sister, there's something I must talk to you about."

Sister Janine's smile faded just as I had expected. "Annie, what is it?"

The pent-up words came tumbling out. It was the first time I had voiced my conflict. "It's my vocation, Sister! I'm not so sure I want to be a nun! I can't sleep at night. I'm so tormented." I looked pleadingly into her eyes, hoping she would somehow magically dispel my soul sickness.

"I would not have suspected this, Annie. Can you be more specific about what's bothering you?"

Sister Janine honored the long silence that followed, broken finally by my tremulous voice. "I don't know. There is this feeling deep within, a strong resistance to making vows. When I try and get a hold of it, there are only these vague dislikes . . . unimportant things, really."

"Like what? Maybe they aren't as unimportant as you may think."

"Well, to obey without question, Sister! I always have questions! I try not to be so strong-willed . . ."

Sister Janine could not help but smile. Yes, she was aware of this. "What else, Annie?"

"And conformity! I don't like being like everyone else! Every minute of the day and night is decided for me! And when I look ahead and see my whole life this way—everything determined, fixed—something dies inside me." Sister Janine listened quietly, nodding her head, encouraging me to continue. "I can't find the time to be alone—or the place. There's so little time for prayer, apart from community prayer. I feel like I am losing myself rather than finding myself, Sister!"

"Well, remember the saying of Jesus regarding that, Annie! 'He who loses his life for My sake shall find it.' It isn't that these things are unimportant. In fact, they are very important! My observation is that you *are* an obedient novice—and you do conform! I think your difficulties are common to all of us. It's called self-renunciation. It's not meant to be easy, this religious life. I think, however, you have the mettle to make it! Consider these thoughts as temptations. It seems those of us who make the best nuns are the most sorely tried. And, Annie, don't look ahead that way—take a day at a time." Sister Janine's smile returned and she reached out her hand to me.

My cold hand felt her warmth and my being flooded with hope. Perhaps I did have a vocation, after all. "Thank you, Sister, for your encouragement. Even I don't understand why I am so troubled. I'll try, really, I will." I had not mentioned the *taunting* on the bluff's edge. If I had, I believe my life would have taken a much different course.

By nightfall the burden of doubt was again weighing heavily upon me. My anxiety returned with greater force as did the dreams.

Lost, I felt, in a sea of gray, lost among the gray-garbed multitude of souls, gathered this day in the great cathedral. A hushed expectancy hung in the air, heavy, ponderous. One would be chosen! *One from our midst! I felt very secure, nondescript, sitting there on the hard wooden bench, glad for the grayness that blotted out anything singular about me. I had no concern that I was the one. Still, there was a feeling of apprehension, of fear, just in being there. The possibility . . . the hushed expectancy became even more sinister, a breath-holding waiting, as gray faces turned toward the leader. A formidable presence, he rose and faced the congregation, the sea of gray. His eyes too were gray, but darker and penetrating as they roved over the gray-clad figures. I nervously lowered my eyes, not wanting mine to meet his. I sensed more than saw him slowly move down the aisle, a Moses figure parting the sea, though gray. His eyes scanned the breath-holding milieu, glancing now to the right, now to the left, searching . . . searching . . . for the chosen one. His footsteps were softly moving nearer . . . nearer . . . and then stopped, stopped at the bench where I was sitting. I saw his gray-sandaled feet only inches from mine. My eyes were forcibly drawn upward, following the flowing gray of his garment until our eyes met.*

The leader now stood over me as a vulture hovering over its prey. He said nothing but stretched out his gray hand to me. Mind words within said, Me? THERE MUST BE SOME MISTAKE! NOT ME! *He simply nodded his gray-cowled head, his hand suspended in space, waiting.* NO! NOT ME! Why me? I HAVEN'T DONE ANYTHING! NO! *His eyes said,* Yes, you are the chosen one. *The suspended hand came down heavily on my shoulder and I cringed, drawing back instinctively.* NO! NO! *Then gray arms gripped me, pulling me off the bench and thrusting me forward into the aisle.*

No longer lost in the sea of gray, but singled out, chosen, I was roughly half carried toward the sanctuary of the cathedral. My struggle to escape the gray arms was futile. Fear struck at my heart—terror in the realization that I was the chosen one—bewilderment that this should be so. I AM INNOCENT! INNOCENT! I HAVE NOT DONE ANYTHING! *The pitiful, piercing wail filling the vaulted dome of the cathedral was mine, the wail of helplessness against such power.*

Now, in the sanctuary, my eyes saw the stake, a slender reed-like rod, reaching to the heavens. The gray hands pushed me up against it. NO! DON'T DO THIS TO ME! I HAVEN'T DONE ANYTHING! I'M INNOCENT! I DON'T WANT TO BE CHOSEN! *A myriad of satin blue ribbons trailed gracefully from the top of the rod. The effect was that of a festive maypole, deceptively harmless. Gray hands clutching blue satin ribbons . . . gray figures dancing about the maypole . . . wrapping my writhing, resisting body as a gift. Tied with blue satin bows to the slender rod, I was to be sacrificed.*

The strength of terror enabled me to break loose from the ribboned nails fixing me there. I MUST GET AWAY! I MUST GET TO THE DOOR! *I ran down the aisle, feeling the surging gray sea engulfing me. A tall black-garbed figure I recognized as a priest was waiting there, rooted, blocking my escape. Stopping me. His eyes too spoke words,* "You cannot escape being the Chosen One." *I was trapped.* TRAPPED! *There was* no way out. WHY, PRIEST, WHY? *And the booming answer echoed through the vaulted dome of the cathedral:* DESTINY!

My heart pounding, I woke up in a cold sweat with a feeling of doom. I could still see the emblazoned word *destiny* in the eyes of the black-garbed priest. *Who are you, priest?*

Chapter 4

BRIDE OF CHRIST

1954

In the months that followed that first opening up of my inner world to the novice mistress, there was to be many more such confidences. My heightening indecision regarding my call to religious life further split the wholeness I was seeking. Nevertheless, I held on to the belief that I had a vocation and that it was being tested. All the internal struggles were but a sign that I indeed was *chosen*. To be a nun was my *destiny*.

The eve of my first vows, two and a half years after entrance into the order, Sister Janine and I stood together one last time in the now-familiar office. Night prayers were over and the novices were in the dormitories preparing for sleep. It was the sacred time of solemn silence when no word or gesture was allowed except in grave emergencies. Light snow of late winter was falling gently, soundlessly, as though it too was bound by this strict observance. The conflict was so strong within that I dared to approach Sister Janine and break one of the most sacred of rules. I was living with the cancer of conflict—something deep inside saying *no* to what was about to happen and the chorus of *yes* on all sides.

"I can't do it, Sister! I just can't." I felt the tears welling up from that place within. "I know it's time of solemn silence, but I have to talk to you!"

"Don't worry about that, Sister Francis. Are you questioning again?" Her loving concern was visible.

"Yes, Sister, I can't seem to be at peace in my decision to make vows. I continue to be plagued with doubts!" The tears would not be held back, and the band of pressure tightened around my head.

"It's not unusual to experience this the night before profession, Sister. It must be your free choice, though, to make vows. From my experience, you are certainly well suited to be a nun. We've discussed this many times. I think, Annie, you will find peace once you have made vows and put this indecisiveness behind you." She smiled a smile that gave a glow to her countenance and reached out in peace to me.

"I want to believe that, Sister. I don't question it is God's will. And a part of me does want to be a nun. I suppose it is choosing who I will be." My tears came under control and I felt a resolve take over my being. *I will be the bride of Christ. Thy will be done, not mine.*

A cold but magnificent world of white greeted us the next morning. I had put behind me the terrors of the long night and allowed the peace of the silent, fallen snow to be mine. It was the feast of St. Joseph, March 19, 1954. My profession day! The date was inscribed on a silver pocket watch with the words *To Sister Francis—From Mother and Dad. How I wish you could be with me!* I caressed the remembrance lovingly and slipped it into the pocket of my new black serge habit made just for this special day. The pleats of the voluminous skirt reached to the floor in graceful folds. Over a tailored long-sleeve blouse was worn a full, waist-length cape with a high white linen collar. The sleeves were wide enough so that the hands could be tucked inside whenever possible. The headdress was white, of new linen and heavily starched. It was elaborate and distinctive of our order. The effect was that of a nun *contained* within her own private world. One viewed her face through the frame of a finely pleated border upon which set a hood covered with a waist-length veil. The folds on the back of this veil were pinned in the shape of a coffin, and that is what we called it—*the coffin.* We were dead to this world.

I picked up the black ebony rosary and kissed the crucifix as I clipped it to the leather belt around my waist. It had belonged to one of our early members and had been removed from the community relic room to be given to me. All the other novices had rosaries of pond lily seeds. *Why have I been entrusted with this community treasure? What is expected of me? Is it my potential as a religious the reason why I am so tempted?* My cold fingers tightened around the crucifix. This day I was leaving all that behind me. It would be different after I made my vows; the voices of dissent would be silenced forever.

The white-veiled novices moved in procession slowly, piously, up the long chapel aisle, wholly absorbed in the profound spiritual event that would change their lives. "Thee, O God, we praise!" The "Te Deum," flowing from the organ and resounding off the chapel walls, was triumphant, jubilant! *I am the bride of Christ.* I peered into the flame of the slim white candle I carried in my hand. In the soft bluish-gold radiance, a picture came to life, one I had seen in a religious magazine as a child. It had depicted a young woman dressed in a bridal gown with a flowing white veil, descending a staircase flanked by nuns, the candles in their hands illuminating her lovely face. Bride of Christ was inscribed on the glossy colored print. I had looked at it longingly, knowing that one day I would be that bride. And here that day had come! The joy made me forget that there had ever been a question as to my destiny. Sister Janine had been right all along. Peace flooded my soul, and the burning candle I held in my cold hands illumined the smile on my face just as I had imagined. "COME THEN, MY LOVE, MY LOVELY ONE, COME!"

"In the name of our Lord Jesus Christ crucified, I vow to thee poverty, chastity, and obedience for a period of one year." Just before receiving Holy Communion, the heart of the vow formula was repeated by each novice. Kneeling alone before the bishop in the chapel sanctuary, my voice was strong as I pronounced the solemn words of commitment. "I, Sister Mary Francis, vow to thee." I felt the white veil being removed from my head by the mother general of the order and replaced with a black one. I was now a professed religious.

This sacred event marked the beginning of life on the "missions." I would leave the novitiate and go out into a world I had not seen for two and a half years. The only news items that had filtered through my seclusion were the coronation of Elizabeth as queen of England and the election of Dwight Eisenhower as president of the United States. My cloister had been complete.

Chapter 5

THE UNKNOWN

1959

For the next four years I lived the religious life under temporary vows, free to leave the order. Annually, I had renewed my vows of *poverty, chastity, and obedience*, and each time was a crucial decision point for me, never routine and predetermined. The same was true for the order in reassessing my suitability for religious life. Regardless of my deteriorating health, I had always been given the encouragement and blessing of my superiors, and always I chose to continue on the path of a nun. Now I was in my fifth year under temporary vows, and final vows loomed on the horizon when my commitment would be *forever*.

It was going on four o'clock when my superior Sister Therese and I arrived at the medical building in downtown Milwaukee. Nuns never went anywhere alone, by holy rule, which chafed my independent nature. I didn't mind having Sister Therese as my *companion*, however, as she was so supportive and someone I could trust. We also enjoyed being together and could laugh easily at convent foibles. In silence, we made our way through the medical building, hands tucked in our wide sleeves as was customary, eyes down, looking neither right nor left any more than was necessary. "Custody of the eyes" had become second nature to me after novitiate training and years of practice. It helped keep the world in abeyance and thoughts on the things of God. Nuns aspired to this spirit of recollection, as it was called, an awareness of God's presence at all times.

We easily found the office of internist Dr. Fahey, as I had been a patient of his for about a year and visits had been frequent. He was a young man, and his casual appearance made him look somewhat out of place in the streamlined medical office. He came from a long line of doctors, and I felt he was carrying on a family tradition, his heart elsewhere. My initial diagnosis had been scarlet fever, but a series of mysterious ailments had followed. As the months slipped by, there was no accounting for the persistent fevers, severe sore throats, and increasing weakness. I was a problem to this doctor and to myself. It seemed futile, but I continued on this course in obedience to my superior, which always prevailed. It never occurred to me to demand a change of physicians, even though Dr. Fahey had nothing to offer. Pulling medical books off the shelf, he would slam them on his desk out of total frustration and look for answers. Fear of this possibly well-intentioned physician took root and was to impact on my future.

As I entered his office on this day for what was to be my final visit, my heart started pounding, conditioned to the "white coat." Having announced my arrival at the receptionist desk, Sister Therese and I sat down to wait. I came prepared, knowing *waiting* would be part of the visit, and pulled a notebook out of my deep nun's pocket. I would jot down new ideas for class the next day. I may have had doubts about my religious vocation, but certainly not about my passion for teaching. In my preteen years, I conducted my own *school*, and it was definitely compulsory education for the children in the neighborhood. The attic was my classroom in the winter, the rose arbor in the summer. By the time I was in high school, teachers were referring students to me for tutoring. It gave me spending money for Saturday afternoon movies. I loved teaching. I loved the children. It was only natural that I should enter a teaching order rather than one dedicated to nursing. I had happy memories of the nuns who had been my teachers, and the image of chalk-covered black habits was somehow reassuring and even comforting. I grew up believing I would one day be part of that world. It was not only natural; it was also *God's will*.

I had not anticipated the outcome of this last visit with Dr. Fahey. Without any preambles, he went right to the bottom line: he was through with my case and turning me over to another internist. It was the first good news I had had in a long time. My new doctor was an elderly gentleman who had attended our school in his youth. He was kind and compassionate, acknowledging the unknown element of my condition but believing there was a medical explanation yet to be determined.

Beyond that, however, he likewise had nothing to offer. I managed a day-to-day existence only through the theology of the value of suffering. I was one with the crucified Christ and, *in Him and through Him*, was saving souls. I lived on this tenet of Catholicism. *Or was I dying?*

It was now spring, and the snows had passed. This day when the rising bell had sounded at five in the morning, as it did every day, I did not get out of bed. I could no longer carry on as usual. I joined my voice with the muffled voices of the other nuns up and down the hallway, "I rise from this bed of sleep in the name of our Lord Jesus crucified. May I rise on the last day to everlasting happiness." Unmoving, I listened to the shuffling of slippered feet as they prepared for the full day ahead.

I gazed out the window at the one elm tree, barely visible in the dim morning light, and remembered the *premonition* of that late winter afternoon when standing under its bare branches. The past few weeks those branches had filled out with the new green of balmy spring days. The earth was thawing, as were the spirits that sometimes grew cold through long winters. I should have been feeling wonderful and reveling in the new warmth. But it didn't touch the coldness that was now always with me. *Is the premonition coming to pass?* I closed my eyes and tried to sleep. I heard the Jesuit priest coming in the back door of the convent, as he did every morning, to celebrate the six o'clock Mass in our chapel.

Mass was preceded by a half hour of silent meditation. It was difficult in wintertime to sit motionless in the cold chapel. The half hour sometimes seemed long, and an occasional bobbing of heads, fighting sleep, broke the illusion that everyone was deep in contemplation. This warm spring day would lessen the austerity of the religious asceticism. I would be missed. The vacant front pew would speak of my indisposition. My facade of well-being was shattering, shards of me flying off into a dark world.

The shattering had been gradual. I missed meals now and then, sometimes rose late, retired early. There were days when I never made it to the classroom. I simply could no longer keep up with the schedule of religious life and community living. I could no longer maintain the image of an exemplary nun in those external ways. My pride suffered. I feared what people thought of me. I didn't know how to answer the question, "What is wrong with you, Sister Francis?" *I don't know!* The unknowing became a burden heavier than the sickness itself. Like a shadow in the darkness of my soul hovered the threatening label of *psychosomatic*. No one ever verbalized this as a possibility; it was a phantom of my own mind, born of fear. Doctors believed there was an unknown but organic basis for what I was experiencing. My suffering was looked upon as a gift of God by those who advised me, even a sign of holiness. I was *chosen*. *Yes, I was certainly meant to be a nun.* Tertianship, the summer of spiritual preparation for final vows at the motherhouse in Iowa, was now only two months away. Time was running out.

Chapter 6

CHILD OF FEAR

"*Et cum spiritu tuo . . .*" And with thy spirit. Very faintly, I could hear the nuns' responses to the liturgy coming from the chapel below. I tossed and turned, unable to sleep, and finally turned on the light. I would pray the Mass here in my bedroom—alone. My missal lay on the chair next to my bed. I picked it up and opened its gilt-edged pages. Prayer books could be treasure troves of memories, such as holy cards slipped between its pages and commemorating a first Holy Communion or the death of a loved one. I took in my hand a small photograph. Two faces stared out at me, a mother and child. Yes, memories. It had been my fifth birthday.

Grammie was teaching me how to write. I sat at the kitchen table and practiced. A-N-N-E . . . *Anne*. I wanted to please her the next time she said, "Little Anne, let me see your writing!"

The kitchen door swung open, and my mother came in carrying the wicker laundry basket. I kept writing. A-N-N-E. She set the basket on the table and looked at me very strangely. It made me drop my thick pencil, making an ugly mark on my beautiful page.

"Who are you, little girl?" my mother asked in a very stern voice.

"I'm *Anne*, Mommy, your little Anne!" I felt my chin tremble and looked up at her lovely face shadowed in some kind of darkness.

"No, you're not! I've never seen you before. I think you better go home now." She pointed to the door and started folding kitchen towels.

Who am I? Where do I live? Silent tears started rolling down my plump cheeks. I continued to stare at the woman folding towels. *Not my mommy?*

"You cry so pretty, little girl. Well, you better get going!" The woman gave me a look as she snapped a towel in the air.

I slid off the chair until my short legs could reach the linoleum floor. I felt so lost, so lonely with no name, no place to go and, worst of all, no mother. I wiped my tears that would not stop, the silent tears that were so pretty, as I slowly, very slowly, walked across the kitchen floor. I kept looking at the woman folding towels and wished she was my mother. She looked up once and said, "Get along now, little girl!" My slow steps took me through the living room to the front door. My small hand could barely turn the brass knob of the heavy big door. It opened to the sunshine of a lovely day when the towels dry quickly on the clothesline in the backyard. As I walked out the door, I paused one last time to look back—and there was the woman standing in the middle of the living room. Smiling.

"Oh, little Anne, don't you know your own mother!" She held out her arms to me, but still my tears would not stop. *Mother?* "Come here, darling, and give your mother a hug."

Confusion slowed my already slow steps as I closed the heavy door and walked toward her and into her arms. She laughed as she hugged me, saying what fun this was! Something hurt deep inside, and I could not laugh with her.

"Tomorrow's your birthday, Anne, and we've things to do for the big day. You finish folding the laundry and I'll polish your Mary Janes."

"Yes, Mommy," I said in a trembly voice, drying my tears.

In bed that night, I thought of the woman folding towels and wondered who she was. Sleep came slowly as my tummy ached. Finally, I drifted off into the safe haven of dreams.

Bright sunshine filtered through the drawn curtains of my bedroom window the next morning. "Elizabeth, this is my birthday, my fifth birthday! Here, give me a kiss!" I hugged my life-size baby doll and put my lips to her hard, cold cheek. "Stay warm, Elizabeth!" I tucked the blankets about her chin as I slipped out of bed. The dark hallway leading to the kitchen had no windows to let in the light. I made my way slowly, pausing at the swinging door with the little pane of glass. *Maybe the monsters won't come on my birthday . . . I hope they don't come.* Cautiously, I looked up, my eyes hardly open—just enough to know if it was safe. *No, nothing. Just the small pane of glass.* I pushed the door but slightly and peeked through. *Nothing.* I sighed in relief and entered the kitchen, skipping over the cold linoleum floor to the sink, where Mother kept the breadbox. I felt quite grown-up as I made toast and spread it with butter and jam.

"Mommy! Where are you, Mommy?" No answer. This warm and good-smelling kitchen had two doors—the most fearsome one with the little window and another door leading to the living room. This door was ajar, but I still had to be careful. *Will there be a monster behind this door?* I peered through the crack at the hinges. *Nothing.* I tiptoed through the doorway and nothing happened. No monster jumped out at me. *Maybe they won't come on my birthday!*

I went looking for my mother, knowing I would find her in the bathroom. There she stood in front of the mirror, "putting on her face" as she always said laughingly. I stayed quiet and watched her for a few moments, fascinated by the change that came over my mother's already-beautiful face. White powder on her clear white skin, smooth like satin. Rouge shadings of soft pink on her cheeks. Lipstick of bright red covering her thin mouth. I watched each stroke made deftly and with precision.

"I want to be pretty like you, Mommy!"

"Oh, little Anne! I didn't see you there, honey." She came over to me, knelt down, and took me in her arms. "Happy birthday, Anne. My, five years old! What a special day this is going to be!" The feel of her strong arms around me made me feel safe, secure, loved. I hoped that other woman who liked to see me cry would not be here on my birthday.

"Are we really going to ride on the big Red Car, Mommy?"

"We sure are, sweetheart. You and I are going to have lunch downtown! So we better get things done. Your clothes are laid out, Anne. Get dressed while I heat the curling iron. Hurry along now!" She playfully patted my bottom and headed for the kitchen.

I could hear her singing as she moved about, just melodious sounds, light and joyful, that made me feel good. I smiled as I pulled up my best pink panties. "Just in case you're in an accident," as Mother always said. The pale-blue dotted swiss dress with the white collar and wide sash I slipped over my head, enjoying the feel of the sheer, crisp fabric. Mother had buffed my Mary Janes to a high polish, and I held one in front of my face. Peering closely into its shiny surface, I dabbed at my face with an imaginary puff and glided my index finger over my lips—and laughed. *Like you, Mommy!* Mother was calling from the kitchen. Admiring my new blue socks, I pushed my feet into the Mary Janes and buckled the strap just as fast as I could. I didn't want to miss the big Red Car!

"Oh, you look so pretty in that blue dress, Anne! It matches the color of your eyes. Here, let me straighten the collar. Stand still!" I watched the curling iron heating in the blue flame of the kitchen stove as her fingers with their brightly polished nails fluttered about my neck. "There. That's better!" She pulled the kitchen stool up to the stove. "Up you go, little birthday girl!"

The hot curling iron was ready, and I cringed. So as not to get burned, I sat very still while Mother transformed my wavy blond tresses into a mass of tight curls. She chatted gaily as she worked, talking more to herself than to me. I listened, glanced at the little pane of glass just to be sure, and tried not to think about the curling iron.

"Maureen went to school this morning with her nose out of joint! She just couldn't understand why she couldn't come with us today. When you're in third grade, you don't just stay home when you want to!" Mother's voice told me she was unhappy with my big sister. I wondered what was wrong with Maureen's nose. *Poor Maureen!* She and I were constant companions until something called school took her away from me. *School will never get me!*

Mother put her hand under my chin and tilted my head back. "There! Now I can reach these front strands better. Don't move! That scar is still under your chin, Anne. It really hasn't faded much, and that fall was over a year ago! Dr. Smith did a good job of sewing it up, though. My, I'll never forget that morning when I went into your bedroom and saw blood all over the sheets! A big flap of skin was just hanging from your chin. My heart nearly stopped! I'll never understand why you didn't come get me when you fell out of bed! Why, you didn't even cry!"

"I knew you were sleeping, Mommy."

"Well, sometimes, you're just too good, Anne!"

My brow furrowed in puzzlement. *Too good?* "Grammie says Jesus wants us to be good!"

"Your grammie talks to you a lot about Jesus, doesn't she?"

"Yes. She told me Jesus died on a cross. Can Grammie go with us today, Mommy?"

"No, Anne. You know she's not feeling well. Her heart's acting up again." For a moment there was a sadness in my mother's face. "There, all done!" Finally, the curling iron was laid to rest on the kitchen sink and Mother stepped back to look at her handiwork. "Oh, Anne, you look beautiful! Here, give me a kiss." I put my arms around her, loving the feel of her skin, her warmth, the smell of her own perfume. I always had kisses for my wonderful mother.

Tap! My Mary Janes hit the linoleum floor as I slid from the stool. Mother took my small hand in hers and started singing. "It's three o'clock in the morning . . ." On cue, I immediately began *tap-tap-tapping* my latest dance step, and together we moved gracefully across the kitchen floor.

The big Red Car came rolling down the tracks—one, two, three cars linked together—clanging, screeching to a faltering stop like some giant metallic worm whose segments have to catch up with each other. The conductor wore a black suit and cap and had a money changer on his belt. He reached down to help me up the deep steps. "I'm five," I announced proudly. "I don't need any help."

"Five, are you! Well now, that's pretty old, all right!" He smiled, winked at my mother, and helped me anyway.

It was not my first experience of the electric cars whose network of tracks crisscrossed the greater Los Angeles area. The Red Car was not just a means of transportation but also an experience in itself without going anywhere—like a ride on the merry-go-round at Long Beach Pike. Each time was just as thrilling as the last!

"Here, Anne, you sit by the window." The leather seat was wide and comfortable. Mother sat close to me and linked her arm in mine. With several jolts and jerks, the Red Car started moving, and we began our journey to downtown Los Angeles. Once the giant worm got rolling at a good speed, it settled into a rhythm of motion, a gentle swaying side to side. I felt soothed, content. I looked out the window, watching the palm trees march by one by one like soldiers on parade.

"Spring Street!" the conductor called out.

"Now, Mommy?" Seeing the excitement in my face, she smiled.

"Yes, Anne, go ahead." I reached up and pulled the cord over the window, and a buzzing sound signaled the conductor that we wanted to get off. The Red Car jerked, jolted to a stop, and I was slightly thrown forward and back again as the segments caught up with themselves. Even at five, Spring Street was familiar to me. It was where my father owned a men's clothing store and went to work each day. Hand in hand, Mother and I approached the entrance to my father's world. High over the doorway loomed a massive sign—MICHAEL'S.

"Little Anne! Happy Birthday, Skeezie Doodle!" Father leaned down and gave me a big hug. I felt his smooth cheek against mine and smelled the sweet fragrance of the red carnation in his lapel.

"Can you go to lunch with us, Mike?" Mother stood there stiffly in her smartly tailored suit and pillbox hat.

Father released me and straightened up. "No, Lenore, you know I can't leave the store. Why do you ask!" I saw the pain on my mother's face, and something squeezed my child heart.

"All right, Mike . . . just thought because it is Anne's birthday—"

"Please, Daddy?" I wanted to make my mother happy.

"No, Anne, you go have a good time. I'll see you tonight." He smoothed my curls with his hand and smiled down at me.

Mother and I lunched alone. The disappointment of my father's absence quickly dissipated as I stood in the cafeteria line. My large eyes grew still larger, scanning the assortment of foods. *How will I ever choose!*

"We'll have chicken fried steak, Anne . . . and let's see . . . what vegetable . . . remember, no corn . . . The doctor says it's not good for your tummy problem."

"Peas, Mommy—the peas in those little dishes!" Golden beads of butter glistened on the tiny peas, and my mouth watered in anticipation.

Mother managed both our plates on her tray and walked to a small table against the wall. I was close at her heels, my hand holding on to the edge of her jacket. I was enchanted with the white linen tablecloth and the crystal vase with one red rosebud and a sprig of fern—but especially with the peas swimming in butter in their very own little dish.

"We're having our picture taken, Anne, just as soon as we've finished lunch. I want a remembrance of this special day. The photographer is just down the street." She dabbed at her red mouth with a napkin.

"Yes, my fifth birthday! I'd like a picture with you, Mommy—just you and me." And I beamed at my beautiful mother and thought how much I loved her.

We sat on a stool, my mother and I, with broad smiles posing for the picture on this happy day. The photographer walked behind the camera and pulled a large black cloth over his head. *No, not today! The monsters can't come today!* I threw my arm around my mother's neck and buried my head in her shoulder, trying not to cry out.

"What's wrong, Anne!"

"It frightens me—that black thing!" My tummy ached, and I thought of the peas swimming in butter.

"Oh, for heaven's sake, Anne! That's just the man taking our picture! Sit up now!"

Obediently, I sat up and pressed my cheek to my mother's smooth-as-satin face. I looked straight ahead, seeing nothing but a flash of light.

The two faces, cheeks pressed together, stared out at me from the photograph that had survived so many years—a five-year-old with blond curls and the mother in a black pillbox hat. The child's arm is around the mother's neck. The mother's face is beautiful, young—made-up. Both, unsmiling, look directly ahead, very intently, very knowingly, as though they shared some secret. *What was it, Mother?*

I slipped the small photograph back between the gilt-edged pages of my missal and began praying the Mass, united in spirit with my Sisters in the chapel. "*Introibo ad altare Dei.*"

Chapter 7

DELIVERANCE

1959

Tap... tap... tap... spring rain gently tapping on the storm windows awakened me midmorning. The superior was covering my classroom, so I would not see her until the lunch break. Feeling somewhat better, I decided to go down to the kitchen for a cup of tea. It was too much of an effort to put on the habit, so I pulled on my black robe and secured a soft black veil to my white nightcap. All the sisters were at school except for the sister cook, and the convent had an unearthly quiet about it. Unsteadily, I made my way down the long hallway leading to the stairwell. Only the groans and creaks of the old structure spoke to me. I was wishing I could understand its language and be privy to the secrets stored within its walls over so many years.

    I passed the two large bedrooms that were not used unless we had visitors, the supply room with all its nooks and crannies, the small bathroom with its antique tub on scrolled legs, the curtain-stretching room. Even in the fifties, the nuns continued the bygone custom of starching white lace curtains and securing them to wooden frames for drying. A time-consuming task. At the end of the hallway, I reached the enclosed spiral staircase, narrow and steep. Gripping the iron railing, I slowly descended in near darkness, coming out into the gray sunless light of the dining room. I was hoping the cook, Sister Maura, would not be at work in the adjoining kitchen.

Sister Maura was an intelligent, well-educated woman, but her health prevented her from holding down a classroom of lively youngsters. Thus she was assigned to the position of convent cook, her contribution no less appreciated by the community. She sent out pain signals at every opportunity and found small, petty ways to make my miserable existence even more miserable. I felt she was jealous of me and resented what looked like, at least to her, my special treatment.

As I approached the kitchen, I could hear the pots and pans and knew Sister Maura, to my dismay, was on duty, preparing lunch for the nuns. I drew in a deep breath and dared to encroach on her territory. Trying not to get in her way, I filled the kettle and put it on the stove. Of course, we did not speak. There was the rule of silence. Sister Maura let out a great sigh, however, sloping her shoulders even more than usual, and gave me a side glance of exasperation. I had intended to have a piece of toast as well but suddenly lost my appetite. I carried my cup of tea to the dining room and sat at the long mahogany table—alone. The tears deep within began to surface, burning my eyelids, only to be quickly brought under control.

As I sipped my tea, the feeling of depression subsided and I felt less chilled. The high windows looked out across a narrow passageway to the neighboring house. This was so unlike the California bungalows with their grassy lawns and space to breathe. I thought of home and saw in my mind's eye the English Tudor with its white stucco walls, green shutters, and distinctive mullioned windows and french doors. It was on a corner dominated by a huge pine tree and the typical palms. My father was meticulous about the yard, and the cypress hedges were neatly trimmed, the rosebushes pruned, and the lawn a carpet of green. Along the side of the house were massive oleanders with their pink and white blossoms. Hydrangeas flanked the front windows, a mass of purples and blues. Roses and azaleas lined the driveway.

There was a massive oak tree in the middle of our residential street, a gathering place for the children in the neighborhood. A place of secrets and confidences. There we chose teams and played baseball in the quiet street, free of traffic. I was always rounding up a game and the last to quit. My introspective nature seemed balanced by my love of sports and a circle of close friends. I remembered the health I had enjoyed during school years, attested to by a certificate for perfect attendance upon graduation. I was probably the healthiest young woman to go through the portals of the novitiate at the age of nineteen.

"What had happened?" I asked myself. I sighed and looked out the windows, not seeing the mottled, peeling paint of the next house but only the rain *tap-tap-tapping* on the panes. The rhythm of the drumming rain was soothing, relaxing, in its steady tap-tap-tap.

Tap . . . tap . . . tap. I remembered the blackness of that night and the fall of soft, gentle rain. In the far-off distance, the sound of thunder, deep and foreboding, could be heard. My fingers flew over the keys of the Baldwin upright piano, and the strong chords of Chopin's *Polonaise* filtered through the rooms of our family home. Grandmother had introduced me to the piano when my fingers could not yet span an octave and I had to sit on pillows to reach the keyboard. It was an interest sustained over the years, and even now with all the involvements of senior year in high school, I continued to practice each night. Along with the chords, my mind was given wings to soar the world of fantasy. *Why perhaps I would be a concert pianist!* Suddenly, I was on stage in a flowing formal gown, sitting at a shiny grand piano reflecting the footlights. *What was that! Did I hear something?* I stopped playing to listen. *No, nothing . . . just the thunder and a light rain against the panes of the french doors, lightly tapping. Tap . . . tap . . . tap.* The piano was in the corner of the living room, and the bench on which I sat was angled slightly toward the french doors that opened out to the rose-arbored patio. I peered into the darkness but could see nothing—only the shiny small black panes of the french doors. I continued to play.

There it is again! What is it! Again I stopped playing, again hearing nothing but the light rain. *Tap . . . tap . . . tap . . .* now distinct, growing louder against the small black panes of glass . . . louder . . . louder . . . gripping my whole body in a paralysis. I couldn't move! I was paralyzed with fear, fear as black and cold as the night.

Tap . . . tap . . . tap. My eyes, as with a will of their own, broke through the paralyzing fear and turned toward the french doors, toward the shiny small black panes—drawn by a hand. A hand was pressing against the pane, its fingers tapping, tapping. Then a face moving toward the small pane, coming closer, closer . . . a face pressing against the glass. *No . . . no.*

I was frozen in fear. I could not move. Screams deep within, far off like the distant thunder, could be felt—silent screams only I could hear.

Mommy! Mommy! Where are you, Mommy! It was a baby voice, and the hands suspended over the piano were baby hands—only it wasn't a piano, but the tray of my high chair. My baby eyes, large, blue, staring at the small pane of glass—not the glass of the french doors, but the kitchen door! The small pane of glass in the kitchen door!

No . . . no . . . the faces at the little window . . . they frighten me so! Mommy! I'm so cold, Mommy . . . Please come back, Mommy . . . Where are you, Mommy?

The silent screams were silent no longer but, like the chords of the *Polonaise*, filling the large rooms and reaching my father, who was relaxing with the evening paper in his den. The screams coursed through my whole body, freeing it of the paralysis that tied me to the piano bench. My eyes still fixed on the face pressed against the small pane of glass. I jumped up and ran, but before I could get to the door, my father was there.

"Anne! Anne, what's wrong?" Seeing my state of terror, he drew me to him. "Tell me, Anne, what is it?"

My constricted throat gradually loosened, and between sobs, a few words came out, words of hysteria. "The window, Dad . . . the small pane of glass, Dad . . . can't you see? Can't you see the face at the window!" I gestured toward the french doors, but my face was buried in his shoulder. *I am afraid to look!* "Look, Dad . . . the pane of glass!"

"Oh, for heaven's sake!" He released me and rushed across the room to the french doors and angrily pulled them open, the wind bringing cool air into the room and the sound of rain. I shivered.

"Get in here, Lenore, and take off that mask! What do you think you're doing!" My soft-spoken, mild-mannered father was screaming into the blackness of the night. I could hear his anger, but not the words.

Mother? The face and hands . . . the face and hands that had pressed against the small black panes . . . were the face and hands of my mother? Yes! There she stood in front of us, her rain-dampened hair clinging to her cheeks crimson with excitement, her eyes dark like the night and laughing, laughing.

"Oh, Mike!" And more laughter. "Really, Anne, don't you know your own mother!" *Don't you know your own mother?*

No! Don't come near me! No! Silent words. My body was trembling. *Why am I trembling so? It's only my mother! Why am I so afraid . . . so cold?* Mother's laughter faded as she walked through the house to the back bedroom.

"Anne, come in here and sit with me awhile. It's only your mother. You know she does things like this—always did!" It was my father's voice, once again quiet, soft-spoken, though still edged with anger. "Just your mother, Anne." I felt someone taking my arm—guiding me to the couch in the den—my father's strong hands. We sat there together, his arms around me, until I stopped trembling and grew still—and silent. Always? *Why didn't you hold me* then, *Daddy, in the kitchen? I needed you then.*

The screams were once more locked deep within, silenced, and the french doors with the shiny small black panes of glass were again locked for the night. The light rain continued to fall. *Tap . . . tap . . . tap.*

Tap . . . tap . . . tap . . . rain on windows—not openings as they should be, but constrictive, making it hard to breathe. So much rain, symbolic tears beating silently on the windows of my soul. Unshed.

The teacup was cold to my touch. My hands were trembling as I carried it to the kitchen. A profound weakness made the ascent of the spiral staircase more than I could bear. Pressure weighed on my chest as I drew one deliberate breath, and then another.

Rather than the familiar convent bells awakening me the next morning, it was a cold thermometer thrust into my mouth. It was difficult coming out of my deep, drug-induced sleep. *Where am I? Oh, yes, the hospital!* It had all happened so quickly. With effort, I recalled the day before. By noon, when Sister Therese had checked on me during her lunch break, I was burning up with a high fever. A fire raged in my chest, and each breath was labored and painful. I could barely speak. A new doctor had been called, Dr. William Berry. He was highly regarded in the community, and his skill as a physician had a wide reputation.

Listening to my heart, Dr. Berry asked how long I had been ill. Quite matter-of-factly, I replied, "Ever since I had scarlet fever—about a year ago."

He shook his head with disbelief. "Do you know you have a heart murmur?"

"No, Doctor, I don't. I've been told there is nothing wrong with my heart." I answered with a finality beyond any hope.

He was there only a few minutes, but I immediately felt confidence and was grateful for this new presence in my life. I was desperate for help. Before evening, I was in a hospital bed and subjected to a battery of tests. It was familiar territory to me as this was my fourth hospitalization in one year's time.

The nurse removed the thermometer and smiled, keeping the information to herself. Then the usual questions that I had come to loathe, as the answers came with great difficulty. I was not accustomed to talking about my symptoms, but rather concealing them. The doctor would be in shortly. And she was gone.

For the first time, I took in my surroundings. As usual, I had a private room as nuns usually did. It was a lovely room, which I assumed was in the new wing, judging by its modern decor. There was even a television on the wall. The window looked out to a stretch of blue sky with billowing white clouds, the rain having cleared in the night. I tried to relax but was too apprehensive. My fear was not of what terrible illness I had but that there was nothing wrong with me. There was nothing to do but wait.

For several days I waited. There were tests and more tests. Dr. Berry came each morning, and my confidence in him was strengthened. I was dismayed that I continued to react in fear, however. It seemed I could not shake that response to the medical world.

And then finally, the waiting was over. Dr. Berry came into my room and said the tests results were in and, he felt, conclusive. I had acute rheumatic fever. There were complications of heart disease, bacterial endocarditis. In the past, it had nearly always been fatal, but there was treatment now and he believed I would get well. The drug penicillin was prescribed for an indefinite period. I didn't know what to feel. The explanation for what I had been suffering this past year was clear enough, but somehow I couldn't absorb the words. Psychic pain doesn't diminish with the words of a moment. I had nothing to say. Nothing to ask. Then I was alone, allowing what I had learned to slowly sink in.

I got out of bed, put on my soft black veil and robe, and left the hospital room. Gripping the hand railing for support, I inched my way down the long hall to the chapel. It was empty and immensely quiet. I went in and threw myself on my knees. Incense was still in the air from the morning service. Light filtered through the stained-glass windows. Suddenly, I realized tears were flowing down my face. Tears of relief. Somehow, I felt freed of bondage. The great oppression of the unknown had been lifted. *I know what is wrong with me!* It was the answer to everything. A peace I hadn't known for a long time flowed through my entire being. I wasn't aware of pain. I was in another world in the presence of a merciful Christ. My only emotion was gratitude. I gave thanks for deliverance.

A tapping on my shoulder brought me back to the hospital world. It was the nurse with a wheelchair. "Sister Francis! Don't you know you shouldn't be out of bed! Dr. Berry has ordered complete bed rest."

I should have felt reprimanded, but I was impervious to what seemed an inappropriate solicitation under the circumstances. "Yes," I said with the usual smile, "you can take me back to my room now." Feeling shaky and weak, I was glad to be helped into the awaiting wheelchair, recognizing my independence was slipping away from me.

Chapter 8

VOCATION

Days grew into weeks, and progress was slow. I adapted to hospital routine that demanded nothing of me. It was a tremendous relief not to have to keep up with a schedule. I learned what "complete bed rest" meant and resented the feeling of dependence. There was nothing to do but acquiesce and, at the moment, was being subjected to the ritual of the bed bath. The nursing profession had it down to a fine science. Jean and I chatted over the basin of warm water like it was a cup of coffee.

"Why did you become a nun, Sister Francis?" It was a common question put to nuns. People asked out of curiosity, unable to imagine why anyone would choose such an extreme lifestyle unless there was something wrong with them. "You are so attractive!" Often, this comment went along with the question, inferring only unattractive girls enter convents. It always amused me. *Why? Why is anyone what they are? Why is the universe? Did it simply evolve over time, or did it come to be in one cataclysmic explosion?*

Jean's question tapped a sensitive depth within and echoed my own struggle for truth. I gave her an answer that was viable but wanting. "Well, Jean, I had the desire to give my life to God and was drawn to a life of prayer and service." It wasn't that the answer satisfied her any more than it did me, but we both left it at that.

Her question stayed with me long after she had gone. There were many shaping forces I could have shared with Jean. The long, silent afternoon gave me time to ponder just what they had been. "Why *had* I become a nun?" After seven and a half years in the order, it was a timely question. The day of final vows was fast approaching, less than two months away. One of the strong influences, I knew, was that of the nuns who had taught me in the parochial schools.

The choice to become a nun had demanded much of me at nineteen—just ripe for the usual path. I had watched my big sister, Maureen, put both feet on that one eagerly: dating, marriage, moving out of the family home, having babies. It was all there waiting for me as well. From the very beginning, however, *from the mother's womb*, I knew my path would be different. It was as though an angel had appeared and pointed the way, allowing no room for dissent. I had been *chosen*. I had a vocation. If there had been any "vision," it was of the nuns themselves, the women in black wearing a habit of heavy serge with deep pockets and very wide chalk-smudged sleeves. It was the wide sleeves in particular that I remember. Like wings of a blackbird, they would sweep across my desktop, correcting my fledgling attempts at writing or numbers. I knew when a nun was approaching, winding her way down the narrow aisle between rows of student desks. It was the gentle sound of the rosary beads that hung at her side, whispering, whispering, announcing her angel presence. That warning sound, it reminded me of the surf's last gentle brush of the sand before it disappeared into the vast sea. It was with a mixture of spiritual joy—and fear—that I looked up into her all-seeing eyes.

I read in those reflecting eyes what I had known since birth. They knew the unspeakable that *I had been chosen*. It was in her smile too and the light tap of encouragement on my shoulder, her too-quick reaching into the deep pockets to retrieve a holy card portraying a beautiful fair-haired saint and handing it to me, bridging the vast gulf between us. Something we could share, even speak of—"It's St. Philomena, Anne. Pray to her every day for your vocation." *Vocation* meant a *calling*—and I had better answer. I knew that much, even as a first grader. Yes, it must begin early. You'd think I would have been better behaved, more in keeping with this *calling*. But no. I was good at setting it aside for later. Of course, I would pray, hold St. Philomena close, and contemplate her lovely hair. Since the days of parochial school, St. Philomena has been removed from the list of saints, relegated to wherever such fallen-from-grace saints go. Something like a nothing place of nonexistence, a now-familiar place.

I could not explore the roots of my vocation without thinking of perhaps even a stronger shaping force than those blackbird wings: Uncle John, my mother's brother, who was a priest. We had a close relationship—very simply, I adored him. He was tall, quite handsome, and blessed with charisma. A spiritual man and eloquent speaker, he was very much in demand for retreats. He had quite a following. If he hadn't been a priest, he surely would have been president of a large company or a successful politician. Uncle John was my confidant, the only person with whom I discussed my innermost thoughts. I considered him my spiritual adviser from my earliest years.

"Take my hand, Uncle John. I'll teach you how to dance." I was not yet six years old. Five and twenty-five. I arched my neck and looked up into his immense height until our eyes met. Uncle John loved little Anne. It was there in the clear sky blue eyes clouded with the mist of shining priestly goodness. And I loved Uncle John. *It will always be that way. Always!* Suddenly, I felt shy and shifted my gaze down to the shiny blackness of my patent leather tap shoes tied with black satin ribbons. *Tap . . . tap . . . tap, tap, tap . . . tap.* I gripped Uncle John's hand tightly, my small hand lost in his, and critically watched his oh-so-large black shoes keep rhythm with mine—clumsily, heavily, but then this was just the first lesson, the beginning. Uncle John learned quite well, and we became a dancing team, performing for any willing audience whenever he was home from the seminary.

His return to his studies to be a priest was always heart wrenching for me. He would swoop me up in his arms and kiss me good-bye, telling me how special I was to him. *My favorite niece.* I still felt sad, but then I had his letters to watch for, letters that spoke of Jesus and his love for me and how I should trust him. I wrote back in my scrawly handwriting, "Dear Uncle John . . ." and always closing with "I love you." The hand matured as the years went by, as did my love, and soon Uncle John was ordained a priest and returning home to his boyhood parish to celebrate his first solemn High Mass.

"Come then, my love, my lovely one, come." I stood in the vestibule of the old church, watching the early morning sun furl ribbons of soft color through the stained glass then coming to rest gently in benediction on the large congregation of family and friends, giving them rather an ethereal presence. There was a hush of expectancy, and the organ sounded the processional hymn. I placed my satin slipper on the white runner of the aisle leading to the altar. As I moved into the ethereal colored light, the shiny white satin of my bridal dress became a myriad of dancing colors, its swirl of folds undulating with its own life. Slowly, I approached the altar, the weight of the long satin train resisting my every step. The orange blossom crown hugged my array of curls, and the white net veil fell gracefully in clouded mists about my shoulders.

My bridal "bouquet" was a white satin pillow trimmed with rows and rows of delicate lace. On its smooth surface was painted a white host elevated above a golden chalice with streaks of light and bordered with clusters of purple grapes. Resting on this pillow was my offering, a wreath of orange blossoms entwined with pearls. This thing of beauty came from the artistic fingers of my grandmother, Uncle John's mother and now a mother of a priest. She was proudly positioned there in the front pew, beaming at me as I moved closer and closer to the sanctuary.

Grandmother had talked to me of this privileged moment the night before as she gently wound my hair in rag curls and tied them in knots that pulled at my scalp. "You will be the bride, Anne." I had been chosen. "*She is the darling of her mother, the favorite.*" And then, as she tucked me into bed in her sweet and gentle way, she raised her hand, bringing it down on my forehead. There she wrote, firmly with her index finger, "I-N-R-I," the invisible letters tangible in the strokes on my child-soft skin. Grandmother was re-creating the enactment of the Roman soldiers nailing a sign to the cross upon which Jesus was dying, the sign that was a testament to the world as to his identity: INRI—"Jesus of Nazareth, king of the Jews." Grandmother always did this when she tucked me in. I wondered, *Who am I?*

I was but nine years old and a bride. *Whose bride?* I asked myself as I moved through the open gate of the altar railing and into the sanctuary, feeling as though I were trespassing on holy ground. I felt in the company of angels as I glided across the marble floor to the single prie-dieu, where I eased myself down on the satin-covered kneeler, letting out a great sigh. I felt very strange and alone there in the vast sanctuary—not unlike the shining tall holy candles and flower-filled golden urns that graced the altar. Fixtures. Symbols. The doll I wanted for Christmas came to my mind, a bride doll dressed in white satin and lace with a long net veil, standing alone on the shelf in the toy store. There were no "groom dolls." *Whose bride is she?* I wondered. Two bride dolls, sharing an unreality in a little girl's world. It was pretend, make-believe. "*Our sister is little: her breasts are not yet formed.*"

"*Introibo ad altare Dei.*" I will go unto the altar of God. Holy Mass was beginning. I had placed the satin pillow on the chair behind me and now clutched the olive-seed rosary that was my most treasured possession. Uncle John as a seminarian had made the rosary for me, which made it very special. It had arrived in a small gold box with a note, saying, "Happy birthday to my favorite niece." My sixth birthday. Every birthday was remembered by Uncle John, if just with a little note that said "I love you, little Anne." As the years went by, I was not so little, and Uncle John did not seem quite so immensely tall. At nine, as the bride, I did not have to arch my neck so much to look up into those shining eyes. I always saw Jesus there and wanted to know more about that. Now my uncle John would be "Father" to all the world. I wasn't so sure I liked having to share him that much.

I watched his priestly figure bowing reverently over the altar, now genuflecting, now raising his hands, performing with great exactitude all the rituals and rubrics of the solemn High Mass. I watched with great intensity, my whole body poised in waiting for the moment when I was to rise from the kneeler and walk with grace to the altar steps.

"*Sanctus, sanctus, sanctus.*" Holy, holy, holy. The altar boy rang the bell three times. That was my summons. "*I trembled to the core of my being. Then I rose to open to my beloved.*" I stood up straight and tall, turned, and picked up the satin pillow from the chair behind me. Holding it reverently as the treasure it was, I walked to the altar steps, barely breathing. My eyes were drawn to the great cross suspended above the altar. Jesus was looking down at me, at the bride, in a most loving and sorrowful way. And then it was Uncle John's face, Uncle John's eyes, as he approached me, leaned down, and gently lifted the wreath from the satin pillow. *How I love you, Uncle John!* He smiled down at me and I felt my world was complete, full of love. *There is no need for a groom doll,* I thought.

Back at my solitary prie-dieu, I watched as Uncle John placed the wreath over the chalice and bowed low over the altar. I too lowered my head in adoration, knowing Uncle John was uttering the most sacred of words given to us by Jesus. It was the most solemn part of Holy Mass, the Consecration. The hands that had plucked pennies from my ears and then made them disappear were now anointed hands empowered to change bread and wine into the body and blood of Christ. "*Hoc est enim corpus meum.*" This is my body. "*Hoc est enim calix sanguinis mei.*" This is my blood. Uncle John's voice was barely above a whisper but reached the most-remote corners of the big church that seemed fixed in a timeless, soundless space.

Soon the Mass was over, as was the day. Along with memories, the satin pillow was wrapped in linen and laid to rest on the top shelf of Mother's closet to be forgotten.

My relationship with Uncle John remained, though it was to shift and change with my growing years. He was always the center of my life. Quite sufficient. No one else could measure up to Uncle John. He was my ideal. He was perfection. No one could be as tall, as handsome—and perhaps, most importantly, as fun to be with.

Memories of Uncle John are memories of saltwater and sand and smell of seaweed. Each summer during my teenage years, Father would rent a beach house right on the sand. A rambling white-frame house with a deck shaped as the bow of a ship, giving the illusion of being at sea. From its broad bay windows, we could watch the rolling surf, the tides telling the time of day. The demands of Father's business prevented him from being with us except on weekends. Friends and relatives came and went, including my high school friends. Uncle John seemed always there. With Uncle John in my life, I really didn't feel the need for any other companionship.

We spent the summer days in and out of the surf, swimming out beyond the breakers, resting on our backs, and then swimming back to shore. It was a time before surfing was popular, but Uncle John taught me to ride the waves, timing the breakers and catching them at just the right moment with outstretched arms. When we missed, it meant being helplessly caught in a swirling force, tossed head over heels, tumbling, scraping the sand-bottom sea, tossed and thrown up on the beach, sputtering, laughing, and ready to try again. Only a satisfying sense of exhaustion found us sunbathing on beach towels, side by side. So often this was the time to speak of serious things, such as God's love for us, his divine providence—and my vocation.

The wind blew in from the sea, and the whitecaps danced like white-laced ballerinas. "Uncle John!" My voice sounded thin and distant to my ears, somewhat strained. "It is God's will that I become a nun. I know it!" The heat was growing more intense as the sun peaked in the noonday sky, baking the sand beneath us. "But I'm not so sure I want to do that!" Encouraging a suntan, I rubbed my arms with lotion while I talked. Uncle John's brow furrowed as he listened to what I was feeling about my vocation. I went on, "There is always this duality within me—I feel I'm being called to religious life, but on the other hand, I feel a deep resistance!"

Uncle John looked at me with his translucent blue eyes, and I knew that whatever he said would be the closest I could come to hearing the voice of God. "Desire is necessary to a vocation, Anne. You must *want* to be a nun. But you can foster desire, you know."

I wasn't so sure I wanted to know. My fingers combed my sun-streaked hair as I considered this. "Well," I finally asked, "how's that?"

"I advise you to get to Mass every morning, say the rosary every day—*ask* for the desire. We can't always go by what we feel, Anne."

"But, Uncle John, it's so hard to get to morning Mass! I have to leave for school by seven o'clock!"

"You can do it, Anne, if it's important to you. And you know I'll remember you in my Mass every day. You have your senior year ahead of you, so there's time to find out what you really want to do with your life. Meanwhile, trust in God and his blessed mother—they won't fail you, Anne." As Uncle John spoke, an expression came over his face that reflected some desirable, spiritual place unknown to me. I wanted to enter more into his world, that world of the spirit, so I was drawn. His face was to be obscured in time by that loving, sorrowful face of Jesus looking down at me from the cross. At times, the faces were indistinguishable. "*I have found him whom my heart loves.*"

Chapter 9

DEATHBED LEGACY

1949

It was the night of the dying grandmother. A different kind of night—with friends, relatives, Uncle John, all wanting to be close to the dying grandmother, crowding the sickroom, spilling out into the hall and kitchen . . . the odors of anointing oils and burning candles spilling out also along with the dirge of murmurs . . . whispers . . . cries . . . undecipherable.

I stood next to Uncle John by the side of the frail old woman lost in the big brass four-poster bed. *My Grammie. My Grammie is dying!* Watching Grandmother die tore at my heart and I felt the silent tears within. Reaching out, I took her bony, lifeless hand in mine—cold, cold with approaching death.

Her eyelids fluttered but slightly and then opened wide, and she looked up at Uncle John. Her eyes glowed with a proud, shining light, bathing her countenance with a beauty not of this world. Seeing her son, who was a priest, standing there gave a sense of purpose, of meaning, to her long, holy life. The thin wisp of a voice breathed, "John!"

Then the proud, shining light moved from Uncle John to me, standing there, watching. Her pale blue-gray eyes were strong with love as was her voice, her thin blue lips forming words with the strength of one not dying. "*Anne, your arms are outstretched on the cross with Jesus. You will help priests by your suffering. You are special, Anne—chosen.*" Taking her son's anointed hands, she placed mine in his. The eyelids fluttered again, and the proud, shining light flickered like the flames of the holy candles on her nightstand.

Deathbed words! The coldness of her hands seemed to close about my heart. *No, not that! Anne doesn't want to suffer. But this is a holy death. These are holy words. All last words are. It must be true!*

All energy drained from me, drained by the deathbed legacy, I moved as a sleepwalker from the sickroom into the adjoining bedroom, my parents' bedroom, that special place not open to us children. But this night was different and doors would open, doors that should have remained shut. The dirge of murmurs, whispers, cries, undecipherable, spilled out, followed me. I muffled my own wracking sobs in the pillows as I threw myself on the wide bed, its chenille spread rough against my skin.

Whose death am I mourning? Grandmother's? Or mine? My arms outstretched . . . suffer . . . help, priests. The heaviness of it all weighed on my soul, oppressed my spirit. And then the nail that fixed me there, You are special, Anne, chosen, Anne. *You know what this means . . . You know what you must do.*

"You know what you must do, Anne," my mother's voice, not muffled and indecipherable, but hard, distinct, cruelly clear, intruding on my quiet, wrenching sobs. She had entered my room stealthily, as one about to steal. *Is it my soul?* "You know what you must do, Anne . . . Anne, do you hear me? You know what you must do, Anne . . . Anne, do you hear me? Now is the time, Anne, now . . . tonight . . . you must!"

I rolled over on my back, slowly, my body a great weight, and looked up at my mother standing over me, her height a column of strength, of overbearance. "No! Not tonight. No!" This was *my* secret, embryonic, not yet fully formed within me, not ready to be exposed—especially to the fetid air of this night. *How can she ask this of me any night—but tonight!* There had to be a sense of timing, an intelligent, emotion-free judgment, of *when*. The hysterics of this night said it was *not* the time! "No, don't make me, Mother. No, not tonight. Even if Grandmother did say . . . You know what he will think . . . what he will say . . . not tonight . . . and besides, I'm not sure, Mother . . . not sure." I sobbed.

"Tonight, Anne . . . tell your father tonight that you are going to be a nun . . . You know you are going to be a nun, Anne . . . You must tell your father . . . tonight."

"What are you talking about, Lenore? Tell me what?" I heard the edge in my father's voice, his stooped figure darkening the doorway unexpectedly. The fanatical undertones of the religious drama surrounding my grandmother's death offended him, repulsed him.

No, not now! My mother said nothing, but looked at me in her commanding, soul-stealing way.

And I did her bidding. I told my father when I knew I should not. And she knew.

"Tell him, Anne."

The night of the dying grandmother was not over, however, as Grandmother fiercely hung on to life. Each time Death approached, she turned and fled, always staying just beyond the reach of the Grim Reaper. Had her time not come? Or was she rejecting its wisdom? So the watch continued, though the watchers dwindled like the melting wax of the holy candles into extinguishment. The reality of exhaustion was seeping into the watchers' bones, and they departed one-by-one into the night, leaving the watch to the immediate family. Even *their* whispered murmurings hushed into quietude. Grandmother herself grew still and lay there in the whiteness of Death's shadow.

I was young and strong, and my tears had long dried in the desert of my soul. I would continue the watch. I would stay with the dying grandmother. "Get some rest, Mother . . . Dad . . . Uncle John."

I went into Grandmother's room. Her large double brass bed was just inside the doorway. Entering, I paused at her bedside and took her bony, lifeless hand in mine. "Grandmother," I whispered, "I love you, Grandmother." She did not stir or open her eyes. I secured the blanket about her chin and went to the far corner of the room and sat in the comfy big chair. The dim light of the bedside lamp cast shadows on the still form of Grandmother within easy view of my watch. Watch—watch the ebbing of a life that was so precious—so precious to me. How many times had I kept such a watch over my grandmother as she nursed an ailing heart? "Rheumatic heart disease," the doctors had said. She bore the sickness nobly most of her life, living often on the edge of eternity—never quite there, as now. Was I not yet three when I began my watch?

My mother had errands to do or helpful tasks for grandmother. Little Anne could be trusted to be good, to sit by the bedside of the ailing grandmother hour by hour. The clock ticked by the moments loudly in the heavy silence of the sickroom. Traffic could be heard in the far-off distance and the arrhythmic, heavy breathing of Grandmother there in the big brass bed so close to me. Hour after hour. I twisted and turned in the big chair, my child legs turned under me. There was nothing to do but study the pictures on the wall of Jesus wearing his crown of thorns and Mary wearing hers over her heart. And I watched—until I could watch no more. Then a small, faint voice, not wanting to disturb or offend, said, "Grandmother, Grandmother, aren't you ever going to wake up?"

I looked across the room at her now. *Are you, Grandmother, going to wake up this time?* I sighed, and closed my eyes, feeling too the exhaustion of the night. I felt my body relax into the cushioned chair, the tensions of the night easing into the relief of shallow sleep, a part of me continuing the watch.

I was to witness my grandmother's final death struggle with unseen forces that night, gripping the crucifix, moving her lips in silent prayer. She looked over at me from her bed of suffering with a wildness in her eyes, pleading for I knew not what. It was an arena not yet familiar to me, but I instinctively knew Uncle John with his priestly powers should be the one to engage in battle with her.

I found him in the kitchen, sitting there quietly in the nook, hunched wearily over a cup of coffee. "Uncle John! You must come! It's Grandmother . . . She needs you!" One look at my troubled face told him all he needed to know, and he moved quickly. It was as though I could *see* him stepping into his priestly power. He was ready, imbued with *knowing* and strength, to do, to *be*, whatever this night would require of him in the name of Jesus.

I watched as Uncle John put the purple satin stole around his neck and armored himself with the crucifix. "I will go alone," he said, as he moved toward the door of the death room.

I remained behind, knowing the watch was not yet over. I heard the door shut firmly behind Uncle John.

Chapter 10

CLASH OF WILLS

The seeds of vocation. Who is to say what all the influences were that shaped my destiny? I only know they were planted deep within my soul and broke through the hard ground of my resistance, flowering into the desire required of me. I wanted more out of life than simply "settling down." I wanted a broader stage for whatever was to unfold. The convent seemed to offer that, surrounded by mystery and having some kind of exclusive access to the spiritual realm. The making of vows gave promise of a cataclysmic breakthrough to a new internal universe. I would make my choice. And I did. I cut through the conflict and questioning and said, "I want to do the will of God. I *will* be a nun!"

The decision would not go unchallenged. My parents, after Uncle John, were the first to know. I don't remember actually telling my mother—it was as though she had always known. We enjoyed an unusual closeness as mother and daughter, alike in many ways. Between us there were unspoken understandings and even psychic communications. My vocation was one of these, I think. Perhaps *she* told me.

It was in the days before penicillin, and Mother was hospitalized with pneumonia. She was ill unto death, and I could not bear losing my beautiful mother—for she was beautiful. Mother had what I would call star quality. An intelligent woman with a stately bearing, she carried her height with great dignity, her head tilted slightly upward. She could command by her very presence, and her voice, equally impressive, was strong, even strident at times, ringing with authority. It was a voice not to be contradicted—*should* not be contradicted because she was *always* right. Black was black and white was white and as she decreed. She instilled confidence, but not without fear. I could not imagine crossing my mother. *What terrible thing would happen!*

Mother did recover from pneumonia and came home to us, though in a weakened condition. No one, I believed, rejoiced more than I. On those languid days of recovery, she told stories as she was wont to do, made-up stories and true life stories. She was a master storyteller and could weave a spell on us children. This day, Mother and I were alone. She told me of an experience she had in the hospital. She knew she was dying, she said in a wistful voice. She felt lifted out of herself, leaving her body, and hovering high above the hospital room. There was a long tunnel through which she was propelled with great speed into other worlds. She had visions. One was of me.

> *I saw you, Anne, as a nun. You wore an elaborate starched headdress and a white habit. You were bustling down a cobblestone street. It may have been a foreign country. There were many children surrounding you. It was like you were shepherding them. Yes, Anne, I did see you . . . I did see you as a nun. Perhaps a missionary.*

This vision became mine and confirmed my feelings of being *special* in my mother's regard; when she was dying, her thoughts were of me! The vision fed my thoughts of vocation as well, and I put much store in it. My mother was always right, after all. So there really was no need to tell Mother *anything*. At the same time, I knew it tore her apart to think of me leaving home and going to what then was a great distance, some two thousand miles away, perhaps never to return.

My father had no such visions but just ordinary dreams for me of marriage and a family. I believed I was no less special to him. Mother always said of my father, "He is such a good man." Goodness as defined by hard work, integrity, devotion to duty and family. The "old-fashioned" values. An Irish Catholic, I would describe my father as being more spiritual than religious. He saw beneath the surface of things to the soul of matters. As he was introspective by nature, it was not unusual for him to simply sit and look off into a space filled with things we could not see.

In the evenings I waited patiently for Father to finish his late meal after a long day's work and join me in the den, where I was already busily doing homework. There, huddled up to the radio with him, I would enter into his space. Together, we enjoyed some broadcast, read the evening paper, or simply sat without need to talk. At times, we took late-night walks under the stars, a comfortable silence between us. I felt safe, loved, in his presence, a presence that instilled respect and even fear. I always felt there was some great, brooding storm within his soul about to break. So it was not without trepidation that I approached him that Sunday afternoon.

The french doors to the rose arbor were wide-open, letting in the fresh spring air. The white roses climbing the trellis were in full bloom and their fragrance I perceived as a special blessing on this day. From the living room, I could see my father sitting on the canopied swing, cigar in hand, enjoying the little leisure that was his. The *Sunday Examiner* was at his side, unread. Father was simply looking into space, lost in his own thoughts, enjoying his well-earned solitude. I hated to intrude—no, I *feared* to intrude. *But I must . . . I must do what I must do!* I was sitting on the white brocade couch, rosary in hand, praying to the Christ on the flower-papered wall. *Help me, O Christ, help me to do this. I can't do it alone! Be with me. Please make Dad understand!* I rose from the couch, braced myself, and walked through the french doors out into the patio, grateful my mother was not there. She was at the store, buying freshly baked french bread and peppermint-stick ice cream for Sunday night dinner. *Help me, O God.*

My father's face lit up when he saw me and put his hand out, motioning for me to sit next to him which I did. We said nothing, just enjoying being together and the silence of the lovely spring day. *Help me, O God . . . help him.*

"Dad, there's something I want to tell you." The somberness in my voice caught his attention, and he turned on the swing and looked directly at me.

"What is it you want to tell me, Anne?"

Drawing a deep breath, I went on, groping for words to soften what I knew must be said. "I mentioned it before, Dad—but you wouldn't listen to me. You remember, the night grandmother was dying."

I could feel my father grow rigid, could see the muscles in his face tighten. "Oh, *that* night! You were all upset—you didn't even realize what you were saying—"

"Well, I do now, Dad," I broke in. "I want to be a nun. I *am* going to enter the convent as soon as I finish college." There—I had said it. I held my breath and waited, seeing the storm rising on my father's face.

"Never! Never will I give permission for you to be a nun! I'd rather see you go to the grave first!"

"I'm not asking your permission, Dad, I'm *telling* you. My decision is made!" I heard the tremor in my raised voice.

"Telling me!" His voice too was rising in pitch. "Well, I'll tell you something! It's an unnatural life you're wanting! You don't even know what you're giving up! What do you know about marriage?"

"I know enough to know I don't want to get married! I have a vocation, Dad, a calling—"

"A calling! A calling!" He spat out the words, his face growing red with rage as he rose from the swing and stood over me. "A calling from whom—UNCLE JOHN!" The words were screamed at me. "I should have put a stop to that long ago—stay away from him, Anne, do you hear me! I don't want him around here—I'm warning you!"

I too was now angry, fighting to keep the tears back. "This has nothing to do with Uncle John! Please, Dad, please try and understand—"

"No, Anne, *you* understand—not one penny, not college, no support, nothing! I'll not waste a dime on you—do you hear me? You do this and you do it alone. I'll never support you in this decision. In fact, I'll have nothing more to say to you, ever—nothing." His voice broke, in anger as much as in sadness.

"I am going to do it, Dad, even if I am no longer your daughter. *Nothing . . . no one . . .* is going to stop me . . . and I'll not ask for any money. I'll forget college, go to work, earn my own way. In fact, I'll enter the convent this fall—September! College courses are offered in the novitiate—I can still earn a degree. I don't need you, Dad." My voice was back in control. My course was firmly set. I now stood, face-to-face with my father. We looked into each other's eyes, seeing tears, feeling tears, recognizing the lines were drawn, the stubborn lines of determination, righteousness, defiance, and estrangement. Locked in our difference, neither of us could bridge the chasm stretching between us. I turned and walked through the french doors into the house, hearing my father's plea. "Anne! Anne, don't do this to me! Don't leave me, Anne!" And a sob.

I had only heard my father cry when his mother died, when his father died, when his brother died—and now me. I was dead to him. Suddenly, the brightness had left the spring day and I felt only a darkness, deep, gripping my soul. *Dad! Dad!*

Chapter 11

GRANDMOTHER'S SONG

1950

I have to get out of this house! Inside, a wild frenzy was building, a force to crush the grief I didn't want to feel. *DAD! DAD!* The keys to the family Buick were on the kitchen table. I grabbed them, my purse, and slipped out the front door. Within minutes, the car was rolling down the tree-lined residential streets, fresh with new spring green and always the flowers—hibiscus, roses, hydrangea, even the jacaranda trees were in bloom, their clusters of deep-purple blossoms forming fantasia clouds overhead. At any other time, the beauty would have put a smile on my face, but not today. I gravitated to the Catholic church, my only place of refuge, only a few blocks from my home. I had been baptized in its holy font, received my first Holy Communion at its altar steps, been confirmed as a soldier of Christ kneeling in its sanctuary, sang in the choir loft for countless occasions. And then there were the times I simply stole precious minutes, hours, to enjoy the solitude, as now.

I parked the car at the main entrance and walked hurriedly up the front steps. The white stucco walls, red tiles, and wrought iron gave the structure the stamp of Spanish architecture. Through the high carved oak doors, I entered this familiar place, coming into semidarkness and a hushed quiet, an unearthly silence that said, "*Peace, be still.*" The odor of incense was still in the air from morning benediction, and the light coming through the stained glass threw beams of color on the highly polished pews. I walked up the main aisle and knelt down in the front row. I was alone, and the tears came as I grew quiet within, no longer held back by the dam of frenzy. I fixed my eyes on the tabernacle where dwelt the living Christ—the Eucharistic Presence—always there waiting for me ... always there to help me ... to give me the strength I needed ... always there to listen. I felt at home ... loved.

Help me now, O God! I love my father so . . . I can't bear to hurt him this way. Please make him understand! Give me the strength to do your will . . . Thy will be done, not mine.

My prayer grew silent, and I knelt absorbed in his presence, and the minutes slipped by uncounted. I was comforted. I rose and began the Stations of the Cross, the fourteen stations that lined the church walls in colorless plaster, commemorating Christ's bloody path to Calvary.

First station, Jesus is condemned to death. *Give me the grace to accept my fate, whatever it may be, dear Jesus.* I made my way round the thick carpeted aisles of the large church, station to station, genuflecting at each one. At each station I identified in some way with the suffering Christ.

Sixth station, Simon helps Jesus carry the cross. *I want to help you, Jesus. Give me the strength to carry this cross.* Eighth station, Veronica wipes the face of Jesus. *Veronica! Veronica, Grandmother's name.* I thought of Grandmother and how she had taught me to follow along the Way of the Cross with her when I was a toddler. I remembered how dark the church seemed as we wound our way from station to station, my short legs always trailing behind Grandmother, my hand in hers, learning to genuflect, listening to her words, "Jesus, I will help you carry the cross." It was a frequent occasion for Grandmother and me, an outing like many others—going to the movies, the drug store for ice cream, shopping for my first bikini. *Grandmother! I'll go to Grandmother!*

Fourteenth station, Jesus is laid in the tomb. *I will die with you if it is your will, dear Jesus.*

My tears dried by my fervor and the pain in my heart assuaged, I was back in the Buick, driving the mile or so to see Grandmother. In some ways I felt she had been laid in the tomb. Grandmother had come so close to death, so close that we referred to that night as "the night Grandmother was dying." Her words to me that night I had not forgotten. "You have a mission, Anne. Your arms are outstretched on the cross with Jesus." The words seemed particularly poignant this day, even prophetic.

I pulled up and stopped in front of the white-shingled California bungalow with a sign out front that said simply, "Rest Home." After a series of strokes causing partial paralysis and confusion of speech, Grandmother was placed here as Mother felt she no longer had the inner resources to take care of her. I walked up the rosebush-lined path and rang the bell. "Hello, Ruth, I'm here to see my grandmother." Ruth, in her starched white uniform, immediately ushered me to the sickroom, accustomed to my visits.

"Veronica! Veronica! Your granddaughter is here!" There was no response from the frail gray figure on the bed.

"Thanks, Ruth, I'll just sit with her for a while." The room was small but cheery with fresh linens on the bed, white curtains, and sunshine. A vase of roses was on the nightstand. Ruth left the room to attend to other patients, leaving Grandmother and me alone.

I sat down on Grandmother's bed and took her hand in mine, the thin, lifeless blue-veined hand. Her eyes were closed. I smoothed the strands of hair from her forehead and, leaning down, kissed her on the cheek.

"Grandmother! Grandmother! It's Anne. I've come to tell you something. I think it will make you happy, Grandmother." There was no response, but I went on, believing she would hear me, somewhere deep inside herself.

"Grandmother, I'm going to be a nun . . . I'm entering the convent . . . in September, Grandmother . . . pray for me, Grandmother . . . I need strength to do this . . . to do God's Will." I sat there quietly, believing she could hear me, holding her cold, limp hand—and then it stirred in mine. Her eyes opened, the eyes still blue, and looked into mine. Yes, it was the grandmother I knew, not the one whose sweetness and gentleness were ravaged by strokes, but the dear person who held me as a child and brightened my world with her smile—as she did now. *Grandmother smiled!* I leaned down and hugged her thin shoulders and then felt her hands resting on my head in benediction. *Grandmother is giving me her blessing.* And then she started to sing; her tongue was loosed and the voice strong and vibrant, the words clear, "*Salve Regina.*" Hail, holy queen. The age-old Christian hymn filled the small room like sunshine. I looked at my grandmother, who shone like the sun, an unearthly glow enveloping her. I was transfixed. I was watching a resurrection.

"*Misericordiae, vita, dulcedo.*" The song went on, the lovely strains growing stronger. It was as though the angels had taken over Grandmother's form and were singing to me, saying, "Yes, Anne, God is with you, Anne." I smiled too. Grandmother had heard me—she rejoiced with me.

"*O dulcis virgo Maria.*" Grandmother's voice gradually faded as the hymn came to an end. The light too grew dim, and the angels were no more. Grandmother's eyes closed and she became very still. I knew I would never see her again, the sweet and gentle grandmother of my childhood. I reached down and kissed the parchment skin.

"Good-bye, Grandmother, I'll always love you, Grandmother . . . Pray for me, Grandmother, that I'll be a good nun . . . that I'll do God's will."

I walked out of the nursing home and down the rosebush-lined path to the car, my solaced heart echoing Grandmother's song, "*Salve Regina.*"

Fortified spiritually, my course was set. I was only strengthened in my resolve by my father's opposition. In this clash of wills, we were true to our Irish heritage of stubbornness. His threatening words to disown me took on flesh and became a reality. My name was not to be uttered in his presence. He refused to speak to me—to respond to me. It was as though I did not exist. *Dead.*

Realizing I would not be swayed by this approach, Father thought perhaps if I saw more of the world, I would be less likely to renounce it. It was the Holy Year of 1950, and Uncle John was sponsoring a pilgrimage to Rome. Ironically, Father gave his permission for me to be part of this group and accompany my beloved Jesuit uncle. We traveled extensively throughout the United States and Europe, our tour culminating in an audience with Pope Pius XII, the reigning pontiff of the Roman Catholic Church. Kneeling to receive his apostolic blessing, I prayed for strength to follow my vocation.

I had been away from home for three months and returned with more experience of the world but unchanged in my resolve to be a nun.

Chapter 12

BOUND DESTINIES

1950

The elevator was out of order. The sign saying such hung on its grid, sentencing the small group to the ascending stairwell that wound its way upward, floor by floor, serpentine-like, until it reached death row. I was accompanying Uncle John on a pastoral work of mercy.

My high-heeled summer-white shoes tapped on the steel steps as I followed the armed guard in the serpentine ascent. I could hear Uncle John's heavy steps behind me. This was a different dance we were performing this day, I thought. I wanted to grab his hand and hold tight as we used to do. *Tap . . . tap . . . tap.* And after Uncle John, the even-heavier steps of another guard. The New Orleans Parish Prison was heavy with silence, an unusual silence, and the noisy procession of feet tapping its way upward sounded intrusive. I felt intrusive—out of place—in my green-and-white spring dress of cool jersey, its full skirt swirling about my nylon-stockinged legs as I climbed. I kept looking at the summer-white shoes as though they belonged to someone else—taking me through a place I did not belong, to a destination in which I had no part. But I was there—as unusual as it was—a young woman barely eighteen, trying to keep her eyes on summer-white shoes, trying to hear nothing but the *tap-tap* and wishing she were dancing with Uncle John on the hardwood floor at home instead of climbing, step by step.

Pausing at each landing for breath, I felt the vastness of space around me, exposing me to other eyes—staring eyes that drew mine, the summer-white shoes now still. I looked, but could not see, could not see what I did not know—*not yet*. Haunted, lonely, hungry eyes—dark, dispassionate, wondering, questioning . . . white-knuckled hands gripping iron bars . . . faces pressing, empty . . . eyes, hands, a colorless blur of incarceration and despair. *Floor by floor.*

And then we were at the top. Death row. The stairwell led to a narrow passageway flanked by single cells. The opposite wall was a colorless gray, its high narrow barred windows well beyond reach. I drew in my breath and braced myself. I was about to meet a celebrated prisoner, one whose name was well-known due to extensive newspaper coverage. I was about to meet Mark—because I was the niece of Father John, Father John who was here to bring solace and consolation to one who was to die. "*I was in prison, and you visited me.*"

"Mark, I want you to meet my favorite niece, Anne. I've told her a lot about you! Anne, this is Mark."

"Yes, I've heard so much—" I paused in mid-sentence and felt exposed, just as I had on the landings. Hands reached through the iron bars and took mine.

"Anne . . . I've heard about you too. I'm so glad you're here." Mark's grip was firm and strong like his voice, the voice of a young man. He was not yet twenty-nine. Would he see twenty-nine? I wondered. *What does it feel like to* know *you are going to die?* I looked up from hands to eyes, not colorless, but blue, blue as the sea on a sunny day, and whose gaze was unwavering. They smiled and were full of light as was the auburn of his hair, like burnished gold in the bar-streaked sunlight that shone through the small windows high on the wall behind me. His whole visage was one of light, a light that seemed to melt something within me, perhaps the hard, protective shell of one who had a destiny.

The guard pulled up a chair for me, and I had not been aware until that moment that my legs were about to give way.

"Tell me about yourself, Anne." Mark now sat opposite me, our knees nearly touching through the iron bars.

"But I want to know about *you*, Mark. How did this happen to you?" And we talked.

"I've been here on death row for two years, Anne. I've forgotten what it's like out there. You remind me." And he looked at me in a way that felt warm, almost as though he had touched me.

"I feel like I've known you a long time, Mark." *Time . . . time . . . there was no time.*

"Do you know . . ." I could not ask *when* because I did not want to know.

"There have been appeals and several stays of execution . . . no, I don't know."

"How hard it must be in this limbo place, Mark! If only I could help." Instinctively, I reached through the bars to comfort.

"You're here, Anne! Don't you realize how unusual this is! Visitors just don't come up here—especially women!" There was emotion in his voice—and charm. And warmth in his hand. I was suddenly self-conscious and felt myself blush. I quickly glanced away and happened to see a typewriter on a desk in the corner of his cell. Seizing the distraction, I asked, "Do you write, Mark?"

"Yes. I'm working on a book actually, under contract with a publisher."

"Is it your life story?"

"No, it's not. I'm writing on prison life and ideas of reform. It grew out of my experiences here—not only on death row but when I was down on the cell blocks with the other guys." There was a proud ring to his voice in telling of this personal accomplishment.

"I'd like to read it, Mark—really, I would."

"Well, it's not exactly something to curl up with by the fire—but I'll see you get a copy. I suppose my life story would make more interesting reading—a convicted murderer believing in his innocence. They say I killed a police officer, Anne. I was on a lark—Mardi Gras and all that. Down here from New York as a tourist . . . a tourist." His countenance darkened.

I wanted the light to return and hastily went on. "I've always had an interest in writing too, Mark. Perhaps I'll write a book one day—about *this* experience!" And we laughed, a laughter that said what was happening was not real.

The bar-streaked sunlight was shifting, moving across the concrete wall behind Mark as a hand on a clock. And we talked.

> *I'm going to die, Anne.*
> *I'm going to enter the convent, Mark.*
> *It must be God's will.*
> *Yes, God's will.*
> *I feel I have not yet lived.*
> *Nor have I.*
> *Pray for my courage, Anne.*
> *Don't forget me, Mark.*

"Mark, do you want me to hear your confession?" It was Uncle John's voice bringing me back to the grim reality of the purpose of this visit. I quickly got up, smoothing my jersey skirt that was clinging to my legs in the humid heat of the mid-June day, a discomfort I hardly noticed.

"I need to stretch my legs—I'll walk this corridor. See you later, Mark!"

My steps felt light—my heart felt light. I felt like quite a different person from the one who had climbed flight upon flight of serpentine stairs. I looked down at my summer-white shoes and smiled. I did belong. When I looked up, they stopped, stopped dead still. My eyes were riveted on an *object* I had never seen before—an enormous chair. I was looking through a glass at an enormous chair in a very small room. Its steel arms were wide and thick, as were the steel legs and the steel crown atop the high steel back. It resembled a throne in some dark way, except for its barrenness, its ugliness, and death-dealing potential. And the straps, wide, thick straps hanging lifeless, suspended, waiting . . . waiting . . . and then I knew, really *knew*. MARK! The reality sunk in. This beautiful man, so young, condemned to death, death by electrocution. Death in this electric chair, waiting. I pried my eyes from what was now an obscenity to me. I turned on my summer-white heels and fled—fled back to the mirage of a young man with a visage of life that said there was a future.

In this other world so temporary, two days passed untouched by time. Two days of talking with Mark, of being with Mark, the bars between us ceasing somehow to exist. I knew I was not to see him again, so impressed his image deeply in my brain, not to be forgotten—his height, as tall as Uncle John; his physique, strong and muscular; his eyes, sky-blue; and hair, burnished gold; the strong, handsome line of his manly face. Yes, not unlike Uncle John.

"I'll write to you, Anne." It was time to leave, never to return. Darkness was descending, the shadow hands of the clock now gone.

"Yes, Mark, you know you will be hearing from me." I felt his strong hands in mine.

The letters did come—each week upon week as summer grew into fall, letters that were tied with ribbons and laid to rest in a secret place. My free hours on Saturday found me with pen in hand, "Dear Mark . . ." Christmas came and went, and then it was the New Year, 1951. We both had our destinies. My plans were firmly formed for entering the convent the fall of that year. I was fulfilling a will higher than mine. In a way, it was not unlike Mark in saying, "Yes, Father, thy will be done," in walking down that corridor to his death.

"Dear Anne—the date is firmly set this time for January 23rd. There will be no stay of execution this time . . ."

And the letters came—each week. "I'm going to die, Anne. I try not to be afraid. I know the Lord will be with me . . . I am innocent, Anne. Pray for me—pray for me when you are a nun. I want—I *must* be strong."

"I will always pray for you, Mark—I will never forget you, Mark. I love—" *NO!* I put the pen down. *How can I speak of love!*

The days of January were gray and overcast, the mornings shrouded in dense fog. I too felt gray, my spirits dampened. I waited with Mark in some secret place, seeing the small room through glass and the chair, the straps hanging loosely, waiting.

January 23, 1951, 5:00 p.m., California time. Mark's last letter was in my hand. "I am ready, Anne, at peace. I want you to be also. Don't grieve for this end that is mine. Somehow it must be God's grand and loving plan for me."

Yes, Mark, I understand grand plans, God's love for us. But how does one not grieve?

And then the moment, the precise and terrible moment—the switch was pulled and I knew Mark was gone. Mark was dead. And I cried long, silent tears through the night and questioned such a plan that asked for such a beautiful life.

"Lord, I believe, help thou my unbelief."

There was one last letter from New Orleans, not written in what had become a familiar hand, but that of the prison chaplain. "Dear Anne—Mark went to his death and to his god with great courage. He asked me to give this to you." A lock of hair, auburn tinged with gold. I held it in my hands for a long time, remembering . . . visage of life . . . Mark. Then I placed the golden strands in my missal between the gilt-edged pages—and wept.

The missal containing the lock of hair was one of the last items to be placed in the black brass-trimmed trunk and checked off the list of required articles for my "trousseau." The trunk had stood obtrusively in the corner of the dining room for many months, a disturbing presence reminding us all of the journey I was about to take. Like an hourglass, it told the passage of time as it filled with the grains of sand of my future. A green leather sewing kit, one silver place setting, white towels, black oxford shoes, a small hand mirror, a wool hand-knit shawl, heavy flannel nightgowns, long black cotton hose, black floor-length petticoats, a set of meditation books, a copy of Thomas à Kempis's *Imitation of Christ*. The list went on and on as did the months. And then it was September, the fall of 1951. The waiting was over, the trunk now full, locked and labeled, ready to be shipped off to the Midwest.

Mother had tried to create a festive air that last morning at home. My favorite raspberry tarts grew cold on the good china plates. Untouched food. Unspoken words. Not unlike a death scene when only afterward one says, "If only . . . I wished I had said . . . Now it's too late." My father's place at the head of the table was empty. So too was my heart. *Who is dying?*

Father did show up at the Pasadena train station, eyes brimming with tears, one last hug, one last plea. "Anne, don't do this." If only . . . His words fell on steel. I had to steel myself against any last-minute weakening. *The Lord is my strength.* I heavily climbed the steps of the Santa Fe, turned to wave a final good-bye. As the train pulled away, the churning of the wheels seemed to grind my heart to powder in the most painful way. Slowly, my father, my mother, three sisters, and a brother, all faded into the distance and, with them, my life as I had known it.

Chapter 13

CONVENT LIFE

1951

September 8, the birthday of the Blessed Virgin Mary, and my entrance day into religious life. I stood on the front walk of the motherhouse, looking up into its massive redbrick structure four stories high. A cross on its pinnacle said this was *the house of the Lord*—and I had come home. My heart was full of joy in having *left all things to follow him*. Walking up the steps to the main entrance, I felt no cause for concern about living the celibate life. The child-bride symbolism of purity and mystical union had taken on a reality within me. I was innocent of what lay beneath the layers of conditioning that had yet to be exposed. For now, without any distractions, I could wholly focus on the things of the spirit. There would be no half measures.

The first six months of religious life was a period of probation called the postulancy. I was greeted by the postulant mistress, Sister Rose, who had the twinkle of Irish wit in her eyes and whose whole demeanor exuded warmth. She was well suited to the role of superior, helping the postulants to adapt to their new life. Though kind and understanding, she was stern and stood for no nonsense.

Sister Rose was entrusted with about sixty young women from all parts of the United States. We were a miniature melting pot of differences, brought together by reason of "vocation." This in itself was a broadening experience—socially and culturally. I was meeting girls who came from Iowa farms and towns in the deep, segregated South and as far away as New York City and Seattle. Much to my surprise, "California girls" were looked upon as a sophisticated breed of their own. One lone black woman was in our midst, which in the early '50s, raised an eyebrow or two. But all this was to change—and quickly. The *differences* would be wiped away like shells swept from the beach at high tide. Personal information was to be kept to ourselves, and we were discouraged from talking about our past. Our conversations related to the *here and now*, and our new experiences gave us plenty of material. And no matter our backgrounds, laughter was a common language.

Our uniform garb as postulants was a black ankle-length dress and a waist-length cape with a stiffly starched white collar. We styled our hair as we wished and wore a white net veil only for chapel. We addressed each other by our given names. I continued to be called Anne. Not until the probation period of six months was over would we receive the habit and religious name.

The vibrant energy of the body of postulants emboldened the one—we were our own support system. Our days were full from five in the morning until ten at night. The schedule was tightly structured and left no room for personal pursuits: daily Mass and meditation, college courses, daily instructions on religious life, domestic responsibilities, community meals and recreation, and above all, community prayer scheduled throughout the day. Early morning walks along the Mississippi River were required even in winter when the temperature would dip to twenty degrees below zero. For newly adapting Californians, it was anything but a leisurely stroll. We hurried along as if our lives depended on it—and maybe they did.

Gradually, we were introduced to the holy rule and customs of the order that were extensive and detailed in proscribing life as a nun. The sacred vows were the steadfast heart of religious life and required the highest level of conformity. Unquestioning *obedience* to our superiors was expected of us—blind obedience, as spiritual writers had coined such submission. Poverty meant we owned nothing personally and were required to ask for whatever was needed. Chastity went beyond the supreme sacrifice of marriage and family. Solid, wholesome friendships were to form over time, but we very quickly learned that there was a strict rule against intimate or exclusive relationships. We were to see Christ in each of our sisters and treat all with equal charity, not preferring or seeking the company of one over another. Hugs were to be reserved for special occasions, such as vow day or after a long absence. Confidences were also restricted. We were not to divulge interior trials to anyone but the superior or father confessor.

The rule of silence was first and foremost, basic to our everyday living in community and did not come easily. We enjoyed one hour of recreation after our noon meal and again in the evening. Solemn silence began after night prayers, and only the direst of circumstances allowed it to be broken. *Custody of the eyes* went against the grain in an even more unnatural way. The expression speaks for itself—*always in control*, eyes down except when necessary in performing a particular task.

The postulancy was a time to determine the authenticity of our vocation, and within weeks our numbers dwindled, but not by many. I felt very secure in my calling and never wavered in my commitment. I was not a model postulant, however. Perhaps the vow of chastity posed no problems, but the vow of obedience certainly challenged me to the core of my inner being. A postulant for only a few days, I wanted to know exactly how our goal of holiness was attained in religious life. On my way to the postulate for morning instructions, I stopped in the library and consulted a reference book on the subject. I just had time to read a short, and to-the-point, paragraph when the bell rang. I took my time finishing the passage and then proceeded at my newly acquired nun's pace to the postulate. Sister Rose was already expounding on the purpose of religious life and stopped midsentence as I crossed in front of her rostrum to get to my assigned place.

"You are late for instructions, Anne! You must learn to answer the bell *immediately*! Drop everything at the first sound. It is the voice of God! Remember that in the future." There was a sharp edge to her normally gentle voice.

"Yes, I'll do that, Sister Rose." I sat down and blushed, embarrassed to be singled out. Sister Rose continued with her lesson for the day. "Let me repeat the question. Does anyone know what holiness is?" Without hesitation, I raised my hand. She looked surprised that a new postulant would be so quick to volunteer such information. "Yes, Anne."

I stood up, feeling I would be vindicated for the public reprimand. "Holiness is union with God in love, Sister Rose."

Sister Rose now looked startled. "Where did you learn that?"

"A book called *The Spiritual Life* by Tanquerey, Sister Rose. I found it in the library—just now." Sister Rose seemed disturbed, and I received no great praise. The answer, of course, was correct, and I was to learn that Tanquerey was a spiritual master and his book required reading. At this point, however, our postulant mistress truly wanted to know what our thoughts were on *holiness*, not hear some quote from a book, especially one *picked up on the run*.

My intent had been well-meaning—I was just in a hurry. I'd take any short cut to holiness I could find. I had my own approach that, to me, seemed the commonsense way. I was assigned to do dishes one morning but left the task to go to the chapel. It was deserted that hour of the morning, and the intense quiet with no distractions made it so easy to pray. And I was lost in contemplation—but not for long, as Sister Rose was in close pursuit and quick to give me a lecture on religious obedience.

That I had disobeyed had not occurred to me. After all, I was here to lead a spiritual life. What did dishes have to do with that? I had certainly done plenty of that at home! I was open, however, and wanted to learn, and after that, stayed with the dishes. Carryover, however, was poor. One day when I should have been in chapel for prayer, I failed to appear. Sister Rose's search ended in the convent cemetery, where I was praying at the tomb of our Mother Foundress, a young woman of courage and vision from Ireland. Identifying with her love of solitude and prayer, she was a great inspiration to me. That day, I was quite homesick and turned to her as a source of consolation—*obedience* obviously not a concern.

"Anne," Sister Rose's lecture began, "you must understand the conformity required by religious life. You just don't do what you want to do!" This was the most difficult lesson of all for me to learn. Obedience tried my soul, especially blind obedience. I always wanted to know *why*. It would take a lifetime to learn the spirit of the vow: *surrender*. The superior's voice was the voice of God. A nun responded immediately and without question. I learned rather quickly that in the matter of spiritual growth, there were no shortcuts.

I was at peace and joyful during the six months probation as a postulant and moved on a straight line to my goal of reception into religious life. I had yet to know the torments of doubt and temptation. It was with peace as quiet and gentle as the spring snow outside our windows that I knelt in the chapel and asked for the *holy habit of the community and the charity of my sisters in religion*. A veil, white as the newly fallen snow, now distinguished me as a novice; and *I was no longer Anne*—but Sister Francis.

What answer would I give Sister Rose now as to the nature of *holiness?* Seven years later, confined to a hospital bed, it would not be so glib, a quote from a book. It was interesting to observe how well I had learned religious life that even in these circumstances, superiors and fellow religious believed in my vocation. They even spoke of my potential within the order in the years ahead. They *saw something* in me. But w*hat?* A heaviness came over me, and I picked up a book to read for distraction, though it was difficult to concentrate. Memories of those early years of religious life kept intruding, unearthing deep emotions. I felt so strongly a familiar loneliness, the missing of my mother, that took me back to the novitiate one late October night.

"Jesus, Mary, and Joseph, may I breathe forth my soul in peace with you. Amen." Night prayers were over. The chapel lights dimmed as I made my way down the narrow aisle, pausing at the statue of the Sacred Heart of Jesus. His arms were outstretched, reaching to me, his heart ablaze with the fires of love. I responded, *One day I will be your bride.* An internal prayer in keeping with the silence of the night, solemn silence, when only the gravest of emergencies allowed for the spoken word or unnecessary gesture. I made my way down the long hardwood corridor, with its enormously high ceiling, leading to the dormitories. The antique grandfather clock was a ponderous presence at the head of the stairs, its chiming of the quarter hours sending great gulps of sound down the cavernous stairwell, reverberating to all corners of the novitiate. I noted it was 9:00 p.m., the hour for retiring, from which we rarely deviated.

My assigned sleeping area was in one of the dorms to the front of the building, a desirable location with its sweeping view of the Mississippi River and the green hills beyond. All the dorms were alike, however, with the same bare floors, high white walls, and shuttered windows with wide, deep sills. There were eight single beds with small commodes upon which set identical washbasins and, at the foot of the beds, identical straight-back chairs. The beds were lined up four against each wall, forming a center aisle. Muslin curtains, yellow white, could be pulled around the allotted spaces at night for a semblance of privacy and aloneness. I approached my alcove, as these spaces were called, and pulled the curtain, the scraping sound of the rings against the rods magnified in the heavy night silence. I undressed, taking care not to expose my body, concealing its nakedness from my own eyes. Pulling the voluminous white flannel nightgown over my head, I let it fall about me as a tent before removing any clothing. Then the long trek down the hall on slippered feet, balancing the basin of water and back again, looking neither left nor right, eyes downcast "in custody." I fell into bed with exhaustion, took a deep breath, trying to let go of the tension and fatigue of the long day.

The day had begun at 5:00 a.m., as it did every day, with the sounding of the rising bell. No private moments to enjoy the waking to consciousness, but an immediate bounding out of bed with the prayer on our lips, "I rise from this bed of sleep in the name of our Lord Jesus Christ crucified. May I rise on the last day to everlasting happiness." For now, I could rest, could sleep. As the clock struck nine thirty, the lights went out and darkness descended. But sleep did not. I pulled the blankets about me against the coolness of the late October night and clutched my rosary.

It was a little more than a year now since I had left my family and home to begin this new life. The lush green of the Midwest had given way to the vibrant colors of the autumn, which was a new experience for me. I was enthralled with its beauty of transformation, knowing that I was changing, going through my own internal seasons. My emotions seemed as variable and transient as the falling leaves. There was a familiarity and warmth about the novitiate, which were comfortable and consoling. There was also a strangeness and coldness, which were chafing and forbidding. This dissonance reflected the polarity within of the ever-present conflict over my vocation.

"Our Father . . ." I prayed the rosary, sleep evading me. I could hear the novices growing quiet, their breathing becoming deep and regular. I stifled a sob. Several hundred nuns were sleeping under this gabled convent roof, and I was lonely. So lonely. It settled like a cold stone slab on my heart. *No, Anne, don't feel it. You've no reason to be lonely. God is with you, Anne.* But the quiet, silent tears came. Crying without sound was always my way, even as a child, especially as a child, on my mother's lap, listening to her words. "Oh, little Anne, you are so beautiful when you cry that way. There now, don't make any sound." She had taught me well. *Mother . . . Mother . . . I miss you so, Mother. I miss Dad too, all the family, but especially you, Mother. We always had such fun together, Mother, with our private jokes and laughter, our long talks into the night, and our secrets . . . We were so close, Mother—no, we* are *close, Mother . . . so close.* The cold stone on my heart lifted and there was a surge of warmth. The tears no longer flowed. *I am coming to you, Mother. I know how much you miss me, Mother. Oh, Mother, I'm sorry.*

The warmth became a swirling internal mass, then growing hot, the motion accelerating until I became a glowing ball of spiraling fire and the curtained alcove dissolved. I was spirited through space, traveling at a great speed, moving faster . . . faster. *I am here, Mother, here with you, Mother . . . I'll never leave you, Mother . . . never really leave you, Mother.* I stood at the foot of her bed in some spirit form, smiling, and reached toward my mother there in the familiar wide bed. My beautiful, loving mother. She raised her head from the pillow, seeing me with some other eyes, unquestioning of my spirit presence, a presence I could not long sustain. Her visage faded and the alcove closed in with its yellow-white curtains. The fiery heat subsided until the cold slab of loneliness, though now assuaged by the extraordinary experience, closed about my heart once again—and I slept, nurtured by my mother once again. *My mother. She will always be my mother.*

The following week, Sister Janine, the novice mistress, called me into her office. It was an airy large room, and the morning sun highlighted the polished floor. I looked beyond her austere figure to the windows framing autumn leaves of fiery reds and burnished gold. *How I wish I could be out there running and feel the wind in my hair!* Her voice intruded on my reverie, "Anne, you have a letter from your mother—it arrived yesterday." I was immediately at attention. The novice mistress had the right to censor the mail, to protect us from "worldliness" or the unexpected advent of bad news. I immediately knew. It was neither one nor the other. *Do I also need to be protected from unworldliness?* I smiled, rather a sardonic smile. Sister Janine continued, "Your mother refers to some rather extraordinary experience she had—she says . . ." and Sister Janine's voice faltered, as though she feared opening a door. "She says you visited her one night . . ." Her voice trailed off, but her eyes continued to speak, dark, piercing, reaching into my soul. "What about this, Anne? Do you know?"

My response came slowly, weighing the impact of my words, wondering how many to let loose. "Yes, I know, Sister Janine. May I please have the letter?" My gaze held hers. Reluctantly, she placed the white envelope with its familiar script in my outstretched hand. Pulling the cloak of silence about me, I said no more, and she had the grace to honor my privacy.

My inner voice was strong, vibrant, clear. *Nothing, no one, can really keep us apart, Mother . . . nothing . . . no one . . . We are that close, Mother . . . inseparable . . . Mother.*

Years later, my mother was reaching for me here in the hospital, but this time through a more natural or normal channel—the telephone. "Your mother . . ." Dr. Berry, on his morning rounds, was leaning over me, calling me out of a deep sleep. "Sister Francis! Your mother called. I just talked to her, and she sounded very anxious about you."

Mother! "Yes, I'm sure she is, Doctor." *I know you are worried, Mother.* There was still another wavelength of communication between us that didn't require a phone line.

"I'm glad I had some good news to give her. The tests show you are much improved! I think we can project your discharge for the end of the week—that is, if all goes well. I warn you, though, there's going to be a considerable time of convalescence." He smiled, quite pleased with his report.

All did go well, but still the slightest exertion left me limp and exhausted. After six long weeks, I said good-bye to the medical staff I had come to know so well and went home to my community.

Chapter 14

CHOICE POINT

1959

My sisters greeted me warmly, even Sister Maura, who was ready with a glass of eggnog. Sister Ambrose opened her arms to me and cried, "Doll! How great to have you back!" Her hugs were as big as her heart. "Doll" was how she addressed everyone, not just the little ones who passed through her classroom over the years, but also the delivery boys who came to the door as well. She had been a nun for over fifty years, and the aura about her made her seem bigger than life, some living proof that holiness did indeed exist. She was greatly loved. Now she took my arm and, in a soothing voice, said, "Here, Doll, lean on me."

Arm in arm, we walked down the long hallway, Sister Therese, our superior, leading the way. Much to my surprise, she stopped at the corner bedroom at the end of the hallway instead of starting up the stairs to the second floor. "Oh, you've moved me downstairs, Sister! Thank you. It will make it easier for me." I also knew it would make it easier for the tray-bearing nuns.

The room was in readiness for me, and I was touched by the thoughtfulness of my sisters. There was an arrangement of lilacs and tulips on the small desk. The white muslin sheets were turned down, and a water jug was on the nightstand. A sizable armchair set in the corner opposite the desk, an afghan draped over it. This digression in custom for my comfort, I knew, was the kindly touch of Sister Therese for the long period of convalescence ahead.

I entered my new room gladly and sat on the bed, eager to be alone and quiet. Already I was feeling a jolt to my system with the abrupt change in environment. There had been a security in the hospital routine, and I was feeling a certain anxiety of withdrawal. Soon the sisters left me, realizing I needed to rest. Instinctively, I looked out the small lace-framed window to look at my elm tree, and it was a comforting presence. Instead of seeing its leafy top branches as I had before from the second floor, my view now was of the tree's lower limbs, sturdy trunk reaching down into twisted roots. *Perhaps the elm is speaking to me*, I mused. I must reach to the roots of my being for answers to questions that need to be asked, no matter how *twisted* they might be. I felt the major illness I was going through was somehow part of the soul-disturbing premonition I had experienced some months earlier on the school playground. Part, but not all. I would have to wait and see just what was to come.

The days were getting longer, and the high humidity made the heat of the summer days even more uncomfortable. Toward evening, the elm was casting long shadows on my bedroom walls and a cooler breeze was flowing through the open window. It had been an exhausting day. I fell into a sound sleep. I would deal with the questions tomorrow.

Tomorrow inevitably came and all the succeeding days. One melded into another with the monotony of convalescence. I devoured whole sets of books from our convent library—the complete works of Edgar Allan Poe, Sir Arthur Conan Doyle, Tolstoy, Dostoyevsky, to name a few, and always the lives of the saints—Catherine of Sienna, Francis of Assisi, Teresa of Avila, the Little Flower, and more. They peopled my days and my nights, filling the small bedroom and my solitude with their spirit presence.

And I began to draw, reviving a hobby of my childhood. I discovered the medium of charcoal, and my hand followed the imagined lines on the rough white paper with bold black strokes, and they too became people—faces of all shapes and visages but always dark, brooding. Landscapes of the soul. Once the lines took the shape of my own face, a self-portrait in the religious habit, ideal for a study in black-and-white. When I saw that landscape, with its sharply defined angular lines, sunken cheeks, arched brows, and black-rimmed, black-welled eyes staring back at me, I destroyed it. *No, this is not me!*

Long since, it had been decided that I would not return to the motherhouse in Iowa, as was customary, for the period of intense preparation for final vows. My state of ill health would simply not allow it. I had not even the desire to do so as I could not face the energy of the young nuns and the vastness of the institutional complex. So it was with relief that I remained where I was. Sister Therese was aware of my conflict, knew me well, and could wisely counsel me.

Sister Georgina, the regional superior of the Midwest convents, would come to interrogate me and determine if I was a suitable candidate for final vows. She was aware of my interior struggles and had counseled me many times over the years. I sensed she was a person who would listen to me without judgment while holding to her own, strong principles and perceptive insights. There was a wholesome earthiness about her that made her comfortable to be with, like an *old shoe*. Common sense was high in her hierarchy of virtues. She would encourage me, "Pick yourself up by your bootstraps, Francis! You think too much! Study Spanish!" Her words fell on rocky ground, never to grow into any harvest of healing.

Through letters and periodic visits, Sister Georgina had seen me through a crucial period, the years of my first assignment on the missions in Southern California. After two years of teaching about seventy second-graders, I had felt totally depleted. Externals were deceiving. It wasn't the teaching of a large class, which wasn't unusual in the fifties, but the internal struggle that had sapped my strength and energy. I loved teaching from the very beginning; I felt born to it. The making of first vows had only temporarily assuaged my conflict over religious life. I could not maintain inner calm and one-mindedness in my dedication. There was a deep inner pull, that *no* that plagued my existence and drained me of vitality.

Finally, Sister Georgina had called me back to her main headquarters in Chicago to make a personal evaluation. I had expected some sort of recovery period, a time to renew myself in body and spirit. Instead, I was assigned to a large Chicago convent and a second-grade classroom. No doubt it was believed I simply needed less time to brood, to think upon the conflict within. I had not made myself heard. For the first and only time in my religious life, I had stood before my superior and said, "No, Sister Georgina, I cannot take this assignment." It wasn't a position of defiance, but rather a desperate cry for help.

My superior finally heard my cry for what it was and reached out to me. "Yes, Francis, I can see you're not up to teaching right now. I'll find a replacement for you." And then she opened doors that no one had dared. It was as though she had pulled back heavy curtains and let in sunshine. "Francis, I think you should go home. Leave the order—you are still under temporary vows. In fact, I've already talked to your mother. She wants you back—the whole family will welcome you."

My eyes could not take the bright light. No one had ever voiced *another way* before. When faced with the reality of setting the habit aside and all it symbolized, fear surpassed fear. "I can't do that! I do have a vocation!" This other voice heightened the conflict; it forced me to deal with realities. I had a choice. The toll my indecisiveness of such long duration had taken on me physically had to be recognized. I did not return home. Arrangements were made for me to go to a sanitarium on the outskirts of Chicago.

Though I was one of many patients in the sanitarium, I felt very much alone. I had a private room, ate at a table for one in the dining room, and did not interact with anyone. I would thrive on the solitude of this new situation. The setting of the sanitarium resembled that of a country club with its rolling green lawns, manicured hedges, and well-tended flower gardens. It was comfortably and tastefully furnished throughout. For several weeks my only focus and responsibility was my personal well-being. I slept around-the-clock, ate well, and took long walks on the grounds. It was my first time to be away from the order and free of community living. It was healing.

After long hours of prayer and meditation, no resolution of my conflict was found. I decided to go on, however, to continue my quest and remain in the order. I would live with the conflict, at least for now, believing the answers would come in time. I chose not to go through the door that Sister Georgina had opened for me and return to the world. Instead, I accepted an assignment to the Milwaukee convent of antiques and harsh winters, the place of premonition.

Chapter 15

VOWS FOREVER

1959

I was now at a crossroads on my spiritual path as a nun. Once again, Sister Georgina was weighing in the balance a decision that would determine my fate. She would interrogate me, asking questions that would go to the heart of religious life; I would have the opportunity to express my torment and my desire to do *God's will.* I knew it would be a critical interview and I would have to be ready to declare myself one way or the other.

I waited for Sister Georgina in my room, thinking of the storm the previous night. It had been a typical summer display in the Midwest of lightning and thunder and a torrential downpour. I had watched the leaves of the elm dance eerily in the stagelike light of the schoolyard. It had fit my mood of apprehension. I did not really know what the next day would bring. Most of the night was spent in prayer, asking the guidance of the Holy Spirit, the help of the Virgin Mary and my companionable saints.

I thought of Grandmother and prayed to her as well, believing she was now among those holy souls. The reality of her death had come as a shock to me when I was a novice. The novice mistress had called me into her office at a strange hour, just as I was going down the hallway to the chapel for morning Mass.

"You've received a telegram, Anne—from your mother." Sister Janine paused as though looking for some right words and reached out and took my hand. *Grammie!* A pall came over my heart. "Anne, your grandmother has died. I'm so sorry, Anne. I know you were very close to her."

Grammie is dead! "Grandmother died a long time ago, Sister Janine. I watched while she died one night . . . but still . . ." My voice faltered, broke, in the realization of some door being closed. Of some lost memories . . . of a time so long ago. *Here, little Anne, hold the pencil this way . . . Sit still while I curl your hair . . . Let's go shopping, Anne . . . Practice the piano every day, Anne, I'll help you . . . Jesus loves you, little Anne.*

I carried the memories of Grandmother to the chapel with me as treasures in my heart. *Alone.* I was alone with my grief and took solace in the Mass. "*Introibo ad altare Dei. Ad* Deum qui laetificat juventutem meam." *I will go in unto the altar of God. Unto God who gives joy to my youth . . . joy to my youth . . . thank you, Grandmother, for the joy you gave to my youth.*

Grandmother had died alone, when no one was watching, no one there to hold her hand. *Anne, your arms are outstretched . . . You will suffer . . . help priests.* I reached for the crucifix hanging at my side. *Yes, Grandmother, I've not forgotten.* "Requiem aeternam." *Sleep in peace, Grandmother.* On her mystic presence, I traced the letters I-N-R-I. Behind the veiled hood of my *coffin, unseen,* I cried silent tears.

I was jolted back to the present by a firm knock on the door heralding the arrival of Sister Georgina. It was time. *Please help me now, Grandmother. Help me to find the words.* I felt energized, mobilized for the moment. She strode in with a confidence suitable to her position and greeted me warmly. She was not a demonstrative person, but on this occasion, she gave me a hug before settling down in the big chair next to my bed. In her matter-of-fact way, she quickly got down to business. She inquired as to my physical progress and easily moved on to matters pertaining to the spiritual life. It was her place to question; she needed to know the state of my soul. She would make a judgment as to my candidacy for final vows.

Through the long night, I had brought my divergent thoughts into some sort of intelligible position regarding my future. I answered with simplicity and directness, which was my way, yet with great difficulty. She knew of my past conflict, and I could not gloss over the duality that was always with me. Then I shared with her the position that was mine at that point regarding my vocation, risking whatever response she might have.

When I stepped back and, as objectively as possible, looked at my life as a nun, it was indeed very positive. The life of prayer and service was always attractive to me. I wanted to serve God and his children. There was no question I excelled as a teacher and loved this ministry of the order. I believed I fit in very well in the community and treasured my friendships with fellow religious. Above all, I had a deep desire to grow in the things of the spirit. Intellectually, I recognized I had a vocation. I had been *called.*

In addition, the fact that my illness had been diagnosed as organic disease took it out of a psychological realm that could have threatened my suitability. I could find no reason to leave the order. All spiritual advisors whom I consulted agreed. I could go on at great length about why I should be a nun. On the balance sheet, there was little to say on the negative side.

"Sister Georgina, I don't understand it. I can't explain it. I can't seem to get a hold of it really. There's just this resistance deep down inside me. It's nameless. I can't intellectualize it. It simply says *no.* It must be a temptation, a test. It proves that I have every reason to be a nun. I want to do God's will. I ask your blessing." As the words flowed out so did a long held tension.

The kindly eyes of my superior looked deeply into mine, reading the spirit of my words before speaking. "Sister Francis, I've conferred with your superior, Sister Therese, and she wholly supports you in making final vows. She tells me you are an exemplary nun. Sister Ambrose agrees, and she has seen many sisters come and go in the order. This period of temporary vows is a time of trial, and you are free to leave, but if you want to continue in this life, you have my blessing. I will not stop you."

Perpetual vow day, final profession, was now less than two weeks away. I had made a decision. I had set my course. There was to be no looking back. Only forward. Anytime I felt any resistance, even faintly heard a dissenting voice within, I firmly pushed it into some dark recess that extinguished its existence until it was heard no more. When the most important day of my life finally came, I was ready.

The sun shone with unusual brilliance and darkness was no more. It was July 16, 1959, the feast of Our Lady of Mount Carmel. I was twenty-seven years old. Leaving my sickbed, I knelt in the sanctuary of the small chapel with my sisters as witnesses and unequivocally dedicated my life to God. There were long-stemmed red roses on the altar, which was adorned with the finest linens. The spirit was one of solemnity and festivity. In a strong voice, I unreservedly made my final vows.

"I, Sister Mary Francis, vow to thee poverty, chastity, and
obedience forever according to the holy rule of the Sisters
of Charity. I ask thy love and thy grace that I may be faithful

to these vows on earth so that one day I may see thee, praise thee, and love thee forever in heaven through Jesus Christ, our Lord. Amen."

"Forever, forever, forever" reverberated through my entire being. My heart swelled with the triumphant music of the "Te Deum" coming from the antique organ. The voices of my sisters were raised in song praising the Lord—and mine along with them. It was finished.

That night, there was no storm. The air was heavy and still. The leaves of the elm no longer danced but hung motionless, silent, waiting.

chapter 16

THE STRUGGLE

1963

I was early for recreation and sat in the community room, looking out at the courtyard. It was spring, and the grass was a rich green. The well-tended roses were in full bloom, and their fragrance wafted through the open windows. *How different this place is!* I was now assigned to a convent in the hills of suburban Los Angeles, where the people we served were accustomed to luxury and abundance. As a community, we lacked nothing, enjoying the contemporary, comfortable furnishings of a modern convent. Personally, however, we practiced the vow of poverty, owning nothing and asking the superior for whatever was needed. Our guideline for acquiring personal items was "Is it necessary?" The contrast to my last mission in Milwaukee reminded me of the thread of continuity in our lives as religious and members of a community. No matter where we served, we were *one* in living the vows and rules of our order. Externals changed; the essence of religious life did not.

I remembered the old convent I had so loved and continued to miss. Since the episode of rheumatic fever, I had never sufficiently regained my health to go back to teaching. Finally, the doctor advised that I be sent to California in the hope that the milder climate, and one I was accustomed to, would end the chronic strep throats that plagued me. After six years in a place that would always hold special meaning in my life, I had tearfully parted from my sisters. As I walked out the door for the last time, I glanced lovingly at my elm and remembered its seasons. It felt like winter in my soul but I had to believe it would lead to a season of new life.

The chiming of the mantel clock brought me out of my reverie. While saying the clock prayer silently, I could hear the footsteps of the nuns on the hardwood floors approaching the community room from various parts of the two-story convent. Like the convent itself, this was quite a different group from the last. Now I was no longer the only young nun, but one of four. We were all in our twenties, and there was a spirit of camaraderie among us. We accounted for 50 percent of the small community, and our youthful joy of life and enthusiasm had an impact. It was a lighthearted household, more relaxed and casual, but no less devout, with strict adherence to the holy rule. It reflected the more liberal, broader culture of Southern California, which had always seemed to be less restrictive than the Midwest.

This was Saturday night, and out came the deck of cards! For an hour or more, we'd nibble on chocolates and try to outwit one another amidst friendly gibes and laughter. The superior, Sister Martha, enjoyed such things as much as we did and entered into the spirit of fun. Unusually sensitive and perceptive, she warmly but firmly guided the small community and was admired and loved.

Sister Martha and I were slowly becoming good friends. She did not make it easy for me to ask for dispensations from the rule, but when of necessity I approached her, she was kind and understanding. It seemed I was asking more and more as time went on. Restored somewhat by the change in climate, I had been assigned to an eighth-grade homeroom and had been teaching now for nearly seven months. I had a free period at midday so I could return to the convent and rest. It was never enough. *If I can just get through June, see my students graduate, then I'll have the summer to rest!* I was vulnerable to spring as that was the time of year for colds and sore throats and low energy, even in sunny California. The low energy was always with me, and everything was an effort. *Has nothing changed?*

Recreation over, I climbed the stairs to my second-floor bedroom, pausing on the landing to catch my breath. At the top of the stairs was a porch, and I went through the screen door to look at the star-studded sky. The San Gabriel Mountains were etched in the moonlight. I breathed deeply and sank down on the lounge that my father had given to me. He wanted to do something to make my life easier, and Sister Martha had approved, in light of my ill health.

I thought of my father and how he had changed. For two years after I left home, his passive resistance to my vocation had persisted. The only letter I received from him was during the postulancy—just a few weeks after my entrance into the order. He said he loved me and wanted me to come home; the doors were always open. I never answered that letter. My mother had to bear his silence in my regard and could not speak of me to him. I wrote home once a month according to custom, but he refused to read my letters.

When two years had passed, Father decided to see for himself what this convent life was all about and if I was happy. In the heat of the summer, he and my mother made the long trip from California to the motherhouse in the Midwest. He was impressed with the strong, spiritually rooted women who were my superiors, and there was no denying my happiness at the time. The doors of communication were opened. We were father and daughter once again. Now, his solicitude was for my health rather than my soul.

I smiled, thinking of the burden that had been unexpectedly lifted from me. There was a chill in the air; I had sat on the lounge longer than I realized. I wearily got up and headed down the hall to my room. Tomorrow was Sunday, and I looked forward to an extra hour of sleep in the morning. Rather than five o'clock, the rising bell would sound at six.

We chanted the Little Office of the Blessed Virgin Mary on Sunday mornings: Prime, Terce, Sext, and None. Gregorian chant filled the small chapel as we sang the Latin liturgical verses. The thread of our religious life extended beyond the boundaries of this century to medieval times. *Quia tu es, Deus, fortitudo mea . . . For thou, O God, art my strength.* The psalms were a source of great comfort to me. Their words expressed what I could not. The spiritual life, the interior life, continued to be the hub of my existence. One thing had changed. I never questioned my vocation anymore. Not since that day I had said the word *forever.* A door had been closed and I had gone on, not looking back. What had not changed was my ill health. I lived on a strength that was not mine. *For thou, O God, art my strength.*

"*Benedicamus domino . . . Deo gratias.*" *Let us bless the Lord. Thanks be to God.* The chanting of None ended. I genuflected and walked down the chapel aisle, through the double french doors, and out into the garden. The smell of freshly cut green grass was a luxury after so many years of concrete in the inner city of Milwaukee. I wanted nothing more than to walk and feel the cushioned grass under my feet and breathe the rose-scented air, but I could not. For some reason, it was becoming increasingly difficult for me to stand for even brief periods of time. A great pressure weighed on my chest, making it hard to breathe; and I felt cold and faint, often on the verge of collapse. It was all I could do to move from one chair to another. I sat on the swing on the patio, which gave me a view of the San Gabriel Mountains, a lovely spot to do spiritual reading, which was required for thirty minutes each day. I was reading *Contemplation in Action*, a classic on the spiritual life by Pierre de Caussade, a seventeenth-century Jesuit priest. He taught that life itself is a prayer, that we *all* are called to contemplation and mystical union with God, no matter how active our life may be, for he is to be found in the very activity itself. It had been a difficult concept for me as I was drawn to the contemplative rather than the active side of religious life and had not solved this duality within myself. Today I was having a hard time keeping my mind on what I was reading as I was too distressed by what was happening to me physically. *What is wrong with me? Why can't I stand up and be on my feet?* And I didn't know how to communicate what I was feeling, even to my doctor.

Change of location had meant a stressful change of doctors. I was now under the care of Dr. Richard Lindsey, an internist. He was a member of the Episcopal Church and had great respect for nuns, considering it an honor to have them in his care. I felt an instant rapport with this dedicated and competent physician. His expertise in medicine was matched by his humanity and compassion. An appointment with Dr. Lindsey was scheduled for the next day, and that too was a distraction from my spiritual reading. Dr. Lindsey's inability to make a diagnosis was obviously of great concern to him. My condition remained a mystery and was so debilitating that I could no longer function normally. The mystery weighed on my soul and oppressed my spirit. I could only cry in the night and wait. Deep within myself, I knew that one day someone would come to me—someone who could help me. I did not know when. This conviction was intuitive and inexplicable—and I held on to it.

My teaching career was over, and I had lost hope of ever returning to a classroom. I did not live the community life, becoming more and more of a recluse. As time wore on, I was confined to my room, to my bed. It was becoming my only safe refuge—refuge from a state of collapse, which embarrassed me, humiliated me before others. Always, it hovered over me; and I had grown to fear its occurrence, which invariably happened if I remained on my feet more than a few moments. And when it did, I would gradually slip into unconsciousness, a fog enveloping me. In this place of Nothing, I couldn't think, I couldn't feel.

I continued to be under the care of Dr. Lindsey, and I considered this a blessing and a comfort in my life. There were many hospitalizations, but one in the fall of the year was to dramatically change my life. I was in a private room just beyond the double doors of the main entrance, and it felt less *sterile* than other hospital rooms I had experienced. The windows faced east, giving me a view of the San Gabriel Mountains, its pines at the ridge clearly etched against the sky. The view was a comforting presence throughout my stay. Those who cared for me were sensitive and compassionate, doing whatever they could to make my suffering more tolerable. I felt a tremendous support system in the doctors, the nurses, and of course, my community. A sign hung on my door, saying, "No Visitors," and this was honored with the exception of my superior, Sister Martha, and occasionally, members of my family.

The night that would prove to be pivotal to my future was as usual with its unique sounds and rituals of a hospital. I could hear the water cart being pulled down the hallway and the nurses passing out the night medications. Gradually, lights would be dimmed and silence would descend. The night had its own peace. It also had its own torment when one was alone and hurting and couldn't escape the descent of ghostly fears. Fitful sleep would eventually come out of sheer exhaustion.

It was still dark outside my window when I was awakened by a slight touch on my shoulder. I heard a deep but gentle voice apologizing for waking me at such an early hour. It was five o'clock in the morning. Even the hospital had not emerged from its night. It was hard coming out of a deep sleep, and I opened my eyes with difficulty. There, sitting next to my bed, was a large man with a shock of white hair, whom I judged to be in his seventies. He wore a dark business suit, and his bearing was one of great dignity. He introduced himself modestly as Dr. Griffith, saying, "Dr. Lindsey has asked me to take a look at you, Sister." I was to learn that he was the renowned Dr. George Griffith, an internationally recognized authority on rheumatic fever and heart disease. He was considered an educator as well as a much-sought-after practitioner and consultant. He knew my history of rheumatic fever and heart disease and was familiar with my current medical records. He asked a few questions, listened to my heart, and took my blood pressure. Then he asked me to do a simple thing—stand up. I did so, and immediately the state of collapse came over me, the place of fog, the unknown . . . Nothing. I vaguely was aware of the blood pressure cuff on my arm and then gentle hands guiding me back down into the bed. It was a few minutes before his visage came into focus. Then that gentle voice that had an authoritative ring to it said, "I think I know what's causing your symptoms, Sister Francis. Your vasomotor system is very unstable! When you stand up, your blood pressure drops significantly and your heart rate jumps. Blood pools to your extremities instead of returning to your heart as it should, depriving the brain of oxygen." Assuring me that he would be talking with Dr. Lindsey, he left the room as quietly as he had come.

The intervention in the early morning had not been a dream. Dr. Lindsey came in around seven o'clock, chuckling to himself. Evidently, the great Dr. Griffith had come and gone like a thief in the night, the only evidence being his entry on my chart. The hospital staff was quite put out to have missed the opportunity of giving this admirable man and doctor the usual VIP treatment.

"It seems we now know why you can't stay on your feet, Sister Francis!" This condition is called postural hypotension and is rarely seen to this degree of severity. We'll have to determine the cause, but at least we have something to go on now. I'll talk to Dr. Griffith and see what he advises." Dr. Lindsey took my hand and smiled, genuinely pleased at the turn of events.

This was a tremendous relief to me as well—the knowing. Now I knew the nature of that *place of Nothing*, the world of fog. I was very grateful that the gray-haired physician of the night had been called in on my case. Little did I know that he would come to be known as *America's beloved clinician.*

My hospital stay grew into six long weeks. Though convinced of organic disease, the exact nature of what was causing my condition could not be determined. Penicillin, which I had been taking for years, was discontinued; and a steroid drug, prednisone, was prescribed. I was told I would have to face an "indefinite period of disability." *Indefinite.*

Arrangements were made for me to be transferred back to the Midwest, where I would be admitted to the order's infirmary, a small hospital and retirement facility adjacent to the novitiate. I said good-bye to my family, my sisters, and my friend, Dr. Lindsey—to all I had known and loved. The familiar *leaving all things* once again. Dressed in my religious habit, I was wheeled on a gurney through Los Angeles International Airport to board a flight for what seemed like my final *Journey*. It was October 1963. I had just celebrated my thirty-first birthday.

Chapter 15

MEANDERING PATH

1963

Death was commonplace in the infirmary. Elderly sisters, no longer able to maintain their independence, went there for that purpose—to die. Now I was to be a member of this community. It was a late November day in 1963 when the ambulance sped down the narrow road along the Mississippi River. Fall had stripped the once-lush Iowa trees of their leaves, and their starkness reflected my despondency. There was such a finality in my destination. The infirmary was located on the river bluff adjacent to the novitiate where I had entered religious life twelve years before. Never would I have imagined I would return so soon and in such a state. It would be my home for the next two uninterrupted, uneventful years. My assigned room was in the original wing of the infirmary with high ceilings, deep oak sills, dark wood wainscoting, and green linoleum floors worn thin over many years. One tall, narrow window threw a shaft of sunlight across the room in the late afternoon, but otherwise it tended to be dark. In the corner by the window was an upholstered armchair where I could sit up for short periods of time and look out at the vista of cornfields stretching to the rolling green hills beyond.

The only time I was to leave the infirmary would be to go to the local and better equipped hospital to visit a friend, Sister Margaret. She was the only nun in the infirmary near me in age—and she was dying. Death was a joyous occasion in the infirmary, as the elderly and infirmed were released from the trials and sufferings of this world and would finally enjoy the rewards so well earned in religious life. But death is death and a holy death is no less. It was hard to watch my friend, Sister Margaret, grow weaker and sicker as fall grew into spring and spring into summer. I saw no joy in her eyes but only wells of sadness and pain. She died, not yet thirty, in a losing battle with leukemia. I envied her. I grew to envy the dying. I wanted release.

Days melded into days again and months into months. I played a new role on the stage of life and played it well. I was now an invalid, dependent on a wheelchair and the charity and kindness of others. I loathed it but conducted myself as was expected of a nun—with fortitude and resignation. As I had been exemplary in living the rule, so was I now in my limitations. I bore what was *my cross* in silence and was not known to complain. It had become a way of life.

The change of seasons marked the passage of time, and it was my second spring at the infirmary. Within, I still felt the chill of winter yet sensed a season was indeed passing. The next day, I was to be transported by ambulance to the prestigious Mayo Clinic in Rochester, Minnesota. It would be a five—to six-hour trip, and a sister companion would accompany me. After two more years, with little change in my condition, it was time for more investigative studies. I strongly resisted my doctor's decision, but thought perhaps, perhaps I could be helped. I looked to the green hills and prayed for fulfillment of hope, an internal spring.

The Mayo Clinic, the most-advanced medical facility in the nation and internationally recognized, exists for the purpose of research and education as well as healing. It is a city unto itself with hallways as long as city blocks, populated by individuals from all cultures and social strata united in catastrophic disease. I saw what destruction such diseases wrought on the human body. This I envied not but wished there were some external validation of my suffering. Other than loss of weight, pallor, and a "moon face" due to medication, my body remained untouched.

I was assigned to a staff cardiologist, Dr. Martin. When he made his morning rounds, he was surrounded by an entourage of student doctors called fellows, sometimes as many as ten. It was especially trying to be under the scrutiny of so many probing eyes. I had been subjected to tests that had become routine for me and to tests wholly experimental—offered only by the Mayo Clinic. And to what avail? After two weeks of testing and psychological evaluation, I was to be released—released with no findings of organic disease, though the condition of postural hypotension was confirmed. I felt like a rubber ball bouncing off the walls of medical opinions. There was not to be any relief from my suffering—not even an explanation. Once again, the medical world had nothing to offer me.

The drug prednisone, which had relieved the symptoms of fever and pain, was discontinued as there were signs of potentially serious side effects. The "moon face" appearance, caused by this drug, gradually diminished; and I looked like myself again. A small exchange—my crutch of medication was withdrawn, my facade of organic disease destroyed. I felt exposed, vulnerable to judgment as a malingerer or worse. I feared the labels that would categorize me, separate me from the *truly* ill.

There was no place for me to turn. My despair of ever being helped overwhelmed me that night, my last night in the Mayo Clinic. The darkness wrapped itself around me and reached into my soul. *My God, let this pass from me!* I got out of bed, lay supine on the floor, and stretched out my arms. *Just as Grandmother had said. Not my will, but thine be done . . . not my will . . . not my will.* I sobbed into the hard, cold floor of my hospital room. Alone. The life that I saw waiting for me, I wanted to obliterate. And the life within. There was no consolation.

The next day, I was transferred to a private sanitarium on the outskirts of Milwaukee. For the first time in the course of my now seven-year illness, I was placed in the care of a psychiatrist. I remembered the dry leaves of the elm in autumn, rustling in the wind as though crying out before silently drifting downward, aimlessly, without purpose to the earth.

Chapter 17

BETRAYAL

1965

*W*arm. *It was very warm, nearing summer. I walked through the french doors of my country cottage into the garden so brilliant with color, almost blinding. I sat down under the elm to enjoy its shade and breathed in the perfume of the air. I felt so at peace, so free—so well. But it was getting so warm. A brook cut through the garden, and its rippling sound was a soothing one. So warm.*

The warmth started at my toes and gradually, oh so gradually, spread through my body. The trembling eased as I welcomed the warmth. *Warmth!* Then I remembered. I had been dreaming—must have dozed off. I wished I could move and felt the restriction of the treatment I was having, and did have, each day but Sunday. From neck to toes I was wrapped in winding sheets that had been soaked in ice water. My arms were pinned to my sides and I felt mummified, as if wrapped in a shroud. A hot water bottle was under my feet and several blankets were over me. The shock of the cold on my naked body I had learned to endure and even to believe that it was somehow beneficial. The warming process of the body's response was relaxing, and as I lay there for several hours, I often dozed, just as I had now.

This hydrotherapy treatment, along with massages and therapeutic baths, were the only treatments I received at the sanitarium. It was an old structure, but well maintained, and in times past had been a fashionable place for ladies of social standing to go for *rest cures*. Nervous conditions were treated rather than mental aberrations. All the patients had private rooms, comfortably and attractively furnished. Meals were served in a communal dining room, much like any restaurant. The food was well prepared. There was a lounge for patients to socialize if they wished and a great front porch with comfy chairs looking over enclosed gardens. A high, thick hedge completely surrounded the property. It was secluded. This was to be my home for eight months. Another cloister, but of a different sort. For the first time in my religious life, I was away from the community for a prolonged period of time.

The comfortable, elite atmosphere was only a shell, for the institution functioned as a medical facility. There were the usual routines of nurses, medications, therapies, and doctors' rounds. There were medical reasons for patients to be admitted and to be treated and, hopefully, to return to society more able to cope with life.

I was there to come to terms with, to learn to live with, what had come to be called, "my disability." My desperation had prepared me, had disposed me, for this experience. I was open and receptive to the prescribed treatments. I continued to believe that help would come to me one day. *Someone will come!* I also believed that the cause of my incapacitating condition of postural hypotension would one day be determined. For now, the mystery remained and I would have to live with it. I believed in my sanity.

I was assigned to the care of an elderly gentleman, Dr. Paul Danson. He proved to be well-meaning but ineffective in his work with me. I expected great wisdom of him from his many years as a psychiatrist working with so many different people, so many different problems. As the months wore on, seeing him almost daily, I was coming to realize my expectations were based on fantasy. No new insights as to my condition were offered, no part of my psyche ever challenged to be different, to change. I was given platitudes and placebos to simply *go on living*. The sessions became repetitive in content, though I continued to press for reasons, answers, explanations. *Why? Why? Why?* Still, no doors were ever opened, and I was never threatened—at least not intentionally.

It was a late afternoon in June. I was particularly eager to see the doctor as I had collapsed in the dining room that morning, much to my embarrassment. I wasn't dealing with the incident very well and was feeling deep frustration and discouragement. Walking down the long hall to his office on the first floor, I realized at the same time that I had improved. I was walking—to a limited degree—but walking unaided.

The doctor's door was open; he was waiting for me. He had already been informed of the morning incident. I sat down and plunged into my need to know, to understand *why* that happened to me! *I can't control it!* Dr. Danson went through what I had heard a million times, though using a term I had never heard before—*a soldier's heart*. *What does it mean? Is there a diagnosis after all?* Evasion was the answer.

I left Dr. Danson's office without answers to these questions but with a deep curiosity. *Soldier?* So much so, that I managed to find an out-of-the-way medical library rarely used and certainly never by patients. Within minutes I had in my hand just what I needed to find answers and what I read went to the quick of my soul, disturbing me profoundly. My anger was energizing, and rather than finding a corner to lick my wounds, I went right back to the man himself.

Not bothering to knock on the door, I burst into his office. He sat there at his desk, head bent over a stack of papers, and looked up at me in surprise. I was livid. I didn't measure my words. "You've deceived me! You've lied to me! Why didn't you tell me?" My words were delivered in a very much raised voice that he had never heard before from Sister Francis. I was relentless in my accusations and unforgiving. Words pent up for so long tumbled out, one upon another in a tirade I had no desire to restrain.

Dr. Danson grew alarmed, stunned. What was I talking about? *That term.* I knew now exactly what it meant. Evidently, so did he—and everyone else. I felt games were being played with my life under the pretense of having my well-being at heart. I had learned that *soldier's heart* was a nervous condition resulting from long-experienced fear on the battlefield. The term had carried over to other kinds of severe trauma in a variety of life situations. How did this apply to me? I was incredulous of what I was beginning to see. I gripped the crucifix at my side and, ironically, failed to remember its symbolism in my life—the *sword*.

Dr. Danson's anger matched mine, reacting to what he thought was a personal attack on him—and perhaps it was. Rather than responding to the issue, he counterattacked—denouncing my behavior. *Battlefield* was appropriate at this point—and I retreated, going back to my room. Throwing myself on the bed, I sobbed into the pillow, giving full vent to my emotions, letting them run their course. Exhausted, I lay on the bed and tried to sort out what I was feeling. I felt thrown back on my own resources, my own wits, my own will. *Who can I trust now! What am I to do! So many doctors, tests, opinions!* Until today, I had not felt labeled a mental case. I did now. How could I possibly cope with my limitations with this seared upon my forehead!

The answers, *my* answers, came slowly in the following months. I found my own construct of reality. It did not include *soldier's heart*. I was not shaken in my belief that I was suffering an organic, though undiagnosed, disease causing the extreme postural hypotension. I did, at the same time, understand *what* was happening to my body, if not *why*. Even now, I did not question my sanity. The overriding fear was how *other* people would judge me. And what information had *they* been privy to, but not me. *It is my life!* Fear multiplied upon fear. My refuge and consolation was my god, my faith. I firmly believed, as well, that one day I would be vindicated, made well. And I would understand. *SOMEONE WILL COME!* Nothing could shake that.

Meanwhile, I was not deterred in moving toward a day of release from the sanitarium. I *honed my mind*, as it were, taking correspondence courses through distant colleges in advanced math. The As I received told me, erroneously or not, that I was thinking clearly amidst so much confusion and anxiety. My body did grow stronger, though a *cure* did not happen and was never promised. It was the fall of the year when I walked down the front steps and out into the world to rejoin my community once again.

Chapter 18

ACCUSATIONS

1968

Two years had passed since my release from the sanitarium—lost years. The postural hypotension was now described in medical reports as "profound and incapacitating." The little independence I had so sorely won at the sanitarium was no longer mine. I had settled into the life of an invalid, but without peace. Something gnawed deeply inside me, something that would not let me rest. Something nameless.

Once again I was back in the suburban hills of Los Angeles. My health prevented me from participating in community life. I felt alone, isolated, living the rule as much as possible within the four walls of my bedroom. The solitude thrust upon me was no longer a solace. It seemed I was no longer moving toward life but toward death. A downward spiral out of control.

The community had undergone dramatic changes. The cultural, socioeconomic changes of the sixties, the period of social revolution, had an impact on the Catholic church and, particularly, on religious communities. Pope John XXIII, through Vatican II council, opened the windows and allowed the winds of change to come into the church. There were no longer religious superiors but, rather, "community representatives" who administered in a more democratic way. Authority and responsibility were shared and decisions made by consensus. Sisters had more to say about the course of their lives—where they would live, what they would do. They moved more into the world and broadened their services. Certain practices were set aside, judged archaic and out-of-date. The religious habit was exchanged for a simple black suit and white blouse, and the religious name for one's given name. I was now not Sister Francis, but Sister Anne. No longer was it desirable to be "set apart" from the people. It was an unsettling time, and membership was falling off dramatically.

I felt an observer to all this, untouched by change. My illness had separated me from the mainstream a long time ago and what had been my world simply continued to be my world. Externals had long since been inconsequential to me. The changes, however, did allow for special consideration in my case. Permission was granted for me to be frequently at home with my mother and father, the home of my youth and my dreams.

The arbor was always so full and beautiful this time of year, white roses in abundance. It was May, and the California summer heat had not yet threatened to dry up the luxuriant foliage that banked the patio. I looked up from my chaise lounge and watched the white cloud formations and guessed what they might be: wings of the habit we had set aside? Or simply a gull in flight? Through the open french doors, I could hear the television—Father was watching a baseball game. Now that he was retired, he had time for such leisure afternoons. Mother, I knew, was in the kitchen, preparing dinner. It was a peaceful hour.

Time has changed so much! I had been a nun now for nearly eighteen years. My brother and sisters too had long since left home. Mother and Father were in a new phase in their married life. It felt good to be with them, to be home, if even for a few days. Somehow it was a release and relieved the loneliness that had become my companion in the convent. *Tomorrow, tomorrow . . . I must go back!* A sense of dread filled my soul and then guilt that I should feel that way. These home visits were becoming more frequent and more extended.

Whenever possible, I filled the hours with my charcoal drawing, flat in bed. The thick black stub moved across the rough white paper, forming faces, always faces. They grew darker, stronger, eyes more fierce. Nameless faces. And I read—Rölvaag, Conrad, Faulkner, Hemingway, and always, the Bible. I was drawn to the God of the Old Testament, to me the gentle Father who "called me by name." *Anne! Anne!*

Once again, I was under the care of the doctor who had become my friend, Dr. Lindsey. His office was not far from my parents' home, which made it very convenient for him to make house calls. He came by regularly, and I was expecting him early the next morning before returning to the convent. I looked forward to seeing him as his visits were always comforting and encouraging. The mystery of so many years remained, however, and he continued not to have the answers. A humble man, he expressed his feelings about this in a letter to the community representative, Sister Celine.

> Treatment of Sister Anne's severe postural hypotension is very difficult and quite discouraging, as we have learned. Problems of this sort remind us doctors how really inadequate we are. I still harbor a secret hope or suspicion that someday perhaps we can put our finger on the exact lesion and find something really constructive to do about it.

Yes, discouraging . . . and I have no hope, Doctor . . . not any longer.

I lay in the dark that night, thinking, thinking about the loneliness I was going back to and how instinctively I recoiled from it. That bothered me. *I shouldn't feel this way! I'm happy in my convent life! If it just wasn't for my physical problems!* I realized I was becoming more and more incapacitated. More and more, the fog enveloped me, robbing my brain of blood and consciousness. My condition had advanced to the point that sitting upright caused the same symptoms as standing. The only relief was to remain flat in bed. And still, I didn't know *why*. I had learned to simply accept what *was*, and so did everyone around me. Blood pressure was considered an autonomic function, one beyond my control. There was nothing I could do, nothing anyone could do. A status quo that had a deadliness about it, as though things would never be any different. *Never!* I no longer had any desire to go on living. I wanted to die, yet could not.

As these thoughts took over my mind and consumed me with despair, I suddenly felt something stirring deep within myself, so deep I could not reach it. Then, like bubbles coming to the surface, slowly, gently, it would be there but taking a shape so fearsome that I hid my eyes and would not see. *That's not possible! No!* And before it could take the shape of words, words that I could hear, it would be forced back into that void within, silenced—for now. This had been happening of late when I was quiet, as in the night. It filled me with fear and loathing.

This time, in the night, that something would not stay in those dark recesses. It rose to the surface with the force of a sea monster breathing fire of accusation. *You are responsible! You are creating your situation! Your physical problems are your own doing! You are making your blood pressure drop! You are guilty! You are deceiving everyone! An impostor!* The tirade was one blast, like an explosion of awareness that was but momentary. And then it was no more. And I escaped into sleep.

The door! The door—something's behind the door! What is it? I crouched on the floor, trembling, clutching the child close to me, the child seemingly dead, lifeless. Don't look . . . I'm afraid to look . . . afraid to look up at the door. It started to open slowly . . . slowly. I held the child tighter still, could hear the creaking of the door . . . slowly . . . slowly . . . and then something was coming at me . . . some dark, menacing form . . . faceless . . . no . . . no . . . faceless.

The morning light was coming through the curtains when Mother came in with the breakfast tray. She looked concerned and asked me if I knew I had been screaming in the night.

Chapter 19

LAST RESORT

1971

As one month slipped into the next, I became more and more immobilized, the fog clouding my mind more frequently and for longer periods. Sitting up was producing the same state of collapse as standing. My despondency increased proportionately. The smile that had concealed so much no longer concealed anything. Dr. Lindsey had advised me not to return to the convent but to remain at home, where my mother could care for me and he could see me more frequently.

Holding on to the crucifix that had hung at my side on the ebony rosary as a young nun, I turned my face to the flower-papered wall and wept. With my finger I traced the lifeless cluster of blossoms, flat without dimension—still life—never to grow though watered by tears without sound. *Like me*, I thought, in my death place of despair. *Grandmother, in this very sickroom, did you weep against this same flower-papered wall, have these same despairing thoughts?*

It was time, time to call the priest. Uncle John came, wearing the same purple stole around his neck, holding the same crucifix, just as I had remembered *that night of the dying grandmother*. He stood there at the foot of my bed, his eyes tearing when he saw me, knowing I would not be comforted, not this time. He first spoke in solemn tones of trust, of hope, the all-too-familiar words that were now beginning to sound hollow. Already I felt a slipping away, a door closing behind me, leaving my beloved Uncle John on the other side. Another kind of death and I mourned. On the small linen-covered table stood the same holy candles, their flames flickering like the remembered holy, shining light in Grandmother's eyes as she had spoken her deathbed words, "Your arms are outstretched, Anne, on the cross with Jesus." The ritual began, my mother the only mourner as before, *watching*. Uncle John intoned, "*Through this holy anointing may the Lord in His love and mercy help you with the grace of the Holy Spirit.*" I felt the pressure of Uncle John's thumb on my eyelids, making the sign of the cross with the holy oils—on my lips, on my hands, on my feet, preparing me for the final journey. *Your journey was not yet over, Grandmother, when you were anointed in this very room—ahead for you were more years of the death struggle. What of me? My arms are outstretched.*

Just as I held on to the crucifix for strength, I held on to words—loving words of my fellow religious and friends. Just yesterday, I received a note from my former superior, Sister Therese, "You have proved yourself these twelve long years. The Lord is pleased. He will bear you up." I could "prove" myself no longer.

In a final effort to halt the inevitable, Dr. Lindsey had said, "Let's try just one more time, Anne." One more time of hospital tests and evaluation.

It came to pass; I was admitted the next day and subjected to tests I had experienced many times before. One was new to me, however. Strapped onto a "tilt table" and hooked up to a monitor for vital signs, I waited for the consulting cardiologist, Dr. Simon. The table was in a horizontal position, so I was comfortable though anxious about the test I was to have momentarily. I tried to distract my mind by visualizing the haven of the rose arbor that I so loved.

Dr. Simon entering the room brought me back to the sterile, cold world of the hospital. He greeted me warmly and explained the procedure he was about to perform and then proceeded without delay. The table was tilted upright. The fog descended instantly and I felt nothing. I was unconscious. Moments later, the fog lifted and I realized I was back in a prone position. I was then given an infusion of Levophed, and the process was repeated. This time, the fog did not descend. I remained conscious and could talk to Dr. Simon. The medication *did* make a difference. Perhaps I would be helped after all.

An experimental drug was prescribed, and in addition, I was fitted with an elastic support suit that hugged my rib cage and extended to my toes. Even this combination was not totally effective. Years of invalidism had left me without any physical endurance or strength. It was hard to distinguish cause and effect. Now it was possible, however, for Dr. Lindsey to make his next move.

Three weeks had passed when he came into my hospital room to once more shock me out of my world. "Sister Anne," he said firmly, "I think you should go to a rehabilitation hospital. I've discussed your case with the medical director there, Dr. Thompson, and he thinks they can help you. He's done some special studies on postural hypotension with paraplegics who tend to struggle with this problem. It's worth a try—I want you seriously to consider this, Anne."

The whole time he was presenting his rationale, I was screaming no inside. *NO NO NO!* I couldn't face it. More than that, I feared it. Sheer, stark fear welled up inside like a precursor of the sea dragon. *What is my fear!* Dr. Lindsey left me to think about his proposal.

I was obsessed with fear as I lay awake in the dark that night. Something was stirring up inside me. I knew not what. I had this feeling—it reminded me of a feeling I had had in the past. It seemed so long ago. *What was it? When was it?* Then I remembered the elm tree that winter afternoon on the playground in Milwaukee. It was back—the premonition was back. I sensed something was about to happen that would affect my life profoundly. But I knew not what. Then that explosion of awareness happened again and I heard the self-accusations. *It's your own fault. You've wasted your life.* The *no* I had screamed at Dr. Lindsey that afternoon had come from a depth I knew not of. I welcomed the night nurse and a sleeping pill. I *had* to silence the voices.

Far off in the distance, I heard an eerie howling as of a trapped and wounded animal, very faint at first and then growing louder. It frightened me, and I cowered in a dark hole. Then rough hands were shaking me, disturbing the nightmare.

"Sister Anne! Sister Anne! Wake up!" I opened my eyes to see the night nurse looking down at me, fear in her eyes. *Afraid of me?* I was horrified to realize the truth—the howling had erupted from within *me*.

I now know what I must do!

PART TWO

The Psychologist

The Lord is my strength and my shield;
my heart trusted in Him and I am helped.
Therefore my heart greatly rejoices and
with my song I shall praise Him.

—Psalms 28:7

Chapter 20

1971

The Confrontation

This was my first experience of a rehabilitation hospital. Mountain View. I felt quite on the periphery of its activity these first few days. Dr. Thompson, who was my personal physician as well as medical director of the hospital, had said I needed time to become acclimated and to be evaluated. So I remained in bed, was served trays, and slipped in and out of my gray world. Despair filled my soul, and I gripped my rosary as a lifeline to some inner strength.

The sky was clouded and the room in shadows. I looked out the window to the parklike grounds with its green grass and pine trees against the backdrop of the San Bernardino Mountains. *To the hills I look for deliverance.* Suddenly, I felt a presence and turned my head on the pillow, startled to see a bearded gentleman, not more than forty, with dark hair down to the nape of his neck, standing at the side of my bed. His eyes were deep brown and had a look of intensity as though he were fully focused at this point in time on me and nothing would escape his gaze. At the same time, he appeared indifferent, as casual as the sports clothes he wore. He looked rather strange to me and did not fit my image of doctors.

"Sister Anne?" His voice was soft and gentle.

I nodded. "Yes."

"I am Joseph Wright, the staff psychologist. Dr. Thompson asked me to see you. I do an evaluation on all patients on admission. Can you come to my office in the morning?"

I wasn't sure I wanted to see this man. I was afraid. Of what, I wasn't sure. "Well, Mr. Wright, how can I do that? I can't walk. I can't even sit up."

He smiled, and I felt strangely uncomfortable. "If that's a problem, I'll request a nurse bring you on a gurney. OK?"

In other words, no easy way out. I nodded and looked away. The appointment worried me the rest of the day and into the night. I sensed something, but I couldn't quite put my finger on it.

The next morning at nine o'clock, I was being wheeled down the long hall on a gurney. I hadn't seen much of the hospital the day of my admittance and didn't now. I was too preoccupied with what was to come. The sun was shining through the high windows, and the flowers in the atrium patio were in my line of vision. The pure gold of hibiscus. Usually, their brilliant color would have brought a smile to my face, but not now. I wasn't really seeing. I wasn't responding. I had closed myself off in some internal prison where no light penetrated.

The hall gave way to a large reception room serving several counseling offices. One of the doors was labeled Staff Psychologist. It was partly ajar—enough so that Joseph Wright's voice, agitated and with an edge of anger, could be heard in the reception room.

"There's really nothing to talk about, Louise. Talk to my lawyer. I'll repeat what I said last night. It's over . . . There won't be another time . . . You're right about that. We'll talk about listing the house tonight. Look, my nine o'clock appointment is here—I have to go."

The receiver was slammed down with vehemence. If I had eyes to see, I would have recognized the frustration and pain on Mr. Wright's face as the gurney was pushed through the open door and into his presence—a presence that for the moment was involved not with the struggles of his clients but with his own. As it was, I was too contained in my own world to move beyond its boundaries and into that of another. My isolation prevented me from even wondering *Who is this Louise?* That Joseph Wright was wrestling with his own demons of disillusionment was no concern of mine.

"Good morning, Mr. Wright." The gracious manners of a nun never left me.

"Oh, good morning, Sister Anne!" He looked up and our eyes met, locked for a moment. Immediately his features softened until there was no anger in them, and when he spoke, his voice was as gentle as on our first meeting. "I was expecting you." Then, nodding to the nurse, he said, "Thanks, Paula. Return for Sister in about an hour." Joseph Wright and I were now alone. Our eyes held. Mr. Wright was seeing the enlarged pupils, so dilated that they filled my gaunt face like two deep, dark wells, and seeing beyond to the fear that made them so. He didn't hesitate to ask, "What is your fear, Sister Anne?"

I looked at him directly but said nothing. I had but one question. *Are you the one? What makes me think* you *are the one I've been waiting for? Yes, I'm afraid.* I could bear his gaze no longer and dropped my eyes, seeing only whiteness—white hands on white sheets. I studied the blueness of my nails, knowing Mr. Wright too was seeing a death-like visage. I could feel his eyes follow the angular line of my body, a skeletal form, motionless except for an almost imperceptible breathing—in . . . out, in . . . out, shallow, irregular, stopping altogether for moments at a time, hesitating as though the next breath were a decision to be made rather than an autonomic function. In . . . out, live . . . die. *Life is but a breath.* If I had breathed deeply, the acrid air, the musty odor of the tomb, would have spoken to me of death—as it did now to Mr. Wright. I sensed my fragility was intimidating to this psychologist. He reached over to me in a reassuring way, and I felt his hand resting on my shoulder.

"Don't! Don't touch me!" The fierceness in my voice made him draw back, startled.

The intimidation was fleeting, and mercilessly he plunged in. "OK. What are you here for, Sister Anne?"

"You asked me to come, didn't you?" *Two can play this game.*

"Yes, but why did you come?" He was not to be evaded so easily.

"Please, someone help me! I'm dying!" All subterfuge had dropped away; I went right to the heart. Soundlessly, the tears streamed down my face, blurring my vision, preventing me from seeing the compassion in the eyes that held mine. I did hear it in his voice and felt something stirring within. *Perhaps I can talk to this man.*

"You don't have to die, Sister. You can, though, if you want to. It is your choice."

"Choice! I don't have a choice! I can't control what's happening!" Immediately, I was on the defensive. Mr. Wright's words had touched my vulnerability and I drew back as though from a physical touch—rigid, bracing myself for some deeper intrusion on the self. "It's not my fault!"

"Sister Anne, no one is accusing you. Why not just look at everything? I suggest we open all the doors and . . ."

No! Mr. Wright's voice faded into silence, his words now impotent, no longer reaching me. *No! Nothing . . . Nothing.* The shroud of grayness enveloped me. The stillness of death came over me. A space of no sound . . . no feeling . . . no emotion . . . no thing—*Nothing*. Even my body seemed nonexistent. No muscle movement. Breathing only to sustain life. *I'm so cold . . . so cold . . . help me!* The icy cold spread throughout my body and I sank deeper into a comatose-like state. A surcease from anguish, a surcease from pain, from thought, from all that is. Death in life, suspended in time and space. I could look down and see Mr. Wright leaning over me, calling me back. "Sister Anne! Sister Anne!" Medically, he knew what was happening, but this did not alleviate his anxiety. Earlier he had said to Dr. Thompson, "I don't want her dying on me, Curtis!" The medical records there on his desk gave credence to this possibility.

> Profound and incapacitating postural hypotension, an acute drop in blood pressure and acceleration of pulse when in an upright position, resulting in insufficient blood supply to the brain, acute syncope, and collapse. Condition of twelve years' duration.

I frequently lapsed into unconsciousness even on a gurney, as now. I moved between worlds, comfortable in neither.

"Sister Anne!" The voice of compassion was now penetrating my gray world. *Don't touch me!* I must still be alive. I feared to be touched. *No!* I breathed more deeply. The world of reality penetrated the barrier I had created and, with it, the anxiety. It rushed in with all its horror. I was in a hospital—again. *Why can't someone help me! Please help me!* Warmth returned to my body and I grew hot, feverish. The blood rushed to my extremities, compensating for the deprivation. I was back. Fully conscious. I opened my eyes and searched the small office. Yes, I was back. My eyes once more looked into Mr. Wright's—and a heavy silence hung in the air between us. *Who are you?*

Mr. Wright leaned back in his swivel chair, picked up his pipe, and filled it with tobacco, slowly, deliberately. Drawing deeply, he brought it to life and the smoke swirled toward the ceiling, clouding the charcoal drawing of Fritz Perls that hung above his head. *A mentor, no doubt.* I did not know the words of this renowned and innovative psychologist were now giving this therapist direction, "Don't push the river." Unknown to me as well, the stand he was taking regarding my case: *I certainly don't want to get involved in any therapy right now, let alone one that would demand so much of me. There will be no halfway with Sister Anne. I can see that.*

Aloud, Mr. Wright continued talking as though there had been no interruption. "As I was saying, look at all your options. How long have you been a nun, Sister?"

"Twenty years!" I was aware of the fierceness in my voice—my defenses were back. *Enough!* I gave him a piercing look and said, "No more."

"All right, I'm leaving town for a few days . . . going up the coast to Cambria. Think it over. See if you have the courage to open all the doors."

Looking at him directly, I whispered, "You're going to tell me to leave the order, aren't you? You think this illness is psychosomatic, don't you?"

"No, I'm not going to tell you to do anything. I value religious life. I was a minister myself at one time. I'm just saying, look at everything! I don't know about 'psychosomatic.' I don't use labels. Man is a unity. We can't isolate the mind, the body, the soul. Everything is interrelated. We can't talk about anything in isolation." The words were spoken with conviction, and I felt reassured. A sigh of relief I didn't quite understand escaped me.

"I don't know. I'll have to think about it. I know only one thing—I want the truth, Mr. Wright."

"That's all I want too, Sister. And please call me Joseph. Everyone does." He smiled at me as he got up to open the door. He reached out as though to touch me, and then checked himself.

The nurse was waiting, and then the gurney was being maneuvered down the long corridor. I didn't like it that Joseph was leaving town, but I also didn't like the idea of opening all those doors. I closed my eyes, thinking that his words somehow rang of truth. *Truth. Joseph. Are you the one?*

Chapter 21

SHAPES OF FEAR

The long afternoon stretched out before me, though time had become a stranger to me in a sense. There was only a terrible sameness that defied the passing of the hours. My world of fog where I felt nothing, thought nothing, created a darkened inward cave of unawareness. It descended on me shortly after I was returned to my room on the gurney. It was a welcome alternative to dealing with Mr. Wright's counsel of opening all the doors.

As the fog eventually lifted, I felt a foreboding, an inner sense of impending doom on the horizon. There was something familiar about it, as though I had experienced it before. Then it came to me—*yes, under the elm tree!* All those years ago, when I had stood under the elm tree in the school yard, I had had a premonition that something was going to happen that would have a profound effect on my life. For all that had occurred since that day long ago, somehow, I knew the premonition had not been fulfilled. *Why should this feeling flood my being* now? *Joseph Wright . . . does he have something to do with it? Will my decision whether or not to go back to him be critical in my life?* Before I knew it, I was dealing with the issues I so wanted to avoid.

I watched the San Bernardino Mountains become purple shadowed as I lay in bed thinking, thinking with a clarity that I believed essential to my survival. If it had been possible, I would have knelt on the floor and begged for guidance. But I could not. I did kneel down in the chapel of my soul and prayed, *Come, Holy Spirit.* I had tried every avenue of help and found none. Why would this be any different? Yet something told me it would. I always knew someone would come who could help me. *Is this the one? Joseph? But my vocation! I must protect that!* To go back, I felt, would be to make myself wholly vulnerable. It would be to risk everything. Could I do that? My despair of my present condition was fertile ground. *I want the truth!* To go back to Joseph Wright seemed my only alternative to death. And my last.

The room was in darkness, as was my soul. Fear was always my companion, but this night it took on shapes and forms on all sides. I was afraid, but of what? *Ah, the fog! I will go there . . . where there is Nothing.*

"Sister Anne! Sister Anne, where are you?" It was Joseph—returned from Cambria. I pushed through the fog, opening my eyes only enough to see his face looking down at me; I tried to speak, moving my lips soundlessly.

"What is it? What are you trying to say, Sister?"

"I'm coming back, Joseph. When can you see me?" My voice was thin—wispy like the fog from which it came.

"You're scheduled for a patient conference tomorrow at nine. Better make it the next day—ten o'clock! Have a good night." And he was gone as quietly as he had come.

My first patient conference. My gurney was positioned at the foot of a long conference table. All the health professionals who would be working with me in rehabilitation were present—nurses, physical and occupational therapists, vocational counselor, psychologist, attending physician, and the medical director. They were meeting to discuss my case and course of treatment. I was to be included—more than included. Their philosophy was that rehabilitation was primarily the responsibility of the patient and that he or she needed to be actively involved. This was a source of utter amazement to me who had experienced so many depersonalized hospital situations. This new dimension in treatment immediately appealed to me, but my physical and mental states interfered with me being a viable participant. For now, I listened, gave my full attention. Isolated words jumped out of context and hit me forcibly—"therapeutic pool . . . physical therapy . . . progressive tilt table." *So much is going to be expected of me!* I recoiled in fear and resistance.

No time was lost. Early the next morning, I was wheeled on the gurney to physical therapy. I was to experience the infamous tilt table. It was to become a routine morning treatment.

"Good morning, Sister Anne!" It was Dr. Thompson, who I learned was a physiatrist specializing in physical medicine and rehabilitation. The field of physiatry was fairly new in medicine—certainly new to me. At first I confused the term with psychiatry, and it pushed an alarm button in me! Dr. Thompson quickly put my mind at ease, explaining his work with the physically disabled. As he had informed Dr. Lindsey, he had done special studies in postural hypotension with paraplegics, so he had a unique interest in the problem I presented to him.

"We want to get you accustomed to an upright position, if at all possible. With your new medication and support suit, it just may work! Each day we'll monitor what your body can tolerate and increase the degree of the tilt table and length of time."

I nodded. It sounded so simple yet so lethal to me. To be other than flat had become a torture as the blood pooled in my extremities and grayness enveloped me—that Nothing place of oxygen deprivation. I trusted this Dr. Thompson—from the first day. He was warm and friendly and seemed to care. My thoughts were interrupted by Jim, the physical therapist, as he assisted Dr. Thompson in transferring me from the gurney to the tilt table. Strapped in, I was elevated a slight ten degrees.

"I'll check on you in a few minutes, Sister Anne. Jim will be close by." Dr. Thompson patted my shoulder reassuringly and moved on to the patient in the wheelchair nearby.

From the strange vantage point of the tilt table, I looked around the physical therapy room, seeing every kind of physical disability. This rehabilitation hospital was the last resort for many—as it was for me. Patients were here to learn how to be as fully functional as possible and often to rebuild their lives. I remembered my first meeting with Dr. Thompson and the conversation that had remained with me. His words startled me as they were new and revealed an insight that had not occurred to me before. *What was it? Why can't I think . . . I can't think . . . It's getting cold . . . my heart . . . and grayness . . . Nothing . . . Nothing.*

"Sister Anne! Sister Anne!" A voice was penetrating my gray world. It was Jim. He was standing over me, the tilt table once again in the horizontal position.

I wanted to answer but could not. Warmth started coming back—and feeling. I wanted to cry. "Don't do that . . . no more!"

"No, no more today, Sister. But it is a beginning. Even a few minutes is a beginning. Just rest here." Jim was kind. I liked him, but . . .

What was I trying to remember? Oh, yes, my first conversation with Dr. Thompson. I could think now from my prone position. Dr. Thompson had shared his philosophy that there comes a point in illness when one must recognize and accept that he or she is no longer sick, but different, and live accordingly. *Different . . . accept your difference. I was different . . . accept . . . accept . . . but how does one live? Perhaps that's why I'm going back to Mr. Wright.* It was nearly ten o'clock and I was afraid . . . *afraid of* what?

Chapter 22

VOCATION AND CHOICE

The clock on the reception room wall told me it was ten o'clock as I was wheeled into the counseling office. Joseph was waiting.

"Well, let's pick up where we left off, Sister Anne. Why are you here? Why did you decide to come back for this session?"

The question was irritating. *I'm here. Isn't that enough?* I looked at him. *Joseph.* He had said to call him Joseph. He looked very at ease with himself, very self-assured. He made me uneasy—yet I felt a confidence I had never felt before with any doctor or therapist. *Why should this be?*

"Sister Anne? Did you hear me?" His voice intruded on my thoughts.

"Yes, I heard you, Joseph. I'm here because I want to know the truth—as I told you the first time." There was no longer the veneer of a "good nun."

"The truth? The truth about what?" I felt myself tightening up; it was hard to breathe. *What do I want? What is this truth of which I speak?* I tried to reach something in myself. That dark area that loomed up into my awareness in the middle of the night. *No!* "I want to know . . ." My voice was a whisper fading into murmurs. *No . . . I can't.*

"Sister Anne. Sister Anne, where are you? Where do you go?" I could hear Joseph's voice but couldn't respond. I felt his touch and I grew colder. *No!*

The session lasted no more than fifteen minutes. Therapy proved to be a psychological tilt table for which I had no endurance.

Our Father who art in heaven . . . I sat in Joseph's office, waiting for his arrival, the olive-seed rosary clutched tightly in my hand. As the beads slipped through my fingers, they reminded me of the passage of time. A month of therapy sessions was behind me. Each session was a deliberate choice, never routine, always demanding fears be set aside and risks be taken. It was like walking through a psychological mine field, never knowing but quite expecting, that with the next step, my whole world would be annihilated. Still, I kept coming, and there was progress. My tolerance for sitting upright had increased, and for periods of time I could enjoy the mobility of a wheelchair. The ephemeral truth was taking definition but was elusive.

I heard the door opening behind me. It was Joseph. "Sorry I'm late!" He put his briefcase on his desk and opened it, taking out his pipe and tobacco pouch. I watched him as he settled into his swivel chair and quietly, slowly, filled the pipe and lit it, drawing deeply. It seemed to be a ritual, an orientation to the course of therapy. "Have you given thought to my question, Sister?"

"Question? What question, Joseph?" I looked at him as though totally nonplussed.

"You know." He looked up at me and I looked back, unflinching. He never let me get away with playing ignorant, not knowing. It was irritating.

"You mean the question of choice?" I acquiesced.

"Yes. Is it your choice to be a nun?"

"Of course. In a way."

"What do you mean, 'in a way'?"

I drew in a deep breath. *He was absolutely ruthless!* We were moving into, what was to me, dangerous territory. "It's really difficult to sit up this long, Joseph. Maybe I should get back to my room."

"You're OK. What do you mean, 'in a way'?"

"It is my vocation! It is God's will I be a nun!" I heard my voice rise above the low whisper in which I usually spoke and wondered why. "There's really nothing to talk about."

"You can quit anytime, Sister. I understand the nature of vocation, a calling. Did you feel compelled to enter the convent?" He lowered his pipe and tapped the bowl nonchalantly.

"I told you. It was God's will. I didn't have any choice."

"What kind of God would that be? His most precious gift is free will. Did you freely choose to be a nun these twenty years? Look at it, Sister! Did you?" His voice was rising, grating on my nerves.

"Stop! Stop! My whole life . . ." I was growing cold. I slumped forward in the wheelchair, Joseph's hands restraining me from an inevitable fall. *No!*

"Why can't you be touched, Sister? Why are you afraid to feel?" His hands remained on my shoulders.

Oh, this is better. This world of fog, of grayness. No thought. Just Nothing. No one can reach me here—not even Joseph.

Back in my room, I realized the rosary was still clutched in my hand. *Hail Mary, full of grace . . . Hail Mary . . . please help me.* Despair gnawed at the very core of my being. It's true. I never did choose to be a nun; I never wanted it. There was always that resistance deep within, that *no*. It was what God wanted. I simply accepted my vocation as God's will. The disparity struck a discordant note in my soul and in my brain. Could I now acknowledge to Joseph that this was indeed the truth? Such an acknowledgement, I knew, would trigger a course of events, a chain reaction, necessitating, demanding more of me, my very life. Throughout the night I wrestled with myself, trying to find the courage to look at the truth beginning to reveal itself.

"Good morning, Sister Anne! How are you feeling today?" I looked up at Joseph furtively, knowing there was no way I could conceal my fear. It seemed his eyes narrowed as he looked down into that place of gnawing despair, deep within. I said nothing, watching him as he settled down with his pipe, drawing and puffing, filling the silence between us. *The ritual.*

No longer could I contain the cries that had been pent up through the long night. They broke through, my sobs, unrecognizable as mine. The pipe was set aside, and Joseph leaned over to me, asking in his quiet way, "What is it, Sister?"

"Joseph? That question you asked me—about choosing to be a nun. I don't think I ever did." Now I spoke the truth.

"Can you now make that choice, Sister Anne?" His voice was gentle, encouraging me to go on.

"I don't know. But it's all I have—everything." I could feel my heart pounding and my palms grow sweaty. I was terrified. I looked at Joseph and knew he could see the darkness of despair in my eyes. "Help me!"

"I want to help you, but it's up to you. How much are you willing to risk in order to know the truth? Sometimes, for some people, it does take everything."

"I made final vows—forever . . . I can't leave my order. What about my sisters?" Thoughts, questions I never dare let myself think or see the light of conscious awareness were now tumbling about in my mind, one upon the other. So much so fast. My mind couldn't handle it. The world of unfeeling was waiting for me; I could go there anytime—be safe. Though I felt a chill come over me, I remained upright in the wheelchair, conscious.

"Here, I have a book you might want to read." Joseph handed me a slim, soft-covered book. I read the title, *Purity of Heart* by Søren Kierkegaard. Strange book to give me, I thought. It looked like many on our convent shelves.

"Thank you. I'll look at it, Joseph. I really need to return to my room now." This time, he didn't resist and, picking up the phone, dialed the nurses' station.

As I was wheeled down the hall, I noticed the color of the hibiscus was unusually brilliant—yellow, like the sun. Even the roses were blooming. I hadn't noticed that before.

The nurse was waiting for me when I got back to my room. "Time for physical therapy, Sister Anne!" Paula was her cheerful self, a very personable woman I judged to be about my age. Like all the staff at this hospital, she wore ordinary clothes—tailored slacks and a print blouse. There was nothing about her appearance to distinguish her as the very capable, experienced nurse she was. I felt comfortable with Paula and was always glad when she was on duty. She helped me change into slacks and a sweatshirt for the exercise session ahead. I dreaded it. Jim, the physical therapist, exercised my limbs with the hope that one day soon I would be able to do this independently. Jim had a nice way about him, but somehow he bothered me—wasn't quite sure just why.

I looked in the mirror. *Sure don't look like Sister Anne in this outfit!* I tried to really look at myself but quickly turned away. One of our religious customs was *not* to look in mirrors. There was no room for vanity in religious life. I did know I was rail thin, and it showed more in these *worldly* clothes than the billowing habit.

"You look quite like a Barbie doll, Sister Anne!" Paula said, and laughed. She had meant it as a compliment, but I was embarrassed and felt myself blush.

When I stood up to get into the wheelchair, the familiar faintness came over me. "I really don't feel up to going, Paula."

"You'll be all right." Paula was kind but persistent. She guided me into the chair and we were on our way. I had learned it was useless to protest any further.

Jim was waiting for me. He was tall, handsome, a man of few words. All business. "Hi, Sister! Let's see what we can do today." He helped me onto the exercise table. Taking my right arm, he lifted it up toward the ceiling and down again. This was to be repeated several times before he moved to the next limb. He was touching me. *No! No one can touch me!* So I became a stone. A stone that could not feel a touch. Could not feel warmth. And I grew cold—stone-cold.

"Sister Anne!" I could hear Jim calling me. But I was gone. I was safe. Where no one could reach me. I was aware I was being transferred back to the wheelchair, secured by straps, and then wheeled down the hall to my room. Finally, in bed and alone. Finally alone. I fumbled for my rosary. *Hail Mary full of grace . . . help me.*

Chapter 23

SEXUALITY AND CHASTITY

*W**hy does this keep happening to me!* The fact that I had fainted at the last physical therapy session preyed on my mind. *Why? Why?* I glanced at the clock on the office wall. Joseph would be here any moment for our morning session. Impatiently, I waited . . . waited . . . and the same questions pounded . . . pounded in my brain. *Can you look at it, Sister Anne? Can you face the truth? Can you take the next step?*

"Good morning, Sister!" *He was here. Joseph was here.* He shuffled the papers on his desk, glancing my way, waited.

My words were half sobs, choked with terror of what must be said. "All these years, Joseph . . . It can't be . . . no . . . my whole life! What would I do? I'm helpless!"

"We've got to find out why you're helpless. The truth—the whole truth. Remember?"

"To say the words, Joseph, will destroy me." I lowered my head into my hands, as though to stifle words I could not control.

"Destroy you? What is there to lose, Sister?"

The implication made me gasp. I slumped deeper into my wheelchair, covering my eyes so that I could not see.

"Who is crying, Sister? Who is grieving? Who?" As usual, he pressed on.

Who? Who? A cry froze in my throat. Warmth flowed through me, melting the frigid fear. The despair of that inner place was banished, and I felt the trust of a child again. It was comfortable, like putting on old clothes on a Saturday morning. *Who?*

"Who, Joseph?" I released my eyes from their darkness, looked at my therapist, and then smiled. The smile felt warm, natural, softening my features. Joseph leaned closer, and his expression was quizzical. He smiled back. "Yes, who are you?"

"Why, little Anne, of course. I feel I've been away so long . . . so long. I feel such a sadness." *A different kind. How can I tell this gentle man?*

"Why are you sad, Anne?" *Joseph called me Anne! Anne. This is Anne. Yes, Anne! I never chose to be a nun . . . I am still here.* I was afraid to move . . . to breathe . . . the child I felt was fragile . . . near extinguishment . . . ephemeral . . . ghostlike. *I must hang on to her!* I reached out to Joseph . . . wanting to feel . . . wanting warmth . . . life. *I can tell him . . . I can trust him.*

"Yes, Anne, I know you're here. Take my hand. I want to help you." I allowed Joseph's warm hands to encircle mine. "Talk to me, Anne." There was an urgency in the gentle voice, like one calling to a drowning person, standing on a distant shore far off—far, far off.

"My whole life! I should never have become Sister Anne, a nun. So many years . . . gone . . . gone." My voice faded, drowned in the waters of denial. "Joseph, please help me . . . I want the . . ." And the waters closed over until there was only a thin, pathetic wail.

I felt the warmth draining from my hands and I pulled them back, rubbing them together. The coldness was returning—and with it, the despair of isolation, of lostness. The child was lost. *I don't need her!* A strength returned also, like a thick plastic on my being, a cold, thick plastic, sealing the child within. I felt quite nunlike. Sister Anne was back in control. My eyes felt heavy, hooded; my vision narrowed. An uneasiness started to take hold. I felt disconcerted—confused. Joseph sat very still in his chair, staring strangely at me.

"What's wrong, Joseph? I know something is wrong . . ." It was the voice of Sister Anne.

"That's what we're trying to find out. Tell me, Sister, have the vows of your order been a problem for you?"

"My vows . . . a problem? No, no, I don't think so. We take the vows of poverty, chastity, and obedience. Of the three, obedience posed the most difficulty. I've always had my own way of doing things!" My voice grew stronger as I talked, confident in my own perceptions. "I was always a very independent person, even as a young girl. That was probably the hardest thing to give up when I entered the convent—my independence, the freedom to determine my own life. I learned, though, Joseph!"

"Learned what?"

The room swirled around me and I gripped the arms of my wheelchair. My hooded eyes closed completely in an effort to bring the dizziness under control. My answer came out in whispered gasps, "Learned to . . . to conform . . . to do . . . what . . . I was . . . told . . . I am . . . a good . . . nun."

"What was the price!" All gentleness was gone.

My eyes flew open. "Price, Joseph? What do you mean? There wasn't any price!" I felt insulted and heard the defensive tone of my words, no longer whispered gasps but projected stabs at one who dared so question.

"No price, Sister! Look at yourself! LOOK!" Joseph's arm made a sweeping gesture over my wheelchaired form.

How dare him! Opening my mouth, I started to protest. There were no words; they died within, impotent by virtue of what they were. *It is so cold . . . this weakness . . . I'm going to fall.*

"What about chastity, Sister Anne? Was that vow a problem?" Joseph was undeterred by the sudden, visible change in me.

Stop! Stop! The grayness closed in and no longer were Joseph's words touching me, but his hands reached out and caught me just as I felt myself falling forward to the floor. Still he did not stop. His voice, hard, pressing, went on with words I would not hear.

Then silence and he waited—waited. Warmth was returning—and feeling. I straightened up in the wheelchair and opened my eyes, looking into the determined face of my therapist. He would not be stopped. And I was hearing once again.

"Chastity, Sister Anne! You're attractive, you know—beautiful! Men are attracted to you!" *No, stop,* Joseph . . . *please don't.* "And what about *your* feelings, Sister. Do you feel attracted to men? Answer me! Do you?"

The whispered gasps returned. "No . . . no."

"What about Jim, Sister? Why did you pass out at physical therapy yesterday? Why? Don't you want to feel a touch! Don't you, Sister?" Joseph's face was close to mine, unyielding, demanding. I could take no more. I welcomed the grayness. *No, I don't feel anything, Mr. Wright. Nothing.*

The session was over. Joseph knew I was no longer with him, had retreated to that place of Nothing. He picked up the phone and dialed the nurses' station, asking Paula to wheel me back to my room.

Another internal roadblock. Suspicions of Joseph's motives descended upon me as I returned to consciousness. *Why is he raising such questions! He knows my medical history! Dr. Thompson. I must talk with Dr. Thompson.* Whenever I came up against internal roadblocks in my therapy with Joseph and could go no further, I turned to this other voice. I could lay all my questions, my doubts, my fears at the feet of this caring and personable physician. And Joseph encouraged this. He himself was in continual contact with Curt, as he referred to Dr. Thompson. They had a rather rare and unique professional relationship, combining their skills and expertise in the treatment of unusual cases, cases abandoned by the medical profession. For these patients, Mountain View Hospital was a last resort. All else had been tried. All had failed. I was one of these and glad to be part of their exploration of "holistic medicine," bringing together components of body, mind, and spirit alienated by the methods of medical science. It was a new philosophy, a new term, in the psycho medical world. Dr. Thompson and Joseph Wright were pioneers—creative, innovative professionals. They worked as a team, and I observed them to be friends as well. Between them they created a balance in the rehabilitation process, which was to my advantage. I rang for the nurse and requested to speak with Dr. Thompson. *Joseph, why are you doing this to me!*

Chapter 24

GOD OF LIFE

Hydrotherapy was a very important part of my physical rehabilitation and scheduled daily. In my case, the principle was that water gave buoyant support to my cardiovascular system, not unlike the elastic support garment, preventing acute drop in blood pressure.

At first, I had been lowered into a Hubbard tank in a basketlike chair. Its jet system stimulated circulation and toned muscle, muscle grown flaccid and useless. When I graduated to the therapeutic pool, the size of a small swimming pool, I was lowered into the water on a stretcher. Now, the stretcher was left behind and I was tied with straps to rings on the side of the pool. It was therapy I looked forward to, as the warm water was relaxing and my mind could float like my body, without feeling.

The coarse cloth straps stretched across my chest and under my arms, securing me to the side of the pool. I was immersed up to my chin, the water deep enough so that my legs could dangle freely. I was motionless, the still water revealing a shapeless body in a shapeless yellow two-piece bathing suit. I could count my ribs and name the protruding bones—could see the white skin, a whiteness that knew not the sun for many years, stretched taut.

The sun . . . there is no sun in my life. One dies without the sun . . . dies. The skylight overhead admitted rays, but they did not touch me, could not penetrate the grayness of my world. More powerful than the sun was the voice of Joseph Wright, a voice I could not silence.

Do you want the truth, Sister Anne? The water was so warm . . . so relaxing. My body was growing limp . . . limp.

Why did you become a nun, Sister Anne? Why? My body . . . growing lighter . . . so warm . . . lighter.

God's will? Look at yourself, Sister! My body . . . slipping away . . . the coarse cloth straps loosening . . . loosening.

What kind of god is your god, Sister Anne! The warm water . . . crawling up my skin . . . slowly as with a life of its own . . . coming closer to my mouth . . . as a friend.

My god is a god of life, Sister! What kind . . . The voice was growing louder—louder. *God of life . . . of life . . . of life.*

I do not want to live! The water, so warm . . . covering my lips . . . seeping into my mouth . . . the taste of chemicals . . . slipping away . . . without struggle . . . and the grayness . . . deepening . . . slipping.

My god is a god of life . . . life . . . life. The voice fading . . . fading . . . the warm water covering my nose. *I can't breathe . . . no breath of life.* Grayness slipping into darkness . . . and then Nothing . . . Nothing.

My body now slipping into the water's depths, drifting downward, the coarse cloth straps hanging loosely on the side of the pool, as merciful arms releasing me.

"Sister Anne! Sister Anne!" Faintly, far off I could hear someone calling my name, calling me back . . . strong arms pulling me from the water's depths . . . the blackness receding. *No! Don't touch me! No!* I coughed, sputtered, feeling the hard, cold tiles of the pool's edge.

"Sister Anne! Are you all right?" It was Jim, the physical therapist—always there. I wished he had not. *Jim, why? It's so cold.* I was shaking. Jim was putting a blanket around me, lifting me onto the gurney.

"You'll be OK, Sister, just swallowed some water—glad I had an eye on you! See you tomorrow!"

Tomorrow. Now there would be another tomorrow—and Joseph Wright's questions.

Who is your god, Sister Anne?

Later that night, I awakened to see Dr. Thompson standing at the foot of my bed, my chart in his hand.

"Didn't mean to wake you up, Sister! Paula said you wanted to see me. Couldn't get away any earlier." He smiled that charming smile that made him irresistible to everyone.

"Yes!" Without the pleasantries, I plunged in, venting my bitterness. "It's Joseph Wright! I have serious questions about him, Doctor. Sometimes

I think he's out of his mind! Crazy! Absolutely crazy! Joseph talks like my condition is related somehow to my religious commitment! You're a doctor! You know my history! So does he! Why does he raise such questions!"

Dr. Thompson's smile faded as I went on, and his manner became grave. Sitting down on the edge of my bed, he responded in a voice smooth, mellow. "The questions have to be asked, Sister. Yes, your vasomotor system is severely unstable. I've never seen such extreme postural hypotension—but why?"

"I don't think Joseph has the answer! I can't listen to him, Doctor! Where is he leading me! I'm afraid!" I covered my eyes with my hands, not wanting to see where that might be.

"My advice to you, Sister, is not to be afraid of hearing anything Joseph has to say. He can't lead you where you don't want to go."

"Yes, he keeps asking me if I want to continue—what impressed me from the very beginning is his complete openness to all possibilities—no preconceptions! I do want Joseph's help, but there are times like this when I question everything."

"I believe Joseph is uniquely qualified to help you, Sister." The certitude with which he spoke told me there was no more room for debate on that issue.

"You are a Catholic, Doctor. I feel you can better understand the issues I'm dealing with. I made final vows—FOREVER!" I knew Dr. Thompson to be devout in our shared religion but to have liberal interpretations along certain lines. I wasn't certain what his position might be.

"Can anything be 'forever,' Sister! I suggest you take one day at a time. Try not to look ahead. Meanwhile, you are showing progress, and I have some good news!" The smile returned. "I talked to the doctors at March Air Force Base today. The medical problems at high altitudes are not unlike yours! They think the principles of the G suit are applicable in your case and are going to come up with a total-body-compression suit to support your cardiovascular system. Worth a try—it would mean you might be walking around for longer periods of time. I told them to go ahead. What do you think?"

Total? For a moment I drew back, seeing only more "difference," not less. Then I quickly realized a G suit was less formidable than Joseph Wright. "Yes, Doctor, I'll try anything." *Perhaps there is a way to evade the truth.*

Dr. Thompson was ending his visit on a positive note. He reached down and squeezed my hand. "I think your questions are healthy, Sister. Ask for me anytime. Good night!" He turned toward the door, then paused. "Oh, do take care in the pool!"

Dr. Thompson slipped out the door, and I was left alone with my doubts and my questions regarding Joseph Wright.

Chapter 25

THE SOLITARY INDIVIDUAL

It was Sunday, and I was glad for a day when hospital routine stopped and my time was my own. I sat in the central patio and soaked up the California sun. The warmth on my skin felt unfamiliar yet comforting. It was a touch with life that, of late, was becoming desirable. My bent toward death was almost imperceptibly changing course. It felt good at the moment to *feel*, even if it was only something as basic to life as the warmth of the sun. My eyes were drawn to the brilliant splotches of color along the stucco walls of the patio, climbing red roses, and always the golden hibiscus that I now could see. It was with reluctance that I shifted my attention to the slim volume on my lap that Joseph had given to me.

Purity of Heart. For several weeks now, the book had been gathering dust on my nightstand, untouched. Now I felt an urge to pick it up, at least for a perusing glance. Before I knew it, I was reading, though slowly. The words were there, but meaning came with difficulty. For a long time now, my mind just couldn't focus—on anything, it seemed. The phrase *solitary individual* caught my attention. Immediately, I could identify—that was me. Perhaps this book would help me after all.

As I read on, a shadow fell across the page and I looked up to see a woman crossing the patio in my direction. There had been a restriction on visitors from the day of my admittance. *Who can this be?* She did not look familiar. She was smartly dressed, and her long dark-brown hair swung on her shoulders as she walked toward me. She had the California glow of a suntan, and I saw her as a very attractive woman. For a moment I saw my own drab appearance in contrast. As she drew nearer and approached my wheelchair, her eyes met mine. I had never seen such intensely blue eyes. She smiled and put out her hand. "You must be Sister Anne."

"Yes." And I looked at her inquiringly.

"I'm Louise, Louise Wright, Joseph's wife."

I was somewhat taken aback, for suddenly an almost fictitious figure had taken life and was standing there before me. I knew Joseph was married, but he spoke little of his wife, and I had been curious about her. I felt she was very fortunate to be married to such a man as Joseph. Genuinely, I responded, "Oh, I'm so glad to meet you, Mrs. Wright," and took her hand.

"Well, Joseph has told me about you, and I was here visiting in the hospital and decided to look you up. How are you getting along?" Her interest seemed genuine.

"Better, thank you. Joseph has been a great help to me. I am so grateful to him." I looked into her eyes, so intensely blue, and saw in them a sadness—and wondered.

"I'm glad to hear that, Sister." And then, an awkward silence. "I really must run along now—nice meeting you. I hope you get well." And with that, she turned and walked briskly away.

Watching her retreating figure, I felt a sensation unfamiliar to me—envy of another woman. *That can't be.* And then there was no warmth, no feeling. I was gone. The slim volume on my lap fell to the ground as I slumped forward in the wheelchair, catching the attention of the nearby nurse. I was only slightly aware of someone securing the straps about my chest and being wheeled back to my room.

"What is her blood pressure, Paula?" I could hear Dr. Thompson's voice far in the distance.

"Sixty over forty, Doctor. It's starting to rise, though, as it usually does once she's flat in bed again." I could feel the pressure of the cuff on my arm. I opened my eyes.

"Ah, you're back, Sister Anne! What happened?" Dr. Thompson sounded solicitous; his manner was always soothing.

"Nothing, nothing happened. I was just reading in the patio . . . sat up too long, I suppose, Doctor." I was crying, quietly, without sound. So often I broke down in tears when I came back from that place of Nothing. The shift was a shock to my system, and it never ceased to frighten and unsettle me. "I just want to rest."

"That's a good idea. It's Sunday anyway! I'll see you tomorrow, Sister." Dr. Thompson and Paula left the room, and I could hear their retreating steps down the hospital corridor.

I didn't think of Louise Wright again, and if her blue eyes intruded on my consciousness, I quickly dispelled them. I preferred the fictitious figure, bloodless and unknown.

Much later that night, I again picked up the volume, *Purity of Heart*. There was one passage that leapt out at me, and the words bored into my brain. The "solitary individual" was alone, yes, but alone before God. All other voices were silenced. All voices silenced—no one telling me what I ought to do, should do, was called to do, destined to do. No voice counted but mine, but Anne's. I was answerable to *no one* but God. *Is that possible! So many voices!* And suddenly, they crowded upon me, filling the darkness of the night on all sides.

You were always meant to be a nun, Sister Anne. Always! Your vows are forever. Remember! You're the perfect nun! Your superiors have great confidence in you. You have so much to live up to. Your suffering is precious. You are doing so much good—and saving souls. You're chosen, you know. All this is a temptation. The virtuous are tempted. It's the devil! Shut those doors! Who is Joseph Wright anyway! Don't listen to him.

Then the faces—Joseph Wright . . . Mother . . . Dad . . . Uncle John . . . priests . . . nuns . . . superiors . . . doctors . . . the church. So many! I unleashed them all, gave them all their time. Then, one by one, I crushed them. A strength I didn't know I had surfaced and a long, resounding "NO!" shrieked through the deepest recesses of my soul. And then a silence. The voices gradually receded in pitch until they were no more. *I was alone.* The solitary individual, Anne.

Light filled the darkness that had been my world for so long. I felt a presence, the nearness of someone who loved me and was asking me to be no more than that.

Anne. Anne . . . If I could only reach back to her.

God? God, please help me . . . Help me! The light reminded me of the warmth of the sun. I bathed in it until I slept. *Anne . . . Anne.*

> "Anne Elizabeth, you are now dead to the world. From now on you will be Sister Mary Francis, a member of the order of the Sisters of Charity." I heard the snip of the scissors and saw my long strands of blond hair falling down my shoulders to the marble floor of the convent chapel. "Please don't—must you cut all of it off—all of it?" I leaned down and picked up a strand and looked at it, wishing in some way to hang on to it. As I looked, it changed in color and became a short lock of auburn tinged with gold. It wasn't mine—whose was it? Oh, yes! I

raised my eyes and saw the bishop's chair—no, not the bishop's chair. What chair was that? It was enormous and leather straps hung from its arms. It looked made of steel. Oh, no, not that! Mark, your beautiful hair. Why are they doing that to you, Mark! Mark!

Someone was shaking my shoulders. It was Karen, the night nurse. "Sister Anne! Sister Anne! Wake up! You must be having a nightmare. You've been calling 'Mark.' Is there something I can do for you, Sister?"

For a moment, I couldn't speak. "Mark?" I had to struggle to retrieve the dream. "Yes, a nightmare."

Chapter 26

MARK

Pictures exploded in my brain like flashbulbs brilliant to black, blinding soul vision, though deceptively with momentary flashes of a time long past. Their attempts to bring to light buried memories barely intruded on my therapy session the next morning. Joseph was probing with his sharp scalpel, unaware I was balancing two worlds: part of me on death row, part of me in the now-familiar office.

"Karen reported you had a bad night. Tell me, Sister, who is this Mark? I think I should know." *White summer shoes . . . tapping.* "Sister Anne! Sister Anne, you simply can't keep passing out on me like this! Do you hear me?" *Ascending stairwell, serpentine.* "I'll wait it out, Sister! When you decide to return, I'll be here—and so will the questions!"

I felt warm hands take mine and the shroud-fog felt less fearsome. *White-knuckled hands gripping iron bars.* Someone was holding on to me, not letting me slip completely away, beyond reach. *Staring eyes, haunted, lonely, hungry.* Joseph's words heard only as distant sounds of frustration and despair not unlike mine—frustration and despair over a rare and severely disabling condition, a life of half awareness, sudden and frightening collapse, unconsciousness without warning, comatose-like states—all documented for the past twelve years and the unanswered question, why. No physician had ever determined the cause. Joseph's unrelenting, merciless questions spoke of his determination to pull out all the stops to unravel the mystery, knowing full well there was nothing to lose.

"What is it, Sister? What did Mark mean to you?" *Faces empty, pressing against iron bars.*

Mark . . . what was Mark to me? I felt some age-old wound smarting. Moaning, I strained against the heavy weight crushing my chest and brought myself to an upright position. Breathing came with difficulty in short gasps. My eyes would not open, the lids clamped shut like heavy iron doors. "Mark?" My voice was fog-like, thin, wavering, barely audible. "Nothing, really, Joseph—nothing—"

"Nothing? I don't believe that, Sister. Tell me about him." *Hands firm and strong . . . blue . . . auburn . . . gold . . . twenty-nine.*

"He's dead." *Bar-streaked sunlight on concrete walls.* "Mark is dead." *Murderer . . . innocent . . . smarting wound.*

Through the pain of the smarting age-old wound, I had reached a place within myself long lost, estranged, hardly me. I touched it, and the light remained brilliant for a longer time, freeing my eyes from their hooded prison and lifting the burden from my chest. Warmth flowed through me and even touched my words, softening their edge and giving them life of sound. *Anne . . . Anne.* "Yes, Joseph, Anne will tell you about Mark." I pulled my chair closer to Joseph's and took his hands in mine. I looked directly into his eyes and hoped he saw the slim circle of blue expanding, filling the dark wells with their light.

Joseph's response told me that he did. He gripped my hands firmly and smiled, looking relieved that the session had taken such an unexpected turn. He recognized that Sister Anne was no longer present. "You are more comfortable to be with, Anne. Do you know that?"

I ignored the question but smiled back—it was a smile less strained. "Mark? I guess I loved him. There wasn't time." *Through a glass . . . an enormous chair.*

"What do you mean, there wasn't time? What happened, Anne?"

"I only had two days with Mark—that's all." *Thick straps hanging lifeless.* My voice faltered, hesitated. "We corresponded for about eight months before his death. I knew when he was to die—the precise moment. It was a terrible thing . . . to know." The wound now bled.

"Go on, Anne. How did Mark die?" Joseph's question hung in the silenced air unanswered. I felt the iron doors close over my eyes, the great weight settle on my chest. *Condemned to death . . . death by electrocution.* "You've got to hold on to yourself, Anne! You've got to talk about this! As I said, I'm prepared to wait this out!"

Anne . . . Anne. The light within illumined memories, enabling me to go on. "That dream—I dreamt about it last night. Mark was electrocuted . . . murdered. The two days we had together were on death row. That was all . . . nothing more. But I did love him . . . NO! I don't know . . . nothing more . . . Nothing." *Thy will be done, O God.* I felt myself slipping back . . . back . . . light dimming into darkness . . . then Nothing. *Bound destinies.*

"Anne! Anne! You've got to stay with me! It's OK to love someone, to be attracted to someone. It's a natural experience . . ." As Joseph talked, I began hearing him somewhere in my world of unreality. *Letters . . . always letters . . . Anne . . . Anne! I* must *come back!*

"Joseph! Joseph!" My voice came from the fog place, once more thin, faint, distant. I knew I had lost touch with that far-off place of the lost self.

"Sister Anne, I want you to have another test and."

"NO!" I would not let Joseph finish. "NO! I've had enough! I've had all the tests I'm going to have! NO MORE! NO!" I tore my hands from his.

"Well, this will be somewhat different, Sister. Remember you said you wanted the truth. Do you?" Joseph's eyes looked deeply into mine searching for the answer. Through my fear, I breathed. "YES!"

"At any cost?"

"YES!" My voice now held power.

"OK. This test may help us get at the cause of your condition. Dr. Thompson has given his approval. We've great confidence in a cardiologist, Dr. Larkin, and have asked him to consult with us late in the week. Remember, it is always your choice, Sister. With your permission, we'll go ahead."

"Yes! I've got to know! I can't go on like this . . . but I'm afraid."

"Afraid of the truth?"

"Yes!"

"It's OK to be afraid, Sister Anne. We're into our second month of therapy. I think it's time. I'll be there, Sister." Joseph reached out to touch me but drew back. No one, he had learned, touched Sister Anne.

When I returned to my room, I reached for my prayer book on the nightstand next to my bed. I opened it and flipped through to find . . . to find . . . yes, there it was after all these years . . . the lock of hair. It was still lustrous, auburn tinged with gold, belying that day so long ago. It was a remembrance . . . a remembrance . . . *MARK!* How can one hide from love? Was it fear? Fear of being unlovable? Of betrayal of my one course in life to pursue divine love? Even I did not know how deeply I had felt, how deeply I had suffered Mark's untimely and violent death. It only confirmed that I was not to know love in this world. *Remembrance . . . best to forget.*

I snapped the book shut and gazed out the window. The grass was brownish and dry from the long, hot summer. *Everything dies . . . everything.*

Chapter 27

THE TRUTH

The light of the morning sun, barely touching the pines out my window, cast elongated shadows on the grass. I lay in bed, my face buried in the pillow, praying for strength. *The Lord is my strength and my shield.* It was the morning of the stress test. Somehow I knew the sun would rise on a world never again the same. *Why another test! Why? Different? How can it be any different! What greater price can there be!* There was no answer, no consolation.

I dangled my feet out the side of the bed, noticing their blue coloring becoming almost black as they reached to the cold floor. *Cyanosis.* Hanging on to the edge of the bed for support, I turned and looked into the dresser mirror, aware that within moments, the world would turn gray as my blood pressure plummeted and consciousness slipped away. The mirror reflected an image barely recognizable as mine—high cheekbones accentuated by sunken cheeks, lips thin and set, brows arched, eyes hiding the blue-rimmed black wells of fear under heavy, hooded lids. Colorless—like the plaster saints, bloodless, unfeeling, without life. The hospital gown hung loosely over my frame, like a big shirt on a scarecrow. Shapeless. The image in the mirror blurred, and I quickly sat back down on the bed and waited for the world to come back into focus. Then I changed my wrinkled, slept-in gown for the fresh one Paula had left at the foot of the bed. I pulled on a pair of slacks. I was ready. *Yes, I want the truth! The Lord is my strength and my shield.* As I was struggling with the demons in that early morning hour, I was unaware of the forces Joseph himself confronted in the chosen realm of my healing.

The door of the consultation room where cardiologist Dr. Thomas Larkin, coffee cup in hand, was waiting for Joseph Wright swung open.

"Good morning, Thomas! Sorry I'm late." Joseph took a small notebook out of his pocket and set it on the conference table.

"No problem, Joseph. Gave me some time to go over Sister Anne's records. I have some questions about the feasibility of the stress test in this situation." Dr. Larkin's voice, low and ponderous, rang with authority.

"OK, Thomas, let's talk!" Joseph poured himself a cup of coffee and sat down across from Dr. Larkin, ready for whatever resistance would be flung at him. "What's the problem?"

"Well, you and I have administered quite a number of these tests together as a team—and appropriately. The subjects were victims of heart attacks, fully recovered, or type A personalities considered to be high risk. I pretty much knew what was going on. But this! Sister Anne doesn't fit any category! Reading the history of her tachycardia and blood pressure instability to an extreme, I'm concerned! Simply too risky, Joseph. This is a rare phenomenon—we don't know what we're dealing with! And what's the purpose? Her limitations are obvious and treatment just not available." Thomas pushed the file toward Joseph and leaned back in his chair with the unspoken air of "What's there to discuss?"

"Look, Thomas, you've got to trust me. As you said, we've worked together for some time now. Yes, this *is* a different case—the usual just doesn't apply, but we must find out what's causing this debilitating condition—at least, do all I can to find out. I suspect there is a psychological component operating here. This test may give us some answers." Joseph could hear the intensity in his own voice and wished he sounded a bit more detached.

"I don't want Sister collapsing on me, Joseph—you know the risks! I'm the one ultimately responsible!" The cardiologist was not easily convinced.

Joseph realized that Dr. Larkin was feeling the weight of medical responsibility and hurried to reassure him. "Yes, she may—and probably will—collapse, but put her flat and she'll come around. Look, I've been watching this for two months. Agreed?"

Dr. Larkin lowered his head and drew a deep breath, saying nothing while struggling to give himself permission to do the innovative in his scientific world. Joseph waited apprehensively, feeling that much hung in the balance. Finally, Dr. Larkin broke the silence. "OK. Let's go ahead. Janice is assisting me—she probably has everything set up." With that, he got up, gathered his notes, and headed toward the laboratory; his indecisiveness was gone. Once again, he was a man of determination and confidence. Joseph followed, well aware of what he had taken on, and said a silent prayer that he was correct in his assessment.

The laboratory in which the stress test was to be administered was small and windowless. There was a treadmill in the center of the room and, next to it, an EKG machine. I lay on the gurney, a cooperative patient, while Janice applied cold jelly to my skin and attached the suction cups of the electrodes. I was glad for her chatter that demanded nothing of me, that distracted me from what lay ahead. My palms felt sweaty—there was no distraction from my fear.

"You sure don't look like a nun, Sister! Or maybe you do—something like those pictures in religious books. You're too thin—and you look like you've never seen the sun!" Janice's exasperation was not lost on me. If she had her way, I thought, she'd have me out sunbathing on the beach, eating hamburgers! "I can't imagine putting you on the treadmill. But doctor's orders!" Her last comment resolved any question she might have. "Dr. Larkin is such an excellent cardiologist. I'm sure he knows what he is doing."

Just at that moment, there was a knock on the door; and Joseph entered the room followed by an older, grayer man, whom Joseph introduced as Dr. Larkin. Then, walking over to the gurney, he reached out and touched me on the shoulder in reassurance. Fixing his eyes on me in that penetrating way of his, he quietly asked for the final time, "Are you ready, Sister?" I could only nod my head, my words locked in fear. He squeezed my hand, smiled, and turned away.

I listened as Joseph instructed Janice. "Watch the blood pressure readings carefully, Janice. I want you to call them out so that Sister can hear them."

"But, Joseph, we never do that!" Shock showed on her face. "It can be very—"

Dr. Larkin interrupted. "It's OK, Janice, we're going along with Joseph on this one."

Janice acquiesced, but her brow wrinkled in puzzlement as well as disapproval. She said nothing more.

I too was puzzled, realizing this was contrary to procedure in my experience. *Well, Joseph had said this test would be different.*

Joseph gave further instructions, saying, "Sister may collapse, so be alert. If that should happen, just put her down flat on the gurney. I realize this is rather unusual, but bear with me." Joseph pulled out a small notebook from his coat pocket. Joseph, obviously, was ready. *Am I? The Lord is my strength and my shield.*

Dr. Larkin took over. "OK, Sister, Joseph and I will help you onto this treadmill. We'll have to be careful not to detach any of the electrodes." Each took an arm and carefully lifted me onto the treadmill. I felt my body stiffen and knew this response to being touched did not go undetected.

I felt the ridges of the rubber mat through my stockinged feet as I was put down on the treadmill. "Grip these side bars, Sister, and we'll start the treadmill—slowly. We'll keep a slow pace. Don't worry about falling—we're right here." Dr. Larkin's voice did not betray his own doubts, which he had set aside in the making of a professional judgment only moments before.

The treadmill was turned on, and I started walking with the slow rhythm of the machine. Joseph stood close by my side and, glancing at his notebook, started asking the questions he had so carefully devised for this stress test.

"Do you know you are very attractive, Sister Anne?"

"Blood pressure rising . . . One sixty over one twenty." Janice's voice sounded detached and professional.

"Joseph, please . . . please don't do this to me!" I pleaded, my voice anguished and face contorted, suddenly realizing the nature of the test. *Different . . . I had not known!*

"Do you really want the truth, Sister?" The answer stuck in my throat. "Shall I go on, Sister Anne?"

I kept the slow pace of the treadmill, the moving rubber floor kept on . . . and on . . . and so did Joseph Wright. "Shall I, Sister?"

He read more than heard the whispered "YES, I WANT THE TRUTH!"

"You have a very sexy walk, Sister!"

"Blood pressure dropping." Janice and Dr. Larkin reached out to me protectively, fearing a state of collapse.

Joseph's next question came unremittingly, "Are you attracted to Jim, Sister?"

"Blood pressure sixty over forty . . . and dropping. Pulse one eighty." Before Dr. Larkin and Janice could move, Joseph asked, "Were you in love with Mark, Sister?"

There wasn't time for Janice to call out the blood pressure reading. My knees buckled—my body fell forward—my hands slipped from the side bars. I felt plummeted downward, caught in the eddying black spiral down . . . down . . . down . . . the small laboratory spinning . . . fading . . . to gray . . . to black . . . a cold, dark, inky substance enveloping me. THEY WERE CAST INTO OUTER DARKNESS! My whole life was but a flash of humiliation . . . shame. *I AM AN IMPOSTOR!* I felt exposed . . . violated . . . branded like the adulteress, a vivid *A* searing my forehead for all to see. *Weeping and gnashing of teeth.* Then no thought . . . no prayer . . . no feeling . . . no pain . . . no anxiety . . . nothing . . . the place of Nothing. Hands reaching to me . . . lifting me up . . . up . . . loving hands . . . the cold, dark, inky substance falling away from me . . . the black . . . gray . . . fading into light. I could see my body form being lifted from the treadmill and laid down on the gurney as one is laid in a tomb . . . lifeless . . . motionless.

I could hear voices in my place of light, could see Dr. Larkin's alarm as he leaned over the body form. "Goddamn! I've seen blood pressure gradually drop, but not like this! Bottom simply dropped out! Nothing is registering—zero zero!"

And Joseph, concerned but believing. "It's OK, Thomas, she'll come around."

"Blood pressure rising." Janice's voice sounded high pitched, nervous.

The light began to fade . . . the beautiful golden light. *Anne, your arms are outstretched . . . No . . . Grandmother . . . mercy . . . mercy . . . Do you want the Truth, Sister Anne?*

The blood pressure cuff felt tight on my arm. The body form was once more possessed by my spirit. I shook with cold . . . gasped for breath. A frantic bird felt trapped in my chest, its wings fluttering wildly against the walls of my heart.

Joseph was standing next to the gurney, holding my hand. "It's OK, Sister. It's over. You'll be all right. We'll talk later."

"Blood pressure returning to normal . . . pulse still rapid," Janice intoned. There were audible sighs of relief. I felt tears on my cheeks and I could not stop trembling. *Now I knew the price.*

Just as I had trembled with cold, my extremities numb, I now burned as with a high fever, the blood throbbing in my feet . . . my hands . . . my head, an overreaction or compensation in the cycle of severe vasomotor instability. I was suffering my "reentry" into life and consciousness. I slept fitfully that night, dreaming dreams that were beyond dreams.

> *March 19, 1954—profession day. The novice mistress, Sister Janine, stood next to me in the sanctuary of the novitiate chapel, smiling. I knelt on the cold marble floor, holding a large crucifix of brass and wood. The words formed in my brain, I, Sister Francis, vow to thee poverty, chastity, and obedience. I opened my mouth to give them life, moving my lips to form sound, but nothing came out . . . nothing. In the silence, Sister Janine continued to smile, believing I was making a sacred commitment. I had given the appearances of making vows, but had not. I WAS AN IMPOSTOR!*

As the day wore on, my circulation returned to normal and I could rest more comfortably—though the impostor remained on the edges of my consciousness. *Will my soul ever be at rest!* A tray of food set untouched by my bedside, and the blinds were closed for the night. In the darkened room, the nightlight cast an eerie glow. Joseph entered quietly, not wanting to disturb me, my form vaguely outlined in the bed, motionless, as though sleeping. I turned my head and fixed my dark wells of despair on him. The despair was tangible, lurking about my bed, mingling with the darkness. I said nothing, made no sound. Joseph impulsively, it seemed, leaned down and kissed me. Then, startled at his own behavior, he drew back, turned on his heels, and left.

It was not a time for words, only the prayer for mercy—the psalm, *Miserere*:

> "Have mercy on me, O God, in your goodness . . . wipe away my faults . . . wash me until I am whiter than snow . . . let the bones you have crushed rejoice again . . . do not deprive me of your holy spirit . . . renew my joy . . . Save me from death . . . Sacrifice gives you no pleasure . . . my sacrifice is this broken spirit, you will not scorn this crushed and broken heart."

The prayer for mercy became my own, indistinguishable in its expression of remorse and despair:

Oh, my God, help me! It can't be true! No, God, no, it isn't possible. Please don't let this be! All those lost years. My whole life, a waste. Where are you, my God? *I didn't know.* Have mercy on me, O God. *Miserere.*

Chapter 28

FEELING

The stress test had ripped the veil from the temple of my inmost soul, leaving me stripped, shamed, and with nowhere to hide. This soul I wrung out with Joseph in session after session—the terror, the remorse, the guilt, the innocence. *I DID NOT KNOW!*

I could no longer deny that there was a psychological basis for my disabling condition, no matter what the diagnosis had been, no matter how many high priests of the medical world had believed otherwise. And led me to believe. When I had held on to the belief that someone would come, someone who would help me, I had not expected someone like Joseph, or the help to be in such a soul-searing form. But there was nowhere to run, to escape the truth that I had sought with my whole being. There was no decision to be made; it had simply evolved: *I never should have become a nun*. I had no vocation. I never really wanted it. But I had succeeded at the expense of my own *self*, of Anne. I was now trying to get back to her.

I continued to lapse into unconsciousness only to wake to the unbearable agony of awareness, hearing my cries and the screaming *no* as though coming from hell itself. This hell became a pit from which I clawed myself out, day after day . . . session after session . . . threatening Joseph, "If you should leave me here, *you know what I will do!*" Thoughts of death, of dying, of killing the little life I felt within me, hovered over my waking hours. But I was not left there. I was not abandoned. Joseph went into the pit with me and risked everything on his side. It was one late September afternoon . . .

"Sister Anne, don't you think you should tell me more about this Mark? What was he *really* to you?" Joseph's question hung in the air, lost in the heavy silence.

I said nothing but looked into the empty space between us, seeing into the past. A sense of grief went through me, as one mourning.

Joseph tried again. "We both know *now*, don't we?" The implication of the *now* was not lost on me. *The stress test.* It had unleashed so many demons demanding confrontation. Even the spirit of Mark had been summoned as a witness to the truth.

I refocused my eyes on the present and looked at the countenance of this man who had pulled me back from that place of Nothing when the chasm was about to close—*forever. No, nothing is forever.* My voice was still weak and barely threading the silence to reach him.

"The sadness, Joseph, is that there truly *was* nothing. I can't say I didn't love Mark—not now—but I can't argue with what happened during the stress test. It's as though my body knows more, remembers more, than I do about my inmost self. How strange." I stopped talking, bit my lip, preferring to leave my thoughts in the realm of darkness.

"That's true, but what's so strange about that, Sister?" Joseph sensed I was holding something back.

"Strange how one can cut oneself off so completely from knowing . . . from feeling. Not until I realized the implications of the stress test did I *really* know what I went through back there . . . so long ago." I went into the dark place of my thoughts and again there was silence.

Joseph drew on his pipe, waiting, relentless. "Sister, tell me what you're thinking."

"What it was like . . . what it was like to know the exact moment Mark was to be executed, the exact moment when someone you loved was going to be murdered. I believed he was innocent, Joseph." I looked up at him, knowing the pain was fresh on my face. "It was a terrible thing to know the exact moment the switch would be pulled. Can you imagine? To see it in your mind? To feel the jolt? The abruptness of it? And perhaps the most terrible part, the waiting—two years of waiting, of building to that moment . . . and then the 'stays' of execution." Suddenly, a panic stirred within me.

"What is it, Sister?" Joseph could see the fear in my face.

"I hope that is not where I am right now . . . that this is *not* just a 'stay,' that nothing is going to change in the end. I've known so much waiting. I understand wanting to end the waiting no matter what the outcome."

"It's up to you, Sister. Is that what you want? Of course, there is a final death awaiting all of us—there's no denying that! It's going to be up to you whether you choose life or death, day by day, choice by choice. It's putting one foot in front of the other in the direction you want to go that we've talked about so many times. And remember, *all* the doors are open—you can always *choose* to go back to the convent."

The waters shimmered silver, grays, and black . . . There were figures on the shore, nuns standing as silent sentinels, looking to me as though waiting. The haunting dream of years past no longer a dream. "No! No!" I drew back, fear enveloping me. "I don't want that! I can't walk that path!" *I would be no more.*

"No matter—whatever direction you choose, I believe you can now follow through in peace—because the choice will freely be yours, Sister." Joseph spoke with conviction, and I wanted to believe him. Even though I shrank from the thought, I also recognized that the *idea of vocation*, of convent life, still held a powerful attraction for me.

"I'm so cold, Joseph, so cold." I hugged my sides and shivered.

"Will you accept my warmth, Anne? Here, let me take your hands." He reached out and pulled my hands away from my sides. Something in me yielded. I let my hands rest in his. They felt so warm, so good . . . human warmth. I wanted more.

"You say you want to get well, Anne, to learn to feel. I want that for you too. You know I care a great deal for you." I liked that he called me Anne. I felt his hands slide up my arms to my shoulders and pull me toward him. I again yielded—willingly. Suddenly, I was in Joseph's arms, held tightly against his chest. I wanted his touch . . . wanted to *feel.* I wanted to know I was *alive.* His hands moved down to gently fondle my breasts through the thin material of my blouse. I yielded again. I wanted it. And then the hooks of my bra were being loosened and Joseph's loving hands were on my virgin breasts, the caresses growing stronger till feelings entirely unknown to me were unleashed like a gushing spring that had been buried in the deepest recesses of the earth. *Yes, I want it, Joseph! I want it!*

"You are beautiful, Anne. Your breasts are beautiful." Joseph lowered his head toward my breasts . . . something in me snapped. *NO!*

"No! No, Joseph! No, it's wrong." I drew back abruptly, shoving my therapist roughly away from me. Then the horror of what I had done swooped down as a black vulture waiting to devour me. I threw myself on the floor. "Don't come near me. Don't touch me." My whole body stiffened in fear as I pulled my blouse to cover myself and crossed my arms over my breasts. I crouched in the corner of the office that had become so familiar to me, and now so threatening. Sister Anne was back. She was protecting the life that she felt ebbing from her control.

"It's OK, Anne. You didn't do anything wrong!" Joseph cautiously moved toward the door, saying in a firm but quiet tone, "No, I won't touch you. I'm going to get Dr. Thompson. Stay here—I'll be right back."

Time didn't exist for me as I sat huddled on the floor, afraid to move. I felt the returning cold and pulled my blouse more tightly about my shoulders. *I must leave! I'll go to that place, that place of fog, where I feel nothing, Nothing—it's still there for me . . . always waiting . . . yes, I'll do that.*

"Sister Anne! Sister Anne!" It was Dr. Thompson's voice, calm, soothing, nothing frightening. I didn't move or speak. "Joseph has told me what happened. He wants to help you. He also really cares about you." His voice went on and on, words with no meaning floated about the office but just the sound of them reassured me. *What was he saying? Joseph cared? Helping me? I don't understand.*

"Can you open your eyes, Sister?" I sensed Dr. Thompson kneeling down on the floor next to me, drawing closer. Still, I could not speak, tell him. *No, I won't open my eyes. I won't look. No, it didn't happen! Sister Anne wouldn't do anything like that.*

"Here, Sister, let me help you up off the floor." I felt a hand on my arm.

My tongue loosened. "No! Don't touch me."

"It's OK, Sister. This is Dr. Thompson. Here, let me help you up. Paula is here with a wheelchair."

Yes, I'll let her help me. "Take me out of here!" I reached out my hand to Paula, a lifeline, and blindly trusted her to guide me to the wheelchair. My eyes were still closed. And I was cold. I felt miserable. There was some deep, gnawing misery.

I did not show up for my therapy session the next day—or the next. I needed time to sort things out—alone. To look at Joseph Wright with discerning eyes, wide open, and to look within. *I had* wanted *to be touched!* I had not resisted, but welcomed the experience of my sexuality. Yes, I wanted to feel *alive*, but alive as a woman. I could not hide behind *victimization*.

I would be guided through this process by someone from "my own camp," so to speak. Dr. Thompson introduced me a friend of his, a Dominican priest, who was a teacher of theology at a nearby college. Another "voice"—another perspective on the road that seemed so fraught with deception. I recognized another choice point: *What am I to do? Who am I to trust?* Instinctively, I knew that Joseph had helped me. The shock of being touched opened doors that had to be opened. It had served its clinical purpose however unconventional. I could be touched.

I could *feel*. I came to understand that the unorthodox touching was not cold, isolated in the clinician's bag of techniques or exploitation and abuse. It was in the context of true caring and seeing what was *required* for my healing—even at great risk.

I also came to realize more fully to just what extent I had shut down my body. *A DISEMBODIED BEING!* The thought was far more reprehensible to me than the memory of the touching that had propelled me into such depths of guilt. My response was now one of anger that this disembodiment should have happened to me. *Indeed, this is the far-greater sin!*

My wise and experienced Dominican guide had listened well. Like Joseph, he kept *all* the doors open, never pushing me toward one or the other and honoring my freedom of choice, wanting only what was best for *Anne*. No judgment. I was spared the palliative words I had heard so often of "God's will" aimed at dissolving all conflict. By the week's end, I was ready to go on. Without the pain of embarrassment or shame, I returned to the familiar office with its spiraling smoke—and Joseph Wright. The touch barrier broken, no more did I recoil from his gentle hand reaching to me in reassurance, in encouragement. *I am touchable! And I am good.*

Chapter 29

AN INVITATION

Late September continued to bring warm days, drawing me outside in my wheelchair under the pines. I could now enjoy the sun, could feel its warmth. Acknowledging the unfolding aspects of the truth had released a reservoir of strength and determination. The heat of battle was mobilizing. As the weeks slipped by, great strides forward were made in my rehabilitation. I was now exercising without assistance and walking with the help of parallel bars. The walker was used more often than the wheelchair, giving me a greater degree of independence. The state of collapse was less frequent though the world of fog at times did continue to descend—even then I was learning my way back from that place of *Nothing*. No one could predict the level of well-being possible for me to attain. I set no limits. The downward spiral toward death was reversing itself.

Internally, realizations were slowly taking hold—visions beyond the ripped veil to the realities facing me. And I did not draw back as at first. In however unorthodox a manner, Joseph had touched some long-buried place within that gave hope that I could change. *Is it possible I am desirable as a woman?* I was beginning to have faith that there was a life ahead for me—and I did *not* want to live that life alone.

Sitting under the pines of the hospital grounds, I looked up through the sun-streaked branches to the unseen heavens and prayed to the god that had brought me to this point in time. *Thank you for revealing the truth, though I may never fully understand it. Thank you for restoring me to life. Please let there be someone with whom I can share this life.* I sat there motionless, a blank slate before God, allowing my prayer to take deep roots within me. *I want to share life with someone . . . Please let there be someone.*

Joseph had never crossed my mind.

It was a Sunday afternoon and I was restless, feeling a growing desire to break through the hospital barriers and spread my wings. I was feeling sufficiently well enough to know boredom. Of course, Joseph noticed this. *Joseph notices everything!* He invited me to his home for the afternoon, having cleared it with Dr. Thompson and the nurse on duty.

As we walked across the hospital grounds to the house next door, I wondered just where we were going. "I thought you lived in the foothills, Joseph." I paused on the pathway, leaning on his arm for support, and looked up at him. The walker had been left behind, giving me another level of independence.

"I did live in that area up until a few weeks ago. I moved . . . here," Joseph said, unlocking the door of the small white house with gray shutters. Again, I was puzzled, seeing no signs of life.

"Isn't your wife at home, Joseph?" I had expected the lovely young woman I had met in the hospital patio to greet me at the door—but no, there seemed to be no one in the house.

"No, she's not. Louise and I have separated." Momentarily filled with emotion, a cloud came over Joseph's face.

"I'm sorry to hear that. I hope things work out for you. I'm sorry." Something clanged within me, jarring my sense of propriety that I should find myself in a situation such as this.

"No, it's beyond that. Louise has already filed for divorce. It's been a long time coming, Anne. Now, it's just a matter of a legal settlement. Enough of that!" Joseph motioned to the couch, saying, "Sit down, take your shoes off, and put your feet up!" The cloud was gone.

I sank down on the deep-cushioned beige couch, quiet for a moment with my own thoughts while Joseph puttered about the kitchen. The revelation surprised me; I had no idea that Joseph himself was going through his own crisis. For the first time, I was seeing an *individual*, a person with a unique history, struggling with life issues. Just as I was. *So! We're to be alone!* Perhaps I would not have accepted the invitation if I had known. But I had accepted it and I intended to enjoy myself, though it took me a few moments to reassess the unexpected situation I found myself in and say *yes. Anne, you know you are glad. You know you want to be alone with Joseph!*

The living room, I observed, was unpretentious but comfortably furnished. There was an oval oak coffee table and thick, colorful cushions on the floor. Coming from the kitchen, Joseph settled down on one of these and lit a cigarette rather than the usual pipe. I was glad the ritual had been set aside, for a change. It all felt so strange to me, but then everything did that was not of my convent life. Even the clothes I wore: the same pale blue slacks and matching top I wore often for therapy sessions.

"How about some music?" Joseph bounded up and was at the stereo against the wall, pulling out his reels of tapes.

"Yes! I'd love that! I'm curious about what's popular today. You know, the sixties are a blank for me, as though I did not live through those years. I'm not referring just to my convent life—nuns were involved in the civil rights movement—even in the march on Washington with Martin Luther King. My real cloister was my illness." I talked as though to a stranger, and indeed, he was in some respects.

"Well, this afternoon, you're going to hear music of that decade. Time you're exposed to that big world out there!" I observed, from the expression on his face, that Joseph enjoyed sharing with me something important to him. Now, it was the fall of 1971, and the lyrics of Simon and Garfunkel coming from the Altec speakers poetically expressed feelings that were mine. "When darkness comes and pain is all around." It was difficult for me to understand the words—I simply didn't have the "ear." I heard enough, however, to know I would never forget the song and its association with this moment . . . "like a bridge over troubled water."

The afternoon progressed with Joseph sharing more of *his* music: Stevens, Diamond, and Dylan in particular. I immediately identified with Dylan's words "a rock feels no pain," and momentarily felt a squeezing of the heart in the realization of all I had missed. We found it easy to talk, easy to be together on a purely social level. We even laughed. Louise was not mentioned again, nor was any reference made to my therapy sessions. We talked as any two people getting to know each another.

"You mentioned you had been a minister at one time. What denomination?" Suddenly, I wanted the person sitting across from me to take on life dimensions. He already knew so much about me. Now I wanted to know about him.

"Actually, I still am an ordained minister in the Church of the Brethren. I had a pastorate in the hill country of West Virginia for several years. Rode horseback to serve several counties." He rested the cigarette on the ashtray and blew smoke in the air.

I couldn't help but smile at the image of my therapist galloping into the hollows! "Must have been quite an experience," I said, genuinely interested and wanting to know more. "You must have a lot of stories to tell, Joseph."

"You're right there! There's one I love telling about moonshine and how I got the guys making it into church. Even got my hat shot off by an old codger! But if I got started on my stories, Anne, I'd never get you back to the hospital on time. We'll save that for another time." *Another time.* Joseph walked back to the kitchen, and I could hear the perk of the coffeepot, a familiar sound that made me feel quite at home. Returning with a tray of cheese and crackers, he pulled the cushion closer to the couch and sat down. His closeness I found comforting.

"Why did you leave the ministry?" I was very curious about this, thinking there might be some correlation with my own history.

As Joseph talked about himself, I began to realize there was more of a correlation than I would have surmised. He too had felt "special" as a child, marked for some spiritual mission in life. Influenced greatly by his mother, he aspired to be a minister of God and a healer. At sixteen, he responded to his calling and was ordained. At that time, he did not question his destiny. It sounded all too familiar.

"I've been down my own path of self-discovery, Anne. I came up against some personal problems, as we all do. I began to question—and to look for answers. My very identity seemed challenged. 'Who am I?' 'Where am I going?' Beliefs that I thought were in concrete had to be altered or discarded all together. Each new insight required me to make changes in my professional and personal life, not unlike what you're going through now." Joseph paused, flicking the ashes from his cigarette, as though weighing just how much he should say. "I recognized I had to leave the pastoral ministry. I have no regret over those years, however. In fact, the Brethren's belief in an individual freedom of conscience actually helped me through that time. To this day, it is a core belief of mine. Guess I'll always be a Brethren at heart."

The perking of the coffeepot became a sluggish growl; the coffee was ready. Pausing in the telling of his personal story, Joseph made a trip to the kitchen. It gave me the opportunity to pick up the slim paperback on the coffee table. *Courage to Be* by Paul Tillich. I opened to the title page and saw in a scribbled hand the words "The dust of my illusions is the ground on which I stand."

Accepting a cup of coffee, I said, "Thank you. Did you write this?" I held the book up, pointing to the inscription.

"Yes. The words pretty well describe what we're talking about, don't they? If there is any one statement I would make about myself, it is that—*the dust of my illusions is the ground on which I stand.*"

The words called for no explanation. I immediately understood and was beginning to see the complexity of this man whose life evidently had not been a simple, straight line. I put the book back on the coffee table. "You know, from the first time we met I recognized we shared some orientation to spiritual realities—so I listened to you! I can see why." I sipped my coffee thoughtfully.

"I felt the same way. It is as though my life has prepared me to understand you, Anne. I'm not saying it is easy!" I could only pretend to be insulted by that remark; we both knew.

Joseph continued to share his own quest for truth, one that he pursued academically, studying the various life-related disciplines—theology, philosophy, education, and psychology. I was beginning to realize just how fortunate I was to have come into the hands of this unique therapist who could relate to me from such diversified points of view.

"You've certainly run the gamut in your studies, Joseph!" Not wanting to get too serious, I made light of his accomplishments but remembered seeing the framed diplomas on his office wall.

"Working with you, Anne, requires me to mentally turn the pages of all those books!" He shook his head and smiled.

Laughingly, I said, "Do I give you a hard time?" Then, in a more serious tone, I added, "As I told you before, Joseph, I waited a long time for the one who could help me."

"It's more than me. It's the Zeitgeist, the spirit of the times. I don't think it could be happening in any other space." Joseph rose and walked over to the stereo, turned up the volume. "Let's *hear it!*"

"Rolling, rolling . . . rolling on the river." The music of Creedence Clearwater washed over me, making it wonderfully impossible to think of anything else. My feet spontaneously moved with the beat.

"You know, Anne, I've never heard you laugh the way you have this afternoon! You really have a hearty laugh!" Joseph was obviously delighted at the revelation.

"I guess I haven't done much laughing lately! Comes quite naturally, if you can believe that." As though it would explain everything, I added, "I am Irish, you know."

The hours were but a moment. I had forgotten myself and had entered another's world. It was a new space for me where roles were dropped. We related as two individuals, not therapist and patient. I felt a well-being I hadn't experienced in many years, a freshness of spirit. I did not want it to end. I was glad to hear Joseph say, "Let's do this again, Anne. I've really enjoyed being with you." *Yes, Joseph, yes!*

Chapter 30

AWAKENING

That freshness of spirit, of well-being, stayed with me when I returned to hospital routine. I continued to relate to Joseph primarily as my therapist, but the relationship was subtly shifting to that of friends, and we knew the pendulum could swing dramatically one way or the other, day by day. One evening I was sitting in my big chair reading when Joseph appeared in the doorway. "It's great to see you up like this, Anne!"

"Sure feels great to me, Joseph. Thanks again for the other afternoon. I did enjoy getting away from the hospital." That was putting it mildly.

"Good! Because I'd like you to take a drive with me Sunday afternoon. This fall weather is great. Well, how about it?" He smiled encouragingly.

Joseph wants to spend time with me? For a moment I was taken aback and hesitated—but just for a moment. "Oh, I'd love to!"

"Fine—I'll clear it with the nurse on duty. Pick you up about two o'clock. Have a good night, Anne." With a wave of his hand, he was off to see another patient.

Sunday afternoon could not come soon enough.

The day dawned clear and bright, the San Bernardino Mountains sharply defined against a cloudless sky. Long before two o'clock, I was ready and waiting for Joseph. He did not disappoint me but arrived promptly and walked me to the car. There were times, like now, when the walker was no longer necessary.

"It's a perfect day for a drive into the mountains. How about it, Anne?" His voice had the lilt of joyous expectancy.

"I think I'd be happy driving anywhere—but yes, that sounds really great." Joseph helped me into the GTO—as a sports car totally lost on me—and in a short time, we were climbing the mountain that I had viewed from afar. My mood was one of exhilaration, and Joseph seemed to share in it, vicariously enjoying my new freedom.

"You know, Anne, one reason I like being with you is your enthusiasm. It's as though you're seeing the world for the first time—and I am seeing through your eyes." His hands were firmly on the wheel, but he would look over at me frequently as he drove.

"Yes, that's just how I feel. The first time! It reminds me of the sensations one experiences after a heavy rain has cleared the air—everything is so fresh, so pungent. The senses seem heightened." I was acutely aware that the same energy that went into the destruction of life I was now pouring into creating life. *So much lost time.* I winced, remembering the many years.

Joseph pulled the car into the turnoff and parked at the precipice overlooking the San Bernardino Valley. "There, Anne, is a feast for your new eyes. Fantastic view, isn't it, especially on a clear day like this?" My eyes scanned the valley, a world in miniature. I could identify the hospital, an insignificant small box from which I felt separate, free. "Yes, it is lovely, Joseph. How can I thank you for—"

"No, no thanks," Joseph quickly interrupted. "I'm doing this for *me*! I really needed a break."

Hearing something in Joseph's voice I hadn't heard before, I turned and looked at the man sitting next to me in the car. Feeling my eyes on him, he turned toward me and met my gaze. For a few moments, we simply looked at each other as for the first time and then quite naturally, without thought, were drawn together in an embrace. Joseph's arms were around me, holding me close to him, and I knew it was not the touch of the clinician. He pressed his lips to mine, and while I wanted to respond, the old tapes clicked in. *No, I can't . . . my vows . . . It's wrong . . . I have called thee by name. Thou art mine . . . a choice, Anne . . . always a choice.* This time, I did not push Joseph away, did not retreat into the place of fog, but chose the *voice* I would listen to and returned his embrace, his kiss. Then, releasing me, he simply held my hand, my hand no longer cold. For a time we said nothing. The silence was comfortable, allowing for the awakening to full awareness of what was happening between us.

"I'm attracted to you, Anne. You must know that. I think about you—I want to be with you. It's hard to say when I first realized this." My mind absorbed his words in silence, but I was listening.

"From the first time we met, Joseph, I recognized something about you. We were on the same wavelength, spoke the same language, shared some soul space. But I never thought of any romantic involvement—not until that afternoon in your home. Even then, I didn't think you could ever see me in that way." Somewhat embarrassed at this admission, I faced the window and studied the few rather-withered poppies at the bluff's edge that had survived the summer heat.

"Well, I *do*, Anne. If we're both open to it, wanting it, I'd like to have time with you outside the hospital." There was a tentative, uncertain tone in his voice that told me he was insecure as to the response he would get.

Amused, I turned back and laughed. "Want it! There's no question about that, Joseph." His arms were around me again, and again he kissed me. The real question was if I could give myself *permission*.

Coming down from the mountaintop, we had little to say, holding hands and enjoying the pines and vistas that passed by our car windows. Before we reached the valley floor, unrest was growing within me. I felt an urge to destroy the beautiful thing that was happening. An indefinable darkness came over me, blotting out the sunlight of what had been a lovely day.

I turned and studied the man driving the sports car. *A strong profile . . . high forehead . . . like Uncle John . . . No, nothing like Uncle John . . . certainly not as handsome . . . as tall . . . nothing like Mark . . . no auburn tinged with gold . . . how can I be attracted to this man?* I drew my cold hand away from Joseph's and moved closer to the window.

Destroy . . . destroy.

Abruptly, Joseph stopped the car by the side of the road and turned to face me. "What is it, Anne?" His voice was hard, his eyes probing, the clinician's eyes. I wanted to jump out of the car and run—hide.

"What do you mean, 'What is it'!" There was anger in my voice.

"You changed—there has to be a reason. What's going on?" The lover was gone.

"Are we having a session right here, Mr. Wright!" I slumped down in the seat, looking out the window indifferently.

"Looks that way!" Joseph grabbed me by the shoulders. "Look at me, Anne! You want to destroy this, don't you? Too much good, Anne? Can't take it? Have to suffer?" The questions came with staccato force.

"Stop it, Joseph, stop it!" I screamed. "Yes, I do want to destroy it! How can I be attracted to you? You're not anything like Uncle John!" The old *measuring stick* pierced the mountain air like a lightning bolt.

"Oh, so that's it—not good enough for you! Well, I'm available, Anne. I'm real—no fantasy—and I want you. But it's up to you. You've got to fight for what you want or just give in to the demon voices. It's not enough, Anne, to *choose life*. You've got to decide how you're going to live, who you're going to be." Joseph released me and I slumped down in the seat, my head in my hands.

"Oh, Joseph, I do want you—I do! Help me! I don't know what comes over me. You're right. I did want to destroy what's happening between us. Please, please don't go away!" I reached toward him. "Hold me, Joseph. Hold me."

"I'm not the one going away, Anne. I'm ready to fight this thing—are you?" He put his arms around me.

I drew back, looked up at him through hooded eyes. "I don't know."

The next day, Joseph had an appointment with Dr. Lindsey, who had referred me to Mountain View. He had followed my progress, but this was his first visit, and the long drive had been considerable. I had been asked to join them but did so with some trepidation.

"Oh, Dr. Lindsey! It is so good to see you!" And it was. He had seen me through so many desperate years of illness and hospitalizations. Spontaneously, we hugged each other in the joy of meeting under such different circumstances.

Dr. Lindsey stood back and looked at me, smiling broadly. "Anne, I can't tell you how wonderful it is to see you on your feet."

"I never thought I'd be thanking you for sending me here, Doctor! Yes, it is wonderful. It's slow, but I am so much better, as you can see." We sat down opposite Joseph in the small office. I noted the ritualistic pipe resting in the ashtray, the thin swirl of smoke in its usual ascent. "Joseph has told you what's happening here, Doctor?" I spoke in veiled terms, hesitant, somewhat embarrassed.

"Yes, he's filled me in—I'm so glad you're getting the help you need, Anne. I knew I didn't have the answers. When I pressed you to come here, this was my hope." His voice was still gentle as I had remembered.

"I didn't *know*, Dr. Lindsey, really I didn't." That was the closest I could come to saying the words. My voice broke in the realization of the long years this kind physician was at my bedside.

"Anne, I know that!" He put up his hand, a gesture that said I need not say more. "You've got to put all that behind you now and go on. You're such a fine person, Anne, and I believe you have a full life ahead of you."

Joseph broke in, "That's what I'm telling her, Dr. Lindsey, but sometimes she thinks she doesn't even have the right to live. She's got to fight for what she wants!" Joseph paused and looked questioningly at me. "You're not so sure about that, are you, Anne?" I glared at Joseph, sensing he was about to expose me more than I wanted him to. He went on. "What's that destructive streak in you, Anne, that lashes out when things get too good?"

That did it! Impulsively, I kicked Joseph in the shin to stop the threatening flow of words. Then I realized what I had done. My face flamed with embarrassment. I glanced quickly at Dr. Lindsey, hoping my aggressive act had gone unobserved. But no. Dr. Lindsey looked startled, then leaned back in his chair to enjoy a good laugh.

Joseph only smiled, but I could see he was enjoying my discomfort. "Dr. Lindsey's never seen this side of you, has he, Anne?"

"Joseph, why are you doing this!" I was angry that I could not sustain my Sister Anne image for Dr. Lindsey.

"Because Dr. Lindsey has a right to know—and because he cares! You need all the support you can get, Anne, but none of this phony stuff."

I bit my lip, restraining any further outburst. I turned away from Joseph and faced Dr. Lindsey. "It is true, Dr. Lindsey, there is some duality in me about life. I pull back at times."

"Anne, I've observed this—just didn't know what to do about it. You were so sick! You're in the right hands now—listen to Joseph." Dr. Lindsey glanced at his watch. "I've got to go—thanks, Joseph, for your time." He rose from his chair and patted me on the shoulder affectionately. "Let me hear from you, Anne!"

After the door closed behind Dr. Lindsey, I turned to Joseph, feeling intense anger. "Sometimes you are absolutely infuriating! I could—"

"Could what, Anne? Go ahead, say it! Could what?"

"I've said too much already!" Suddenly, the anger drained from me and a deep fatigue set in. I slumped in the chair. There seemed to be a chill in the office. *No, I won't. I* do *want to live.* "Joseph, I don't want to be this way." I looked up into the piercing brown eyes that saw so much, that reflected so much. *How can I love this man?*

Chapter 31

CONFRONTATION

My mother chattered along brightly about nothing while my father sat silently at the wheel, maneuvering the shiny, new white Oldsmobile down Highway 10. We were headed toward Palm Springs, only an hour or less drive from the hospital. I was on leave, my first since my admittance four long months ago. It was now October, the ideal time for Palm Springs, and I was feeling more alive than I had for as long as I could remember. I tuned out the drone of my mother's voice and went into my own reverie, lulled by the beauty of the mountains, whose stately presence somehow gave strength to my soul.

The car swung into the driveway of the condominium, and I was glad the ride was over, as much as I had enjoyed it. I was tired. My strength was coming back, but it was so slow. My father opened the car door, and I reached out and took his hand. He had my walker ready for me, unearthed from golf clubs in the trunk of the car. With this assistance, I slowly walked to the door, vaguely aware that my parents were having some sort of disagreement. It sounded all too familiar. I knew they would make a special effort these two days for their religious daughter. *Religious daughter.*

The condo was modern but casual and tastefully decorated. When I saw the patio facing the mountains outside the glass double doors, I knew what I wanted to do. My father was carrying in the luggage, and I knew he'd be on the phone, arranging a golf time. "Mother, if you don't mind, I really need to rest. I'd like to enjoy the patio and sleep, if I can. The long ride was tiring."

"Of course, dear." My mother was quick to agree. Her agenda was to please me, not wanting to upset any applecart. "Here, Anne, let me help you. There . . . I'll cover you with this afghan I brought along. Sleep as long as you can. Dad and I will be in the living room. Golf's on TV this afternoon, you know. Just call if you need anything!" I sensed this suited her just fine, and she walked off briskly, leaving me alone—alone with my thoughts. I really wasn't sleepy. I felt too exhilarated.

I looked out from the patio to the undulating long stretches of white sand reaching to the mountains, whose contours were sharply etched against the deep blue of the clear sky. The Sunday afternoon drive with Joseph came to my mind—just such a day as this. Our relationship was deepening with each passing day but always volatile, even tumultuous. *Joseph! Is my prayer under the pine tree being answered?* I raised my hand that had been resting on my mother's colorful afghan and touched my breast. Breathing deeply the clear desert air, I whispered, "Yes, Joseph, I intend to fight!"

After dinner, we were enjoying the cooling breezes of the desert, leisurely having coffee in the patio. It might have been many evenings out of the long-distant past under the rose arbor—Mother with her crocheting, Father with his expensive cigar and the night, the night under the stars of the desert skies. Only once in a while, the silence was broken by some domestic comment by my mother or reminiscence by my father. *I look to the mountains for deliverance.* The words of the psalmist came to my mind as my eyes followed the curve of the darkened mountain, now a foreboding presence breathing down upon us. I knew what had to be said.

"Mother, Dad . . . there's something I have to tell you." Immediately, the calm of the desert air was riddled with apprehension. They both looked at me, barely visible on the lounge under the low patio light. The spectral look, I knew, had not totally vacated my visage, and my eyes were dark with dilated pupils—I was afraid. *I am taking my life in my hands, my own hands. Have I ever done that? How do I look to them now, my parents?*

Surprisingly, my mother said nothing. She waited, looked at me disconcertedly, not knowing what to expect. My father's way was to wait in silence, not really needing to know. Drawing a deep breath, I ventured to plunge in. "A lot has happened to me these past months at the hospital—more than you know."

Now my mother did interrupt, "You don't have to tell us that! You're certainly different—"

"Be quiet, Lenore, and let her talk." I smiled gratefully at my father.

"Well, I've made a decision." I wished my voice sounded a bit stronger.

"A decision!" I could feel rather than see my mother's apprehension.

"Be quiet, Lenore!" My father leaned forward encouragingly. "Go on, Anne. What decision?"

"I'm leaving the order." I didn't mince words, and they had a shock effect. I didn't have to worry about my mother interrupting. For once, she was speechless. So I went on. "I never should have been a nun, really. I've questioned my vocation from the very beginning! I thought the conflict had been resolved before final vows. Evidently, I was wrong. I have come to believe the conflict I have lived with so long has taken a terrible toll on me, on my health." There, I had said it, abruptly, concisely. There was no easy way of saying it.

"Leave the order!" My mother had her voice back. "You've been a nun for twenty years! How can you do that? Heavens, what will people say, Anne! And in your condition . . . who's going to take care of you?" And her voice faded as though overwhelmed at the questions she had entertained.

My father broke in. "We know you're very sick, Anne. But leave the order? What do you know about the world! How can you support yourself? You can hardly get around!" His voice faded too at the question he had raised—support. His vulnerable area, even though I felt he would give his life for me.

It was all I could do to hang on to the newfound person within—Anne. These questions too I had asked and sweated through. They were real. I was thirty-eight years old. I had nothing. Nothing material. No friends. No assurance I would regain my health. I felt an island unto myself. How could I dare to think of beginning a new life! But I addressed myself to their questions, and my voice was strong with conviction.

"All that you say is true, but not insurmountable. The doctors are not telling me I will be well. I may always have limitations, probably will, but there is a way. I plan to get an apartment close to the college and get my California teaching credentials. There is help available for the disabled, financial help, through the state. I'll have a live-in attendant on a full-time basis. I can do it. I know I can. I'm not asking you for help. Just give me your emotional sup . . ." My voice broke and my chin started to tremble. I was terrified. I could hardly deal with my own doubts and fears, let alone theirs. "There's nothing more to talk about. I'm going to bed now." I got up, gripped my walker, and walked out with all the dignity I could muster. My mother didn't follow.

I couldn't sleep, the words that had been said replaying in my mind, never to be retracted. On the edges of my consciousness, I could hear my mother and father talking quietly far into the night. And then silence. I looked out my bedroom window across the patio to the mountain, no longer formidable but a reservoir of strength in the starkness of the night. I picked up my rosary beads, *Our Father . . .*

Intruding on my prayers from afar, I heard faint strains of music. *No, it isn't my imagination!* "When you're weary, feeling small." I recognized the melody being carried over the desert air from the nearby park loudspeakers. I smiled to myself, remembering that Sunday afternoon in Joseph's home, listening to the music of Simon and Garfunkel. "Like a bridge over troubled waters, I shall lay me down." The soulful lyrics coming from afar were the last thing I heard. I was lulled into a deep sleep, breathing the pure desert night air, and whispering the name I had so mysteriously come to love, "Joseph."

Chapter 32

LOVE LETTERS

I awoke with a different name on my lips, the name of *Jesus*. *I rise from this bed of sleep in the name of our Lord Jesus Christ crucified.* My customary way of greeting the morning in religious life automatically rose from my mind and heart. Rather than getting up, however, I settled myself upright on the pillows to look out the window—and to think. The rising sun cast a golden glow on the deep purple of the mountains, and as it spread, shadows formed and shifted, now here, now there, as though some entity were moving across its surface. Somehow, I saw myself a shadow, moving through change, chased by some spirit light as I climbed insurmountable barriers. Yes, a shadow, having cast off internally the *nun-ness*, yet what was I? I picked up my notebook on the nightstand and began to write. Writing always helped me to clarify my thoughts.

> Of what am I afraid? Loneliness—of being alive in a vacuum. Life without meaning—of no truth for which to search, of no identity to find. That there will be a void, an emptiness, conditions for death in life, and never having lived at all.

I put the pen down. There were no words really for what I was feeling. I was watching my life being stripped away. My whole world. By now, my superiors had received my letter, telling them of my decision to leave the order. The letter had been difficult to write. I remembered the words, brief and to the point:

> It has been established to my physicians' satisfaction and to my satisfaction that there exists an interrelatedness between my persistent efforts to live religious life and an illness of more than ten years, causing severe disability. I do not believe the destruction of life can be to the glory of God.

Destruction of life—I winced at the thought of what I had done and fought back the tears. I found myself still fighting the truth I could no longer deny.

The condo started coming alive with morning sounds—the back door swinging shut as my father left for an early round of golf, water running in the bathroom, coffee perking. I visualized my mother sitting down at the vanity table to put on her face. Mother did not know how to be casual. Her makeup and dress were rituals with which she began the day, always ready. *Ready for what?* I wondered. Soon, I knew, she would bring me morning coffee and help me put on the support suit that I still needed for circulation. This morning, I dreaded being with her, which was a new and inexplicable feeling. I picked up my pen again and took out a piece of notepaper. I began writing a letter to Joseph:

> *Dear Mr. Wright:*
>
> *Such a formal beginning! Sister Anne must be around. She comes and goes at will. My dearest Joseph, Anne misses you terribly. There is so much beauty here and I constantly find myself wanting to share it with you—as though it is incomplete without you. You add a dimension unknown to me before in life. I love you, Joseph, and it is so good to be loved. I am anxious to get back—to see it in your eyes, your smile.*

I reread what I had written and was struck by the duality: *Sister Anne . . . Anne. Will I ever be free of it? Who will I be when my mother comes to the door?* I felt a hardness go through me. I knew. No question about it. *Anne* was fighting for her life.

The bedroom door opened slowly, giving me a moment to put the letter out of sight. My mother peeked in, not wanting to wake me if I should still be sleeping.

"I'm awake, Mother, come on in." I smiled when I saw her appearance. So characteristic. Impeccably dressed! Mother had a commanding if not regal presence. When she entered a room, she drew all eyes and attention to herself. Now, she filled the small bedroom as she walked over to my bed.

"Good morning, dear." Leaning down, she kissed me on the cheek. "Have a good night?" She meant business as usual. I could tell her intent was not to rock the boat, say nothing that could offend me. I sensed a new attitude toward me, however. *Is it fear? Does she feel something slipping away from her?* I couldn't quite put my finger on it. But the air between us was different. There was a strain, not the usual closeness, and I drew back from that kiss.

"Can I bring you some breakfast, dear?" She sat down on the side of my bed and stroked my arm.

"No, Mother, I'd rather get dressed and eat on the patio this morning." Even to me my voice was cold, detached.

"Are you sure you're up to it now, Anne?" Her expression was one of concern.

"Yes, I'm sure, Mother." My cold fingers smoothed the bedsheets, smoothed the bedsheets.

"Then let me help you with that support suit. I know how hard—"

I curtly interrupted, "I can do it myself. Thank you, Mother."

"I really don't mind, dear."

"I said no, Mother, please." There was a tone in my voice and a look in my eye that was not lost on Mother.

"Oh, all right, dear. I'd like to go shopping for you, Anne—you certainly need clothes! I saw an outfit . . ." As Mother went on planning my wardrobe, I tuned her out, ceased listening. I grew uneasy, disturbed. Mother's features kept changing, one visage melding into another. *She frightens me! I can't think!* Strength was ebbing out of me. I needed to rest. I closed my eyes and heard my mother's voice, as from a distance. "Anne! Anne!" I felt a cold hand touch mine, limp and lifeless. She sighed deeply, recognizing, all too well, the *signs*. I had withdrawn. *She can't touch me here!*

When I opened my eyes, Mother was no longer there. I knew hours had passed as the shadows on the mountains were gone, cast out by the noonday sun. My first thoughts were of Mother, realizing she was seeing quite a different person from the Sister Anne she had admitted to the hospital that day in July. That person, totally dependent on Mother, was pulling away, and Mother didn't know what to do about it.

I reached for the glass of water next to my bed and saw a letter propped there. *A letter! Mother must have put it there while I was sleeping.* I picked it up and recognized immediately Joseph's hand. I tore it open and began reading.

> Dearest Anne:
>
> My first writing to you. It comes out of my solitude tonight. Memories of you in all the ways we have shared thus far float across my awareness. How much you, Anne, have become a part of my existence! Independent of my own separateness as a solitary individual, you, Anne, have become the most influential *other* in my life. If this should sound too scholarly or clinical, let me say it means in more poetic terms that I love you! That I want to share with you what I am and what I have to give as a person and a man to you, a person and a woman. I feel your absence here at the hospital, but it has given me an opportunity to become aware of your significance to me. I want to tell the world that I love you, Anne!
>
> I hope you won't be too disappointed if your parents can't comprehend or appreciate what you have been struggling with for so long. *Let them go!* Remember, the Lord will provide what you need as Anne.

Joseph's declaration of love was not lost on me. I would reread his words many times just to believe it was true: Joseph loved me. It was his comment, "Let them go," that snagged my mind. I don't want to hurt them; they are my parents! And I love them. *Help me, O God!*
Unless you leave Father and Mother, you are not worthy of me.

I was relieved and glad to return to the hospital the next afternoon. It was a homecoming—and Joseph was there to greet me, his eyes shining. Beyond Joseph, however, I felt a fairly general acceptance of the person I was becoming. A dozen red roses welcomed me as I walked into my room. I picked up the attached card. It was signed simply, "Lenny." Dear, thoughtful Lenny . . . all those attentions . . . how blind could I be!

Lenny volunteered his services at the hospital on weekends and some evenings during the week. A kind, giving man with a big smile for everyone. Out of the goodness of his heart, he carried trays, pushed wheelchairs, and visited with patients. When I needed some assistance, he would be there for me—from the very beginning. I remembered when

I first went to the dining room, it was Lenny who pushed the gurney, talking all the way in an effort to put me at ease. He even extended himself to Mother and Dad when they were visiting. *Dear, sweet Lenny.* I felt comfortable with him, not intimidated by his good looks and size. He was a big man, yet so gentle with me. I felt safe with him and enjoyed his company. Lenny had always been attentive to me, but something had changed when he learned I was no longer Sister Anne. I simply had not recognized it for what it was.

Chapter 33

SISTER CELINE

The warm water of the therapeutic pool felt sensuous this day, the eve of my thirty-ninth birthday. I knew Joseph had something special planned for me, but I could not enjoy the anticipation of the morrow. I was nervous. Today the regional superior, Sister Celine, was going to see me. Emotionally and spiritually, she had supported me through the trying months leading to this hospitalization. This was Sister's first visit since receiving my letter requesting an indult of secularization, of release from vows. I could not help but be apprehensive. I knew she would see me profoundly changed.

I looked down at my swimsuit-clad figure and could not deny my body was changing—just as I was changing. The yellow-print, two-piece bathing suit that had hung on me, shapeless, now revealed curves though I did not have the eyes to see the changes taking place.

I moved through the water with a few easy strokes, reveling in the freedom of movement. Water supported my cardiovascular system, enabling me to make slow but steady progress. I had been walking across the pool, submerged up to my chin, long before I could walk down the hallway. Now I could swim several laps of the pool's width.

I remembered the time, some months back, when I had flirted with death as my body had slipped from the straps that secured me to the side of the pool. My attempt to drown the voice of Joseph Wright: "Who is your god, Sister Anne?" I could answer that question more definitively now, and I was glad that there would be a tomorrow, my thirty-ninth birthday. A celebration of life!

I turned over on my back in the water, allowing my legs to float to the surface. I could see the rays of light coming through the skylight and piercing the water's depths. I could feel their warmth on my skin that was now the color of living flesh. *My god is a god of life!* The water lapped about my chin, splashing my face, splashing my mouth, my nose, flirtatiously mocking my memories of death. The waters of life.

I changed position and swam to the other side of the pool, my last lap. I must be ready to greet Sister Celine.

My hair still damp from swimming, I was sitting on the big stuffed chair in my room, an unopened book on my lap, when Sister Celine arrived. She was dressed in a conservative black suit, and her short graying hair was simply styled. A tall, slender woman, her bearing was dignified, and her warm smile lit up my hospital room as she entered. Vibrantly alive, she had the glow of goodness, a solid goodness, her feet firmly planted on the earth, her eyes seeing beyond. I knew her to be a woman of wisdom and sound judgment who could follow through with practical decisions. She was a person I could trust. *Why can't I be like you, Sister! Why can't I be a good nun! You are so alive! I tried . . . tried . . . why?*

Sister Celine strode across the room confidently, leaned down, and hugged me. Her caring was real and genuine. I did not draw back. She always simply called me Anne, as she did now.

"Anne, you look wonderful!" I knew she wasn't referring to the light-blue slacks and matching top or the few pounds I had gained. The change went much deeper than that. *What do you see, Sister Celine? If only I could tell you!*

The audible words were "Thank you, Sister, I feel so much better! Really, I'm so glad you're here."

"What beautiful roses, Anne!" She leaned over the crystal vase on the dresser and sniffed their fragrance, gently touching the velvet petals. She was sensitive enough not to ask who sent them, and I volunteered nothing and never mentioned Lenny. "Well, we have an hour or so before my appointment with Mr. Wright. There's so much you and I have to talk about, Anne. I received your letter."

Fear clutched at me, fear of words that I had heard so often in the past. *It's a temptation . . . You know you have a vocation . . . God's will, Sister, God's will.* Fear prevented the flow of words bottled up in me for so long. *No! I will not listen!*

The strong, soft voice went on, Sister Celine unaware of my internal dialogue. "First of all, Anne, I want you to know that I support your decision entirely. So does our president, Sister Gregory. We are happy for you, Anne—not that we want to lose you—we just want you to be well and have a full life. And we will do anything that we possibly can to make . . . Anne, do you hear me, Anne?"

Happy for me? Support my decision? Yes, I was hearing. I smiled, a smile that came from the roots of my being. This time the doors would remain open. I reached over and hugged Sister Celine again, feeling tears, but now tears of joy and relief. *Finally, there is someone who can hear me . . . can see.*

"Oh, Sister, thank you . . . Thank you! I love the order—I always will. I have so many friends—"

"Your friends will still be your friends, Anne. Those who go away were not real. They are no loss."

I knew the person sitting across from me was real, would always be a friend, as at this moment. I envied her calling, her vocation—a calling and vocation never mine. *Why? Why can't I be like you—like so many others?* Many are called, but few are chosen.

We talked of many things—those of the spirit and the practical. Sister Celine assured me of the order's financial support until I was independent, standing on my own two feet. My request for an indult of secularization would not be granted until that time, perhaps a year—for my protection. However, I should consider myself an adult woman with freedom to make my own decisions, to choose my own lifestyle. I was not to be bound by the vows during this time.

The hour sped by swiftly, leaving some things unsaid. There was one area within that I kept hidden, out of fear. I could not risk telling Sister Celine of my personal involvement with Joseph. I gave myself this right to privacy, to remain silent as an independent human being. Though I had come to claim this right, to do so was to underestimate this woman bringing me so much love and support.

"I've got to run along, Anne. I don't want to be late for my appointment with Mr. Wright. I'm so glad we had this time together. Think only of yourself now and grow strong and well. We'll be in touch." A parting hug and she was gone.

Her supportive, life-giving presence further strengthened my resolve to continue on the course I had chosen. Even so, I was apprehensive that Joseph would divulge his personal involvement with me.

"Ah, Sister Celine! I've looked forward to meeting you!"
Joseph put out his hand in welcome.
"I'm glad to meet you, Mr. Wright."
Cordially, they shook hands, and Joseph motioned to the empty chair opposite his desk. "Please, sit down!"

Even with Sister Superior, Joseph began with the ritual of his pipe. Caressing the wooden bowl, he asked, "You don't mind, do you, Sister?"

"No, of course not, Mr. Wright. Our pastor smokes—I'm quite used to it."

"Thank you." Joseph proceeded to slowly fill the wooden bowl, tapping the tobacco with his finger, striking a match—the ritual set the mood, the smoke swirling toward the ceiling, incense-like, bespeaking the sacred. The conversational tone became reverential, subdued, as whispered words in a cathedral, speaking of things not casual or rarely spoken. *Sotte voce.*

Joseph began the session. "I'm glad you're here, Sister. Anne needs your support—emotionally. Have you seen her?" Joseph's eye searched Sister Celine's face, as though reading what may be unspoken.

"Yes, the change in her is phenomenal! Anne looks like a different person. Tell me, Mr. Wright, what were your perceptions of Anne when she was admitted here?" Self-composed, Sister Celine sat back in her chair.

"Well, she came for her first appointment on a gurney, reluctantly. She was emaciated, extremely pale, and very frightened. I would say in a panic—fear state—terribly confused as to what was medical, what was psychological, terribly concerned about her integrity . . . desperate for help . . . in real soul despair. In Anne's words, 'wanting the truth—at any cost.' I concurred with Dr. Lindsey that she could not have gone on much longer, Sister Celine." The memory of that first meeting still had an effect on Joseph. His expression was grave, troubled.

"I agree with you, especially this past year. I saw such a decline in Anne's health." Sister's voice dropped to an almost inaudible level. "Mr. Wright, some spirit went out of Anne—she became so depressed, withdrawn—and her physical condition! She grew frailer and incapacitated, helpless, slipping more and more into that comatose-like state. I didn't know what to do to help her, Mr. Wright. Dr. Lindsey didn't know what to do. It was terrible just to watch . . ." Sister Celine stopped midsentence, at a loss for the words to describe the helplessness she had felt.

"When I first saw Anne, Sister, I too had no idea what to do. To be honest with you, I didn't even want the case! Anne's extremity was intimidating—even to me!" Joseph smiled, remembering his initial reactions. "I think she was leaving this world in a very real sense, slowly dying, physically dying, and psychologically withdrawing from reality."

"I suspected such . . . I tried to reach her, but it was futile. Well, it seems she is in the right place—that you, Mr. Wright, have been able to reach her. Tell me, how much longer do you think Anne will be in the hospital?"

"It's hard to tell—perhaps a month or so. As you said, the change in Anne is phenomenal. Emotionally, she has a ways to go—certain cues trigger setbacks and symptoms recur, but she is learning how to handle this."

"You know, Mr. Wright, I see her mother as a very difficult person, creating problems for Anne. What is your opinion?" Sister Celine looked directly at Joseph. She too was making an evaluation.

"There's no question about that, and this issue, more than any other, may determine the length of Anne's recovery. It is so difficult for Anne to question her relationship with her mother—it's love-hate and fear of losing her. I think there's still something we don't know." Joseph's voice revealed frustration and puzzlement.

"Another question, Mr. Wright." It had become apparent that Sister Celine had her agenda. "What am I to tell the sisters? They are asking about Anne."

Joseph sighed. "That's a tough one. Very simply, just say that by temperament and personality, Anne is incapable of functioning in the religious life and her efforts to do so have severely affected her health. They don't need to know everything. In fact, there is still the element of mystery, Sister, in Anne's illness and recovery, and that mystery must be accepted—by all of us—even by Anne herself. There will be the doubting Thomases—those we must not worry about."

Sister Celine laughed softly. "Yes, Mr. Wright, well said. They do exist, but in the minority, thank God! There is one nun in particular right now who was very dependent on Anne—she is angry and hostile, refusing to accept Anne's decision. I've instructed her not to communicate with Anne. Do you agree?"

"Absolutely! Anne can't handle any more right now—she's dealing with enough issues. She needs all the support she can get—that's why your visit today is so important to her, Sister."

"Well, she has a lot of love and support from many sisters. She always will."

"I want you to know, Sister." Joseph shifted in his chair, drew on his pipe. "I want you to know that Anne has my love as well." Joseph looked at Sister Celine for signs, but she did not flinch. He continued, "There is a personal involvement. I want to be open about this with the appropriate persons who have a right to know, such as you. All along, our medical director, Dr. Thompson, has been aware of the relationship developing between Anne and me. I don't know the direction this will take, however. Anne has to create her own place in the world, tough as it will be, and my own situation is rather complicated at this time."

Sister Celine smiled, responding without hesitation. "I appreciate your confidence, Mr. Wright, and I also suspected such. Perhaps that is part of Anne's healing."

"No, Sister, it was Anne's own courage. I think that's why I fell in love with her, was so drawn to her."

The sonorous mood lifted as Sister Celine rose to go. "I so appreciate this exchange—thanks so much, Mr. Wright. Call me if anything should come up."

"Yes, of course. Good-bye, Sister."

Their parting words were spoken in normal tones, and the smoke of the pipe was dissipating, now only a thin line hovering at the ceiling.

Joseph entered an account of this crucial meeting in the hospital records. He described Sister Celine as "very understanding, showing a great deal of psychological sophistication, and most importantly, a genuine concern for Anne as a person."

Chapter 34

FIRST BIRTHDAY

Having obtained leave for an evening out through the proper channels of the hospital, we sped down the freeway toward Laguna Beach. Joseph and I were celebrating my thirty-ninth birthday together. I noticed he had dressed for the occasion and was looking quite sharp in a white turtleneck sweater and navy sports jacket. It was a relief that our relationship was no longer to be hidden from those who had a right to know. My decision behind me, I was determined to live in the world and poured all my energies into getting well. Intensive psychotherapy sessions each day, coupled with physical therapy, were showing remarkable results. The threat of collapse was still there, but I would not let it rule me. Anne, more and more, emerged as the dominating personality, and she was the one holding Joseph's hand as he fought the rush hour traffic.

"Joseph, I haven't been to Laguna since I was a teenager! It was one of our favorite hangouts in high school. I've never been so excited! I am a bit nervous, though. It's been so long . . ." My voice trailed off; I didn't like to admit my fear. *Always the fear!* I wasn't going to let it spoil the evening. Joseph said nothing, only squeezed my hand, and we lapsed back into the silence with which we were both comfortable.

Finally, we arrived at our destination, driving down the steep driveway to the oceanfront Beach House Restaurant. Turning the car over to a parking attendant, we walked, arm in arm, through the patio entrance and into the low-lit lounge. I caught my reflection in the bar's mirrored background. *Do I look like a nun?* I had yet to learn what was stylish in clothes and had no idea if the black jersey pants and striped tunic I wore were fashionable or not. My mother had selected the outfit for me. *Mother! I'm not going to think about her tonight!* My hair was quite short, and I had made some effort to curl it, without much success. I didn't feel free enough yet to try makeup. I wondered if I ever would. I felt good about myself, however, and Joseph had this indefinable way of always giving affirmation to my feelings of well-being.

We were shown to our candlelit table on the deck overlooking the ocean under the open sky. It was a balmy October evening, and the sun, slipping into the sea, shot streaks of flame across the sky, as though candles were being lit for what I called my first birthday. Just as our silence had been comfortable, so now was our conversation over filet mignon and Chardonnay. There was always so much to talk about. We had so much to learn about each other. The ocean waves rolled in just below us, like a third party sharing our enthusiasm for newfound life with its rhythmic ebb and flow, a breathing in and out that said, "Live, Anne, live!"

Joseph reached across the small table and took my hand. "I feel so comfortable with you, Anne—you're good for me."

"I'd like to believe I have something to give in a relationship, Joseph." The hollow, empty space within still haunted me.

"Well, you do—you give back—you're not a taker. That's what I want. So often it seems like energy is going out of me and nothing coming back—it's depleting, to say the least."

"That would be deadly! I don't think it could last long either." I took a sip of wine, thinking of that empty place so familiar to me that suctioned out the self.

"That's my experience. I'm going through my own self-exploration in working with you. You know, this process of staying with one's personal integrity or truth, as you call it, is never over. In this sense, everything I'm demanding of you I'm demanding of myself." Pain crossed Joseph's face as a shadow, such as I had seen before that Sunday afternoon.

I set my wineglass down on the table, fingering its slim stem. With directness, I asked, "Are you referring to your break-up with Louise?" We rarely talked about this, but I had a need to know more.

"The sad thing about Louise and me is that we had so much going for us—so compatible, it seemed, in so many ways. I envisioned what I call a promised land and hoped, believed, I would enter it with Louise. But it was not to be. We simply could not resolve our differences on some very important issues."

"Do you still have that vision, Joseph?" I felt somewhat threatened by his words.

"I had really given up the dream, stopped believing I would ever find a woman to share my life on many levels—a peer relationship—until I met you, Anne. At first you were just another patient, though even initially, I was attracted to your courage. You just kept coming back for more! It's hard to pinpoint when I first realized my interest in you was more than clinical. Certainly, neither of us could have planned this!" Joseph's brow furrowed as he pondered the imponderable.

"I never thought I was lovable, certainly not desirable! Deep down, I probably fear if I should love someone, that person would go away." My hand smoothed the white tablecloth as though to erase the thought.

"You're not alone, Anne. Can you believe I have the same fear? After all, the break-up with Louise was a rejection. I've failed in more than one relationship and *you*—I doubted that you could ever be interested in me!" I looked at this therapist, this person, talking about his fears! My feelings for him were suddenly stronger, more real. He went on, "I definitely know what I want in a relationship and what I don't want. We have not yet begun to talk about that."

"I have to find my way. I really don't know what I want! Who will I be? I ask myself. I am so inexperienced, Joseph. I do know my independence is extremely important to me. And my need for aloneness. Another person can never be my whole life—I do know that about myself. It really has nothing to do with being a nun."

"Well, I'm the same way. I want a healthy separateness—only then can two people bring fullness to a relationship. And it must be exclusive, but not now and *not with you*, Anne. I want you to experience your freedom—have other relationships. You need to do that before you can commit yourself to anyone. You've got to find out *who* you are in this world."

"I agree with what you're saying. I know this is important, but for now, I'm enjoying being with you, Joseph!" I wasn't quite ready to take on anything beyond the moment.

"Right! Actually, I'm in no better position to make a commitment than you are, Anne. Meanwhile, as you say, let's enjoy what we have. Happy birthday!" We clinked the nearly empty wineglasses, suspending them for a few moments while our eyes confirmed the feelings of our hearts. The words of the poet, Khahil Gibran, came to my mind—*think not you can direct the course of love. For love, if it finds you worthy, directs your course.*

The buildup of wax at the base of the candle told the passage of the hours. Dinner was over. We carefully descended the worn narrow steps of the deck to the sand below. It was now dark, and the stars were our guide. We sat down on the deserted beach and held each other. Even in the chill of the beach night air, I had never felt so warm.

"Anne, I love you, Anne." Joseph's mouth was on mine, kissing me deeply. One hand held my breast, the other about my waist, pressing me to him. The rhythm of the sea I felt in my own body and abandoned myself to it. My life, as I had known it, was being wiped out by the divine current; perhaps now it would carry me forward.

Suddenly, the night turned cold and a shiver went through me.

My birthday celebration seemed like a dream the next day. I awoke with a new joy in my heart. Indeed, I felt younger, not older. The sunlight seemed unusually bright, highlighting the blackened edges of the red roses now wilting in their crystal vase on the dresser. They had served as a constant reminder of Lenny. His attentions were escalating and he was now letting his interest in me be out in the open. Other gifts followed the flowers—one a silver jewelry box with red velvet lining. It was heart shaped, and I loved it. But I certainly didn't love Lenny. Still, Joseph had encouraged me to be open to other relationships, to experience my freedom. For now, I would enjoy the attentions Lenny was giving me, knowing full well I was not in the least interested. It was a dangerous game to play.

"Good morning, Anne! Can I throw out these roses for you?" It was Lynda, a nurse's aid. Everyone seemed to be calling me Anne, and I had mixed feelings about it. I had been Sister for so long. "And oh, I have a letter for you. Came in this morning's mail."

"Thanks, Lynda. Yes, the roses have seen their day."

"That Lenny sure is a sweet guy, Anne! Looks like there could be a romance in the air!" She smiled and briskly walked out carrying the vase of wilted roses.

I felt irritated by the comment, as though I had been insulted. Sister Anne, a subject of hospital gossip! It suddenly occurred to me that no one was aware of where the romance really was! Joseph and I had gone out of our way to be discreet. Evidently, with success. So much was at risk—especially for him—and without Dr. Thompson's support, quite impossible.

The letter. The envelope told me it was from the president of our order. I ripped it open, not without trepidation, and began to read.

Dear Sister,

Your letter came as a great surprise to me. I was much saddened to read of your decision to leave the order, although I do realize that your health is very poor and that in hopes of restoring it, community membership might well take second place. At the same time, I rejoice with you that you are making such progress. May your recovery continue!

I could not, however, possibly agree to an indult or separation from the order as long as you are in your present physical condition. When you show improvement to the degree that you can take care of yourself, I will move on the matter. Meantime, rejoice in your improving health and keep me informed.

As I read, my heart twisted with a new grief in the realization of my severance from the order, even though it was not yet to be. The legal process was going to take time, as with any "divorce." *Why am I grieving?* I pulled out my notebook and pen and tried to answer my own question.

> The order is no longer *my* order. Yet in a very real sense, it will always be mine. Twenty years of intense living as a nun, or dying, if you will, are not years lost. They are a very positive, dynamic, organic process of growth in the totality of my life existence. "It is in dying that we are born to eternal life." I will not only accept those years in not denying them, but I will also treasure them as producing a situation in which I could grow back into Anne.

I closed the notebook. It was nearly time for my session with Joseph, and I wanted to stop in the cafeteria for a cup of coffee.

I walked down the hallway, thinking of Lynda's remark about a romance in the air. *Nonsense!* Irritation again welled up within me. As I passed the nurses' station, Paula called to me, "Your mother left a message for you, Anne—asked that you call her back."

"Mother? She's not supposed to call me here!" My muscles tightened, my jaw set. I kept on walking. *I have no intention of returning her call! She really isn't interested in hearing what I have to say anyway.* I remembered our last conversation. The "tone in my voice," she had said, had disturbed her and she "didn't like my attitude lately."

Chapter 35

URGE TO KILL

The cafeteria was a bright, cheerful room with wide windows looking out to the patio. Sunlight splashed the seascapes on the walls, bringing them to life. The artist was a former patient, I had been told. I sat alone at a small corner table, not wanting to talk, and sipped my coffee. My eyes scanned the motley group of patients that had become my "community." The spacious room was a montage of gurneys, wheelchairs, walkers, crutches, and even special eating utensils for those who needed them. All this had become familiar, "normal," here in my hospital world. What amazed me more than anything else was that if I closed my eyes, it could have been any café in town, judging by the flow of chatter and laughter—even a sense of joy.

My joy had dissipated when I awakened to the realization that I had collapsed once again right there on the sand the night before. I couldn't shake the depression, verging on despair, that such a lovely evening should end that way. The clock on the wall told me it was time for my appointment with Joseph. There was a sinking feeling in the pit of my stomach, and I wasn't that anxious to see my therapist.

Slowly I walked down the hall toward the counseling wing, feeling a change coming over me. Inexplicably, the depression was lifting and with it the fatigue. I felt quite confident, even cocky. *Joseph, who does he think he is anyway!* My body moved with a fluidity that filled me with an indefinable sensation. I felt taller, straighter, and very much in control.

Seeing Lenny in the distance, I called out to him and waved, laughing, "Hi, Lenny!" Beyond that, I didn't give him the time of day and kept walking, swinging my hips. Knocking loudly on the now-very-familiar door labeled Joseph Wright, Staff Psychologist, I said to myself, "I HATE HIM!"

"Come in, Anne." *Mr. Wright is always ready to see me!* I opened the door and briskly strutted in. "Good morning, Mr. Wright." I hooded my eyes, barely seeing to sit down in the usual chair. I felt my mouth slash into a smile that was actually more of a smirk. *Well, let's see what this brilliant psychologist has to say about last night!*

"Well, good morning, *Sister Anne.*"

I noticed the emphasis that Joseph gave to *Sister*. "My, aren't *you* perceptive this morning, Mr. Wright!" Two could play this game.

Joseph continued, ignoring my sarcasm, though I knew it wasn't lost on him. "Do you remember last night?"

"Last night? Of course. Anne passed out, didn't she! Right there on the sand! You must have been very disappointed, Joseph—at *such* a moment." I smirked again. "You had to carry her to the car, didn't you!" My laugh, hollow, loud, mocking, had a visible reaction on Joseph, which I enjoyed. "She had to do that, you know."

"No, I don't know! You're the one who's screwed up, Sister Anne!" Joseph's tone was entirely uncalled for!

"How dare you, Mr. Wright!" *You bastard!* Joseph grabbed his leg and grimaced, having been kicked firmly in the shin.

"Be glad I didn't kick you someplace else, Mr. Wright." I moved over to Joseph's chair, slowly, sensually, sat on his lap, and put my arms around his neck. His skin felt warm to the ice-cold touch of my hands, the hands that wrapped themselves around his neck, their grip tightening. Joseph remained motionless, looking into my eyes with a wariness that betrayed his fear. *I hate him!*

"I hate you, Mr. Wright, HATE YOU!" The words were intense with hate, and my grip tightened even more. *Joseph . . . Joseph!* I shut my eyes, feeling an ebbing of strength, the loosening of my hands; and I leaned against him for support.

"Why do you hate me, Sister Anne?"

"You've taken everything—everything! I should never have trusted you—never. You're responsible, you know, responsible!" Weakness was taking hold of me, and I felt my body growing limp, lifeless. Joseph's arms were holding me so that I would not fall. "Joseph, help me." *This sadness . . . what's wrong.* I felt the tears, the silent tears.

"It's OK, Anne, it's OK. Talk to me. What's going on?" Once again, it was the gentle, compassionate voice so familiar to me.

"I don't know. Something is happening to me that I can't explain. It is true. I do feel *hate* building up inside, but it's not really about you, Joseph. You know that, don't you?"

"Yes, I know that, Anne, so what is this hate about?" He sat back in his chair, said nothing, waited.

My words, stifled with guilt, were but a whisper, "I've lost everything. It's so easy to blame you. And . . . and now, my mother." The thought of losing my mother choked me with sobs.

"What about your mother?"

"She doesn't like the changes she sees in me! I had a dream about her last night. She kept saying, 'You're shutting me out, Anne.' And I screamed at her—over and over again."

"Maybe that's what you need to do, Anne—scream—scream at her." Joseph was still holding me on his lap, but I was unaware of this, so immersed was I in my memories of mother—and my grief.

There were so many days in the convent when, confined to bed, time dragged endlessly for me. I wanted to pound my bedroom walls until they gave way, crumbling, so I could pass through into some world that wasn't gray. If I could only go home, break the monotony and boredom that weighed on me, if just for a few days. But no . . . that was not *possible*. My mother had not been feeling well. *No, Anne, it's just isn't possible. I just can't take care of you!* She was suffering severe dizziness, imbalance. I saw her as a pendulum swinging out of control, dangerous, not sure what direction she was taking. She did come to see me one day, hanging on to my worried father, her low-heeled shoes shuffling, sliding on the hardwood floor of my bedroom, each step a stabbing pain in my heart.

Why, Mother? Why do you lie? You need not do this, *Mother. Why not just tell me, as you did when I was little, that I don't belong to you?* "Why don't you go home, little girl? Who's your mother, little Anne?" *Why don't you just tell me, Mother, that you don't want me anymore? Did you ever?* The convent walls were not to crumble. There was no way out for me. I was trapped. I had always been trapped.

The sense of abandonment overwhelmed me, crushing the breath from me, and my voice faltered as I tried to share with Joseph the insights that were coming to me. His response went right to the core of the issues.

"Your mother should not be your way out, Anne. I'm beginning to realize your relationship with your mother is a key issue. We all have to let go of our mothers, you know!"

"That's what Dr. Lindsey said in a note I received the other day . . . 'cut the umbilical cord.' But she's all I've got! Without her I will not have a soul in the world! And I'm hurting her—sending her away!" Desolation was in every word I spoke.

"Or is your mother sending you away, Anne? And isn't it time she did! You have to face some cruel, hard facts. I think your perceptions that 'gray day' in the convent were accurate. You needn't shut them down, deny them out of guilt. Trust yourself! Whatever the reasons, your mother did *not* want to take care of you at that time. And yes, she didn't have the guts to face that and tell you so. I'll tell you, though, we have it on record!"

"On record!" I stood up, on the defensive. I was shocked—doubted Joseph's veracity. "What do you mean, Joseph, 'on record'?" My eyes flashed angrily. "Just what did my mother tell you?"

"Here, let me read a report to you." Joseph reached into his file drawer and pulled out my records. "I don't normally do this, but I think you need to know where you stand with your mother. This is from the admittance interview." Joseph began reading. Words jumped out at me, searing my brain, "Extremely frank . . . at times prayed to God that he take her daughter . . . weary of the responsibilities . . . prepared to do whatever was necessary for Anne's welfare . . . in spite of her own fatigue . . . open to alternative suggestions for placement."

Joseph had not spared me. "*Take me?*" Silence hung heavily between us. *Placement? My mother, weary.* "So she didn't want me home. She was tired of taking care of me." My voice was quiet, low, lifeless—the voice of one disillusioned.

"You both have a right to your personal independence. Part of your recovery will be for you to claim that right. You can't worry, Anne, about what's going to happen to your mother. Believe me, she can take care of herself quite well." Joseph took in a deep breath then sighed, choosing not to elaborate on his comment.

"I don't know if I can claim that right. I'm afraid of her, Joseph." I shivered and hugged my sides.

"Afraid of what?" Joseph's eyes bored into mine.

There was a long silence. "Of something . . . something." *Why am I afraid . . . afraid of what?*

There was a sudden knock on the door behind me, triggering an unexpected and strange reaction. *Oh, no! Tap . . . tap . . . tap.* "It's so cold . . . Mommy, don't go away, Mommy!" My voice became that of a small child on the verge of tears, and as a small child, my chin quivered. I began to rock from side to side.

"It's OK, Anne. We'll just ignore the knock on the door. That's all that was." Joseph saw the change come over me, saw a woman with the look and voice of a small child. He reached over and pulled this child to himself protectively.

"It's my mother at the door, I know it! She frightens me! Don't let her come near me!" I buried my head in his shoulder so I would not see. Then I felt myself falling . . . falling . . . and everything fading . . . growing black . . . black and cold . . . so cold. I was only slightly aware of Joseph dialing the phone and asking Paula to wheel me back to my room and to relay an urgent message to Dr. Thompson.

Tap . . . tap . . . tap. What was that sound? Who was coming? The blackness had not dimmed my mind completely, had not stopped my thoughts but only momentarily. I was holding on to some thread of consciousness. *I need to know . . . know what?* I was unaware of passing Dr. Thompson in the hallway as Paula wheeled me down to my room. I did not see his concerned glance or hear his warm greeting. Likewise, I was unaware of the consultation about to take place at Joseph's request only moments before.

Joseph had just finished entering his notes on the therapy session when Dr. Thompson was at the door. "Joseph! Paula gave me your message. What's on your mind?" Glancing at his watch, he added, "I have a few minutes—have a meeting coming up."

"Fine. I just want to fill you in on Sister Anne. I'm concerned, uneasy. I feel she's building to something." Joseph paused.

"What are you saying, Joseph?" Dr. Thompson sat down across from Joseph, a concerned and curious expression coming over his face.

"Well, Curt, I'm not quite sure. I think she should be watched closely right now. I left instructions at the nurses' station about this. I never saw such a dramatic shift in Anne's personality before. Everything about her changes! She talked of hatred building up inside and wanting to kill me. I'm not concerned for myself—but I am concerned about what she might try to do to herself. I'm seeing her first thing in the morning and will report back to you afterwards."

"From what you're saying, I think we've reason to be concerned. This doesn't surprise me. I see her every day. There's been a change of late, I know that. Actually, I think her general condition is worsening in some respects. On the positive side, she has more mobility, but she is obviously in a fear state. It's blocking any further medical help I can give. Her vascular system continues to be severely unstable. Do whatever you can, Joseph. You know you have my support. We'll make an assessment tomorrow. Got to go. Meanwhile, give me a call if anything develops." Dr. Thompson looked grave as he walked out of Joseph's office. His risk as medical director was even greater than Joseph's in this case.

All through my therapy, I had been aware that my physician and psychologist were in close communication, sharing the responsibility for my case, supporting one another and even sometimes contradicting one another. There were no set rules, and in fact, rules were broken. The desperation of my case, the fact that everything had been tried, exhausted, and proved ineffectual, demanded creative experimentation. There was nothing to lose—at least on my side. On their side, all was at risk. Without their mutual respect and trust as healers, my therapy would have been quite impossible.

Joseph now was sensing *something*—but what? He couldn't quite identify the uneasiness he was feeling. It was as though a storm were brewing, but from what direction? He needed Dr. Thompson at his side, to be alerted for he knew not what. *Call me, Joseph, if anything happens I should know about.* Dr. Thompson was always there, available whenever he was needed.

Chapter 36

NIGHT CRISIS

My silver pocket watch said eight thirty, still marking the passing moments of my twenty years as a nun. I was too restless to go to sleep but felt bone tired. I was trying to read, propped up on pillows and fully dressed but couldn't focus my mind. I had felt on edge all day and couldn't shake it. Now, sheer panic was coming over me. *What is it? What's wrong? If only I could talk to Joseph!* Sometimes, he worked late into the evening. Maybe he was in his office now. I decided to find out. The hospital was quiet, most of the patients having retired for the night. The corridor lights had been dimmed, but I could easily make my way to the counseling wing. I was relieved that the doors were still unlocked. There was light under Joseph's door, so with trepidation, I went up to it and knocked. Joseph answered it and stood there looking at me in a surprised way. "Why, Anne! What is it? I thought you'd be asleep by now." He stepped aside and motioned for me to come in.

"I really need to talk to you. Do you mind?" I sat down, sighing deeply with exhaustion.

"No, I don't mind—just finishing up here." Joseph sat back in his chair and looked at me in that caring way of his that cut through my vulnerability, enabling me to open up to him. "Maybe we should talk more about your mother."

"Mother? Well, she was a loving mother." The office seemed unusually cold tonight. Feeling an icy draft, I shivered visibly.

"Then why are you afraid of her, Anne?"

"Afraid of Mother? Did I say that?" My eyes grew heavy, so heavy.

"You're closing your eyes, Anne. Why?"

"My eyes? My eyes." Yes, Joseph was right. I wasn't seeing what was around me here in his office. I had retreated elsewhere, another place, another time. *You have such beautiful eyes, Anne. So blue! So big! Cry, Anne. Mother loves to see you cry. Don't make any noise! There. Such beautiful tears!*"

"Sister Anne! Where are you? This is Joseph talking to you."

"Joseph? You seem so far away. Mommy? Is that you, Mommy?"

Who are you, little girl? Where's your mother? You don't live here, you know. Where do you live? Don't you think you better go home now? Such beautiful tears!

I don't want Mommy to do that! I wish I could talk. I wish I could tell her not to do that! Where shall I go! Oh!

"You're crying, Anne. It's OK. I'm here—Joseph is here. Where are you, Anne?"

"Mommy! Mommy! Don't leave me, Mommy! Mmmmm."

You sit there in the high chair so pretty, little Anne! There now . . . Mother's just going away for a while.

My mommy's going away, leaving me alone. The kitchen is so quiet. It's awful cold. I don't want those others to come. No! I won't look at the door. "That door, Joseph. It has a little window. It's the kitchen door. See! I'm afraid to look!" The worlds had merged.

"That's just the office door, Anne. That little window has always been there."

"No! No! I can't look. They'll come. Listen! There's a noise! Look! Look! At the window! They're coming! Oh!"

"Who's coming, Anne? Tell me. What do you see?"

"Those faces . . . those terrible faces . . . LOOK! LOOK! Can't you see them? There's that red one . . . and the other one . . . a black one . . . They scare me so! They're coming at me! No!"

Who is that screaming? I can hear someone screaming awful. Is that me? I better hide down on the floor . . . here in this corner. I'll hide my face . . . there . . . It's so cold. I'm so afraid. I feel like ice. I better not move. The thick gray fog . . . so thick I can't move through it . . . And no one can reach me . . . no one . . . I am so alone! I can't see anything . . . Everything is going farther and farther away . . . Nothing . . . Nothing. "God, O God, help me!"

"Anne, can you hear me? This is Joseph. Joseph is here. You are not alone! I'm here on the floor with you."

"Don't come near me. Don't! God help me!" *I'm so far away, so far.*

At this late hour, the counseling wing was deserted and the switchboard disconnected. Joseph and I were alone—isolated with the demons of my mind, demons that were taking on perceptual entities and filling our space, a space frozen in time—unending. There was an unearthly quiet, a silence heavy with feelings of dread and terror, terror I could not escape, cringing in the corner of Joseph's office, my head buried on my knees, emerging only to let out one more soul-piercing scream—and one more. *It is the hour of darkness.*

Joseph dared not move. He sat with me on the floor only a few feet away, though my perception was of a vague ghostlike form, shrouded in fog, in the far-off distance. Sweat was pouring down his brow, and his position was painfully contorted. He was talking to himself, telling himself to hold on—hold on, as one hour slipped into the next, and the next. If he had moved toward me, I would have imploded—spun off into some internal place of self-destruction—or I would have struck outward, killed the force coming at me. But he did not, dared not, move.

In time the screams started to subside, to grow less in intensity. Then a most soulful sound, a kind of wail that became melodic—and then a song sung from some unknown depths within me. Anne was singing.

Our Father who art in heaven . . .
Someone is singing the "Our Father" . . . sounds so faint and weak.
Hallowed be thy name.

"I'll sing with you, Anne. *Thy kingdom come, thy will be done . . .* This is Joseph, Anne. Here, I'm reaching out to you . . . *On earth as it is in heaven.*"

Someone is there . . . It's not my mother . . . Are the faces gone? If I could just see through this fog. "Who are you?"

"This is Joseph, Anne. I'm here. We're singing 'The Lord's Prayer.' He will help you, Anne. You are not alone. Here, take my hand."

"Joseph? Joseph?" *I want to . . . I can't move. God, help me! Mary . . . Blessed Mother . . .* Give us this day our daily bread *. . . I can't move. God, help me! There's something in this fog . . . a hand . . . reaching to me . . . Joseph's hand . . . If only I could reach his hand, maybe I could come back . . . I'm so scared . . . so cold. . . . Forgive us our trespasses, as we forgive those who trespass against us. Mother Mary! St. Therese! They'll help me. I'll move my hand. There . . . it moved a little bit. It's getting closer to Joseph's hand. If I only could reach that far . . . so far. . . . and lead us not into temptation, but deliver us from evil . . . I feel our fingers touch . . . A warm hand is closing on mine. So warm . . . Joseph's hand . . . I must hold on . . . I might slip back in that faraway, lost place . . . Hold tight . . . Don't let go!*

Silence . . . holding . . . time passing.

"It's OK now, Anne. I have a hold of you. You won't go away. It's OK now. Let's stand up. I'll help you. There now. I'm going to open the office door. This is the office—you're with me. I've got a hold of you."

"Joseph, don't let go! Take me out of here!" I clung to Joseph's arm, grasping his hand. *I won't look at the door . . . if I can just walk through with him. I'm so tired . . . so cold. Yes, just let me lie down . . . ohhh.* "Don't let go, Joseph!"

"I won't, Anne. Here. I'm right next to you on the bed. The nurse has given you a shot. It will make you sleep."

"I can't sleep! Don't leave me, Joseph . . . Don't let go!"

"I'm not leaving, Anne. I'll stay here all night. Just hold on. I won't let go. Now rest, Anne."

I held on to the warm hand—Joseph's hand. Somehow, it was my connectedness with the universe. It way my one thread holding me to this life. If I should let go, if he should let go of me, I would be lost forever, forever in some world of madness from which there would be no return—no return.

Chapter 37

DIFFERENT WORLDS

I was in a limbo place between worlds, strange and unfamiliar. I held on to a thread, a hand warm in mine with the touch of love. Somehow I knew that. That is all I knew, all that seemed real. There were nightmarish flashes of doors, windows, faces, and screams. I felt needles in my arms and a floating sensation, all thought ceasing, no fears, no pain, just grayness—Nothing. I floated in a safe place of no meaning. And just when I felt beyond reach, I jerked awake and the terror descended—and the piercing screams.

"No! No! Don't let her come near me! Keep my mother away!" I gripped the warm hand of the form sitting very close to me on the narrow hospital bed. Protecting me, loving me.

"It's OK, Anne, no one is going to hurt you. I'm here, Anne. I won't leave you. You're Anne—*Anne.*" The voice was low, hoarse, wearied, but it reached me; and I let go once again and floated off—off into the safety of grayness, Nothingness, until the next time.

The short hours remaining of the night passed fitfully, an ebb and flow of mental tides bringing me to the shores of a changed world. The hospital room was a still life canvas, a flat surface without dimension, dull without light and shadows, colorless. Nothing moved. Nothing had a name. Nothing had purpose. It just was there and I was part of it, an object. The loving form with the warm hand was part of it also, now sitting in the big chair by the window, face cradled in his hands, unmoving. *Still life.*

I closed my eyes as the scene held no interest for me, had nothing to do with me. When I opened them again, the still life had changed. *A face! At the foot of my bed . . . a face!* "Ahhhhhh . . ."

The face of a stranger, another unfamiliar form standing at the foot of my bed. I too was unfamiliar to him. The stranger saw not the Anne he knew looking back at him but a terrifying presence looking out through the dark wells obliterated of light. Fear reflecting fear. The stranger's face slit in some soulless grimace and the mouth moved. Now there were sounds, flat, lifeless without inflections, hollow. The face was made of plastic, unreal, like everything else, flat without dimension. Soulless. *Still life.*

There was no time in this limbo. I drifted in and out of drug-induced sleep. Nothing mattered. I had no thought, no will, no direction, no purpose, no identity. My one connection with the universe was the loving form, the warm hand, always there. I held on to him every time I awakened to see him sitting at my bedside. And always he said the same words, "I'm Joseph. You're Anne." At first they were nonwords, but as the days passed, they began to take on meaning. *This loving presence is Joseph! I'm Anne—ANNE!* And I started saying the words to myself—started believing. The world gradually became familiar again, taking on dimension with light and shadow. *The still life no longer still!* The plastic stranger who had worn a mask of fear now took on an identity, and I called him Dr. Thompson. Slowly, I was coming back, slowly staying in contact. Slowly the world was taking on meaning. I was not lost forever . . . *forever.* Without denying my experience, I again believed in my sanity. In that limbo place of unreality, I had made a choice. Always a choice!

Then one day, Joseph sat on the edge of my bed and took my hand. *Joseph, yes, I know who you are.* "Anne, there's something I need to tell you. Dr. Thompson and I have been very concerned for you—more than you know. We want what's best for you, and sometimes that calls for . . ." His voice faltered, his words hanging in midair ominously.

"What are you trying to tell me, Joseph?" My voice sharp, to the point. I was definitely back.

"It's a decision point, Anne. We think it's time we had a psychiatric consultation. Mountain View may not . . ." His voice faded, old voice, broken.

"No! No!" The thought terrorized me, fearing the outcome. *Iron bars—like Mark!* Deadly images of incarceration floated through my mind.

"Anne, there's no choice here. The risk for the hospital is too great." The strong therapist with the voice of steel, when required, was back.

"Are you trying to tell me I may be transferred to a mental institution! Are you?" I glared at him, anger fulminating at what was being proposed. *Staring eyes, haunted . . . fear, hopelessness.*

"Yes, that is a real possibility. You must be prepared for anything, Anne."

"But I'm getting better, Joseph. You know that!" I felt the situation slipping out of my control. *Thick straps, hanging . . . THE CHAIR!*

"Yes, we know you are—and that's to our advantage. Anne, you know I love you—"

"Are you going to tell the psychiatrist that? Are you?" *Condemned . . . crucified.*

"It's best, Anne—yes, I am. I have to be completely open with this doctor, hold nothing back. Listen, we've risked much already. We can't stop now. The truth, remember?" Joseph leaned down and put his arms around me, and I sobbed into his shoulder. He had not said it aloud, but the risks of which he spoke included not only the vulnerability of the hospital but his own as well. His license as a psychologist was at risk; the stakes were high.

There was nothing more to be said. Yes, I knew he loved me and I saw my fear reflected in his eyes. There was nothing for me to do but accept and wait. I went into my Gethsemane and prayed, *Not my will but thine be done.* All the classic images of the mentally ill in institutions filled my reeling brain. *I am not one of them! Innocent.* I knew if this transfer was to take place, I would never return to this world. *Never.*

> Joseph walked slowly down the hospital corridor to the consultation room, his footsteps heavy with the weight of his mission. All along, he had managed to stay with his professional detachment and think objectively in his treatment of Anne. As part of the medical establishment, he needed affirmation and, at times, guidance, for the unorthodox nature of what he was doing. His integrity alone demanded this of him. Continually, throughout Anne's therapy, he had placed himself at the feet of other qualified professionals to reflect back to him that he was acting in his client's best interest. It was particularly important that he do so now. So much was at stake.
>
> "Good afternoon, Dr. Warren! Dr. Thompson and I had considered bringing you in on Anne's case even before this crisis. We very much want your recommendation." He motioned to the chairs at the conference table and poured two

glasses of water. I understand you met with her this morning." Joseph held his breath while Dr. Warren talked, almost afraid of hearing what he had to say.

The psychiatrist spoke with authority and compassion, describing his observations of Anne and confirming the seriousness of her break with reality. He had taken the time to study her history and current medical records and had consulted with Dr. Thompson. All in all, Dr. Warren had the capacity to see the totality of the case and appreciate Anne's progress—in spite of the critical setback. Then, with confidence in his own judgment and expertise, he gave his recommendation. "I think the present course of psychotherapy should continue, Joseph. Anne should remain in your care. You seem to be the one to help her. She's doing well at the present and—"

"There's something you need to know, Doctor," Joseph interrupted. He knew all the cards had to be on the table at this point—no matter what the risk. "I have more than a professional interest in Anne. There has grown between us a very personal relationship. I believe I am in love with her." *There, I've said it!* Dr. Warren's reply was without hesitation, showing no surprise, as though he had already known and considered this dimension in making his recommendation.

"Continue what you're doing, Joseph. Anne is making phenomenal progress—even physically. To put her in a psychiatric hospital and begin a new course of treatment is not the answer—at least not now."

Joseph was aware that his relief showed on his face. He had held nothing back, and Anne was still to be in his care. Immediately, however, he felt the weight of responsibility that was his. This competent psychiatrist's support, however, relieved his anxiety regarding his status in the case.

The two professionals shook hands, both satisfied with the course that had been set, neither knowing what the outcome would be. Dr. Warren departed, walking briskly down the hall. Joseph stood rooted, waves of relief flowing through his mind and soul. *The course of psychotherapy is to be continued.* The recommendation, he felt, was none less than the spiritual direction he had so needed.

The welcome news that I would remain at Mountain View mobilized me to continue my therapy with Joseph, wherever that may take me.

Once again, a risk had paid off in search of the truth. As so many times in my life, I was now wholly focused—nothing would stop me in regaining my health. I was determined to live.

I will make a new vow: to live and to love in goodness and truth all the days of my life.

Chapter 38

BEHIND THE MASKS

The veils that had become a shroud of unknowing had been pulled back during that long and terrifying night in Joseph's office. Remembering had stirred up the deep, inner levels of my being that had been sealed off for my own protection, my own survival. There was work to do on all levels of my existence. From my hospital bed, I began internally to search out the source of my fears. *How did this happen?* The question burned in my brain, throwing off sparks into the deepest recesses of my life, illuminating the darkness in which I had lived for as far back as I could remember. It became a conflagration of distress, suffocating the life I was trying to hold on to, a cauldron of terror, consuming my last shred of integrity. The question would be asked again and again—and again and again, the answers defied. "How did this happen?" The words were as though suspended in a smoky haze, elusive and haunting.

It was not without fear that I let my mind go back to that night in Joseph's office and look once again. The faces. I conjured them up with great deliberateness in the light of day. One by one and remembered. Remembered what it was like to be small, helpless, dependent, wanting only the comfort of my beautiful mother. But she would disappear, leaving me alone, and then the darkness would descend, blotting out the world surrounding me. There was nothing then but fear and waiting. Waiting in the dark. Waiting for the faces. Now, I could look beyond, tear the masks away, and truly see.

"Finish your cereal now, little Anne. Good girl! You stay here in the high chair while Mommy gets dressed." Mother gently wipes my chin and gives me her beautiful smile. I laugh and coo, such a happy child. Mother is gone and I wait. *Don't go away, Mommy. I want my mommy.*

Mother is getting dressed . . . the long black coat . . . and the face . . . changing faces . . . *false faces.*

Mommy, Mommy! Where are you, Mommy! The small silver spoon is clutched tightly in my tiny fist. I sit waiting . . . watching . . . so quiet . . . quiet . . . *better not move . . . better not make any sound . . . shhhh . . . the door . . . the door . . . watch the door . . . will they come . . . will they come . . . Please come back, Mommy . . . please . . . NO! NO! I hear something . . . something behind the door . . . They're coming!* My baby eyes, large, blue, stare at the small pane of glass in the kitchen door . . . not wanting to see. *There they are! The faces . . . so scary . . . I can't move* . . . the silver spoon suspended, fixed.

Mother comes through the door behind my high chair, the other door. "Oh, little Anne, how pretty you cry! Such beautiful tears, silent tears! There now, come to Mommy!" I stretch out my arms to my mother. *My mommy is back! She is back. Where do you go, Mommy? Why do you always go away when the monsters come? Why, Mommy?* And I cry beautiful, silent tears—that no one hears.

Still under sedation, I slept fitfully throughout the following day. The murky waters were churning and forms surfacing not unlike the nightmarish serpents of my restless convent nights. Memories continued to push through to consciousness, giving me deeper insights as to the truth of what had happened to the child.

Mother of deception: My baby head with its fine gold strands hung over the highchair. My chubby pink hands pressed tightly over my eyes, wet with the silent tears. Dare I look? It is so quiet. I spread my fingers, raising my head a little, and peer through to the little glass window in the kitchen door. Just a pane of glass, nothing more. The monsters were gone. But my body still trembled and the tears still flowed. Then I heard her footsteps. *Oh, Mommy! My mommy is coming. Mommy!* I reach out my arms to her, grasping, clutching as tightly as my baby strength would allow. And the sobs came quietly. My mother liked it that way. "Oh, Anne, you are so beautiful when you cry that way. What's the matter, little Anne? Did something scare you?" And then she laughed in some shrill and sinister way. *You are different, Mommy. Why are you laughing? Don't you know I'm hurting? Don't you know about those monsters that come when you go away? Why do you leave me, Mommy? Don't laugh that way, Mommy.*

I looked at her—so young, so thin, such a pretty mother with her dark coiffed hair in waves about her ears and rouged cheeks and lipstick bright red. She didn't look pretty to me now, though, her straight line of a mouth turning up at the corners in a grimace, her eyes dark and narrow, gleaming with pleasure. She was having fun, I saw, in seeing me this way in my baby helplessness and terror. *Don't you know I hurt, Mommy?* Of course, she knew. I didn't understand that kind of sickness, only that I hurt. I heard the doctor's word, *colitis*, which held no meaning at my young age. I could only suffer it and see the drawn, puzzled brow of the kindly doctor. "I wonder what is troubling this small child," he would say. And my mother's impervious face, impervious bearing, sharing his concern—and her silence. And she knew. And still she laughed.

The good mother: Tumbling in my highchair with giggles and coos, I laugh with baby abandon. *Oh, I have such a funny mother! I love you, Mommy! You make me so happy.* She burst through the swinging kitchen door, her long arms held out gracefully as a dancer on stage—and she was, little Anne her captive audience, my big blue eyes wide-open to see all of my beautiful mother. "Diddi-um-bum-bum, diddi-um-bum-bum . . . Here comes Jim with the mandolin." Her voice, to me, was as lovely and melodious as the bird's song coming through the kitchen window this spring day. Keeping to the beat of the tune, she did an intricate dance step across the kitchen floor on her high-heeled shoes, flashing her beautiful smile at me. She then picked me up and held me in her arms, swinging me around, for the encore, which I demanded. "Diddi-um-bum-bum." *Wheee! What fun! How I love you, Mommy.*

Mother mystified: Wonderful Mother swirled me around and around, and I cried for joy. She held me close to her heart, my chin resting on her soft shoulder. The kitchen was spinning, my vision a blur, but for the light. I let out one loud squeal. The dance came to a stop. My mother turned her head to the side so she could look down into my baby face. I felt the soft shoulder grow rigid, the body that held me so lovingly and securely grow stiff, drawing back. But I didn't see my mother. *THE LIGHT!* I could only see the light, the light that was taking on forms, as it always did, that reached out to me with a love that wrapped itself around my baby flesh like a warm blanket and reached into my baby heart. The arms of light stretched out to me, beckoning me . . . my friends . . . so familiar . . . My face shone too with the light, and I flayed my arms, reaching back. I strained from my mother's arms to get to these friends whom only I could see. My mother held me fiercely and I felt her body shudder. *Oh, oh, the light . . . the beautiful light . . . they love me so . . . Let me go, Mommy . . . I want to go.* I could not see, but I could feel my mother's look, mystified, not understanding—frightened. *Do I scare you too, Mommy?*

Mother the stranger: A-N-N-E. The thick pencil forms the letters as I practice my writing at the dining room table. A-N-N-E. Mother comes in carrying the wicker laundry basket, pausing in the middle of the floor, looking at me strangely. "Who are you, little girl?" Her voice isn't like Mother's, but stern and sharp, not loving at all.

"I'm *Anne*, Mommy, your little Anne!" I feel my chin tremble and look up at her lovely face shadowed in some kind of darkness.

"No, you're not! I've never seen you before, little girl. What is your name?" Mother's eyes say she does not know me, and something squeezes at my heart. *My name? What is my name?* I must have a name, and I wrinkle up my brow, wondering.

"Well, I think you better get along home now, little girl—whatever your name is." The woman starts folding the laundry, not seeing me.

Who am I? Where do I live? Silent tears roll down my plump cheeks. I stare at the woman not my mother folding laundry. My chubby legs slide off the kitchen chair and move toward the front door.

"Where do you think you're going, little Anne!" Mother put her hand on her hip and wagged her finger at me. "For heaven sakes, Anne, don't you know your own mother!"

Yes, I know you, Mother! The silent tears would not come, and the screams were silenced in my throat. *Why, Mother, why?*

The silent father: I'm toddling now, always underfoot as today in the kitchen. It is Sunday, and I hear my father's car crunching on the gravel of the driveway outside the window. He works until lunchtime on Sundays, and I wait all morning, all week, for this moment. I love my father, who dresses up every morning and kisses me good-bye when it is still dark. He smells of things I don't know, like tobacco and aftershave and tweed. I only know I like his closeness. Now he comes through the swinging door, scoops me up, and gives me a big kiss. "How's my Skeezie Doodle!" *What an imaginative name!* I snuggle my head down in the warm curve of his shoulder, a safe place. I feel my little body squeezed tight and then gently placed down again on the hard, unyielding linoleum floor. I toddle over to my small chair against the wall and plop down, my feet curled under me. I watch—very quiet. Father hugs my mother too. "Hello, dear," she says, quite like herself. *What does Daddy say?* He looks suddenly very tired. Then the Sunday smells and sounds. Oh, so good—of melting butter sizzling in the hot cast-iron fry pan and the ham simmering, making popping sounds. My father sings as he fries the ham, turning it over to brown on the other side, "Oh, my darling, oh, my darling Clementine." I listen, quite enraptured, and watch his every move, stealing glances only to look at the small pane of glass in the kitchen door.

Why don't the monsters come when my daddy is here . . . when he can protect me? No, they never do. Why can't I tell him about the terrible things that happen here in the kitchen? How my beautiful mother leaves me, comes back, and how she laughs. Have you ever seen her laugh that way, Daddy? Do you know I don't really live *here? Who is my mother really, Daddy? Why can't you help me, Daddy! Why don't you know?*

Mother now: An older mother—gray, softer, heavier, but still beautiful. Her silver hair piled high, her makeup perfect, her expensive clothes in style. She looms over me as I lay in my invalid bed. Her mouth is open, her lips forming words, many words, and they come tumbling out like serpents, threatening danger. But nothing is said*—I can't* hear *anything. I can't hear you, Mother. Stop! Stop!* But she doesn't stop and the serpents keep coming . . . and the screams start coming . . . my screams . . . and I keep screaming and screaming at her . . . but no words.

Realities merged in these cameo-like dreams that were yet another catharsis of emotion, clearing my eyes so that I could see behind the masks, could see the many faces of my mother—and a glimpse of my father. From the darkness of my hospital room, I continued to allow my mind to roam freely over the landscape of my mother's existence, coming to rest on one most sorrowful event. *Was it your most beloved father's untimely and sudden death that scarred you so, Mother? You were only twelve, a vulnerable age, and his loss changed your whole life. I've heard you say many times, "I've never gotten over it." Perhaps I will never know, Mother.*

Destroy the masks, Mother, crush them in your strong hands . . . Use them no more. You don't need them, Mother. I know you are in there, Mother, somewhere . . . hiding, alone, afraid, wanting . . . wanting what? I do not know, Mother, why you should want at all! You are so magnificent in yourself, Mother—yourself, when you are just you. Only you don't know . . . don't know . . . so you hide behind masks . . . and masks of different sorts.

Chapter 39

IMMOLATION

Mother shared the stage of shaping forces, other performances weaving a cocoon of unawareness as a shroud over my living death. My mind dissolved the hospital room walls and roamed over those illuminations beckoning me into the past . . . *foster a vocation . . . whose bride . . . pray for me when you are a nun, Anne . . . I saw you as a nun, Anne . . . too good, little Anne . . . self-renunciation, Sister . . . not like them . . . always meant to be a nun . . . the Lord is pleased . . . you are chosen, Anne . . . your arms are outstretched.*

I was a new novice. Francis. Sister Mary Francis. I wasn't looking down at the scrawly handwriting of the six-year-old under the rose arbor, but rather at letters inscribed in gold on the black leather cover of my missal, the prayer book used to follow the Mass in Latin with English translation. F-R-A-N-C-I-S. Francis. A new name, a new identity. From my assigned pew in the novitiate chapel, I looked across the sea of white novice veils in front of me to the white altar beyond. A large crucifix was suspended over the tabernacle, and the twisted, contorted, agonized figure of the dying Christ was white with death. The light coming through the stained-glass windows cast a myriad of colors, as though someone had put an artist's brush to a canvas of white. And then the canvas came to life as the novices rose from the wooden kneelers. The chaplain was entering the sanctuary dressed in his symbolic, liturgical robes. Holy

Mass was about to begin, not a symbolic reenactment, but believed to be the same sacrifice that was offered on Calvary. It was the center of a nun's life, the most important part of her day, every day, a source of strength and grace for whatever may be asked of her.

The chapel becomes Calvary. The white veils of the novices fade into the black veils of professed nuns and the novitiate chapel into chapels of many convents where I had been assigned over the years. The Mass was a thread of continuity, a daily drama in which I not only participated, but also lived. It gave meaning to the death that was going on in me. It gave sustenance. As members of the mystical body of Christ, we were meant to continue the crucifixion through what was called the holy sacrifice of the Mass.

"*Introibo ad altare Dei.*" *I will go unto the altar of God. Yes, I too will be sacrificed on this altar. Help me, God, to get through Mass. I feel so sick.* "*Kyrie, eleison.*" *Lord, have mercy on me. Yes, I know I am a sinner. Don't let me fall. God!* "*Suscipe, sancte Pater.*" *Receive, O holy Father, this spotless host. Yes, receive me as a small host on the paten and don't let me take anything back of my self-oblation during this coming day. It's so hard to breathe—help me.* Then silence, a silence of expectation, broken by a small bell ringing three times, heightening awareness that we are approaching the heart of the Mass, the climax—the Consecration. *I must hang on.* "*Sanctus, sanctus, sanctus.*" *Holy, holy, holy. I feel so weak, my god. Help me. Don't let me fall!* The priest bows low over the altar and, in solemn tones, says the sacred words of transubstantiation, "*Hoc est enim Corpus meum.*" *This is my Body.* "*Hic est enim Calix Sanguinis mei.*" *This is my Blood.* I raise my eyes to the elevated host, the elevated chalice. *My Lord and my god! Yes, I will die with you. I stretch forth my arms. Pray for me, Grandmother.*

"*Pater Noster.*" *Our Father, who art in heaven . . . Father, do not let me fall.* "*Libera nos a malo.*" *Deliver us from evil . . . evil . . . evil. The coldness of death comes over me. The moment of union is coming.* "*Agnus Dei.*" *Lamb of God.* "*Corpus Domini nostri Jesu Christi.*" *May the body of our Lord Jesus Christ preserve thy soul to life everlasting.* I kneel at the altar and receive the sacred host. *I vow to thee all that I am . . . all that I have . . . total immolation.*

"*Deo Gratias.*" *Thank you. I did not fall over, did not faint. I can go on. Holy Mass, a healing remedy.* "*Ite, missa est.*" *Go, the Mass is ended. It is over.*

But it is never *over*, I thought. There it was—that same missal on my hospital nightstand. I reached over and picked it up, admiring its gilt edges and colored ribbons. I ran my fingers over those golden letters, *SISTER MARY FRANCIS,* now worn dull and lusterless on the smooth black leather cover, seasoned with many masses through many years. I wanted to wear away the golden letters until they too were black like the leather as though it would help erase the dying years. I wanted to write with golden letters that would never grow dull, never tarnish—A-N-N-E. Anne.

Anne, your arms are outstretched on the cross. I had never forgotten the words of the dying grandmother. They were not just a memory, however, but a way of life fed daily by the Holy Mass. I lived the legacy, fixed to the maypole cross of sacrifice, held in the vise of illusion: *You are special, Anne, chosen.* So much had been shut down, buried with the dead grandmother. *Requiem aeternam. Rest in peace, Grandmother. Ite, missa est. Go, the Mass is ended. Rest in peace, Anne.*

The opening of the mind doors, one upon the other, gave soul space to remember and to heal, but the illuminations of recall were painful, my eyes unaccustomed to the light. For reassurance, I looked around my hospital room that had once again become familiar. Faces, unrecognizable for a time and even terrifying, were no longer nameless—but Paula, Dr. Thompson, Lenny. And Joseph. Joseph had always been there and, though named even in my delirium, had been a formless, loving presence rather than an embodiment of an individual.

I had come back, fought back, and felt alive with a new thrust forward in the healing process. It was as though the sky had cleared after a sudden and ferocious storm—a summer storm, when the sky is rent with jagged lightning spears and dark, ominous clouds move across the illumined sky with deep bellows of thunder. It is short-lived; its intensity could not long be endured. And when it is over, the day is brighter than before.

Chapter 40

FRANCIS

Joseph sat across from me at the unfamiliar desk, lacking the usual projections of himself, obviously feeling somewhat displaced. He fondly cradled the warm bowl of his pipe, which, I had observed, was an object of centering for him. Threadlike streaks of smoke circled slowly toward the ceiling of the unfamiliar office, hovering like some spirit presence above us.

We had resumed our routine morning sessions as soon as I had recovered sufficiently, but I could not bring myself to enter Joseph's office. I could not erase its association with the kitchen of my childhood, which had been peopled with so many faces of terror. We referred to that night as the breakthrough, which indeed it had been for me. I was in a new and stronger place within myself and was more sure of who I was and learning how to claim the right to be that. A smile came more easily to my lips, and there was a sense of joy in my heart. Most importantly, I was beginning to believe that I was lovable. *Anne is lovable!* "Choosing life, choosing Anne!" had become the driving force of my therapy. No area of my life was to escape merciless scrutiny.

"Joseph, I've been struggling with the place of the Mass in my life. I want to go—I've always loved the liturgy—but I'm afraid what might happen!"

"I think we need to talk about that. Why are you afraid, Anne?" As personally involved as we were, the roles of therapist and patient always took over when there was work to be done.

"Well, as the years went on, I couldn't get through the Mass. I would always collapse. I stopped going—it was simply beyond me. I've been looking at this and coming to realize how I used the Mass to feed the death inclination in myself!" I hadn't been aware of this back then, but that did not erase feelings of guilt, innocent or not.

"Then why do you want to go now, Anne?" My therapist had this way of bringing me back to my own questions rather than giving me any pat answers.

"That can't be what the Mass is really about, and I need liturgy in my life. I'm leaving the convent, but God is still all important to me. I'd like to change"—I paused, searching for words to describe what was beyond words—"change that misguided orientation, that twisted conditioning. I wonder if it's possible."

"Of course, it's possible! Anything that can be learned can be unlearned—if the will is there. I agree with you, Anne. Your death is not what the Mass is about! Jesus is not asking you to *die* in a literal sense. The cross was his cross—not yours! This is a misinterpretation of the Mass. So what do you want from the Mass now, Anne?"

"Well, I believe it is actually a celebration of life, not death, and that's how I want to experience it." I spoke with conviction and somewhat defensively, afraid that Joseph was going to discourage the idea.

"If you're talking about going to Mass for a reorientation, I can certainly go along with that, but I'm not going to be party to a death scene! I don't like the idea of picking you up off the floor and carrying you out! OK, let's plan it, Anne. *Naming the demons*, facing them head on—that is your healing. I'll call the local Catholic church and . . ."

Name the demons . . . Name the demons.

F-R-A-N-C-I-S . . . Francis. It was cool in the shade of the rose arbor as I practiced writing my name, my other name. The name I wanted to be mine. I observed my signature and knew it didn't look quite like it should. Big. Scrawly. But then I was only six years old. I kept practicing. F-R-A-N-C-I-S . . . F-R-A-N-C-I-S. Just looking at the name made me feel better—like I could be someone else. When I am twelve, I will be confirmed as a soldier of Christ and take the name of Francis. F-R-A-N-C-I-S . . . And when I become a nun . . . F-R-A-N-C-I-S.

I felt a blow to my chest, knocking the air out of me and I gasped. *I can't breathe . . . no air . . . no air.* The blood drained from my head and the cold descended, the clammy cold, and I shivered. The small office became a blur, swirling. I slumped forward and felt Joseph's arms restraining me and his faint, distant voice saying, "Where are you going, Anne? Talk to me!"

Name the demons . . . the demons. "Of course, I'll talk to you, Mr. Wright." My voice was throaty, deep, strong. I sat bolt upright, pushing Joseph away from me. "Save your stupid embraces for Anne—I don't need them!" I flashed my eyes haughtily, tossed my head back and laughed, a hollow, sardonic laugh, deep, raucous, that mingled in the air with the smoke as though some tangible entity. "Why do you look so startled, Mr. Wright? You're not afraid, are you? This isn't the first time we've met, you know!" I smiled ingratiatingly.

"So we've smoked you out! Of course, I recognize you! How could I mistake you for Anne with your sneers, your insolence! Tell me, what is your name?" Joseph's question rang with authority.

"It's written here—on this paper." I held out a crumpled piece of paper.

"NO!" he screamed. "*Say* it! *What is your name?*"

"You can *read*, can't you?" My voice dripped with sarcasm.

"I am the one to tell *you. What is your name?*"

"FRANCIS! FRANCIS! F-R-A-N-C-I-S!" I spat out my name, spelling it in an exaggerated articulation.

"So! That is what you call yourself! Francis!" Mr. Wright sat back in his chair and stared at me, making me feel most uncomfortable. I could see in his eyes that he perceived me to be what I was—the embodiment of the death and dying syndrome that Anne always had to struggle with. *HE RECOGNIZES ME!*

"Yesss," I hissed. "That's just who I am! How about loving me, Mr. Wright? You'd like that, wouldn't you?" I leaned forward, aware of my sexual attractiveness. Mr. Wright's jaw stiffened, his mouth set in firm lines. I could see that he was ready to take me on. *THE FOOL!*

"What do you want, Francis?" The therapist rushed in!

I crossed my legs, slumped down in the chair, and yawned. "These sessions can be quite boring, you know, Mr. Wright. All this about the truth—finding yourself—all that jargon. Anne's an idiot the way she falls for it! She really had it made, you know. Didn't have to worry about a thing!"

"And you're out to stop her, are you! You're a considerable foe, Francis, I acknowledge that!"

"It takes one to know one, right Mr. Wright?" I made a mockery of his name, emphasizing and prolonging the *I* sound affectedly, and then biting the *T* while showing my nice white teeth. It was very effective—I could see it bothered him. *The weasel!* "Why are you angry, Mr. Wright? Did I say something that bothered you?" My eyes drooped to slits and my voice sounded very seductive. I liked the effect. Now *he* looked uncomfortable! The raucous laugh again swirled with the smoke.

"I asked you, Francis, what do you want?" He slammed his fist down on the desk—to impress me, no doubt.

"It's this Mass thing Anne's into. She thinks she's well enough to go, huh! Well, don't think I'm going!"

"No, you don't belong at Mass, do you, Francis?" Mr. Wright was obviously going to match wits with me. "Mass has nothing to do with dying, as you've led Anne to believe. You don't belong in her life, do you, Francis!" Joseph's voice was harsh, loud. I didn't like it. *He thinks he's big stuff!*

"Not if Anne is into this new orientation bit! Look Mr. Wright, let's level with each other—and leave Anne out of this." I leaned forward, projecting an illusion of intimacy. "You want her. I want her. It's as simple as that. She'd be quite a feather in your cap, wouldn't she! Do you think I've been in control all these years to give up—just like that!" I snapped my fingers for effect.

"You're a phantom, Francis, empty, a vacuum. You're no-life. It is Anne who is rejecting *you*—Anne—not me. But I'll sure as hell do all I can to get rid of you! YOU'RE DEATH!"

"My, aren't we getting heavy!" I leaned back, breathing deeply, as though totally relaxed and uncaring, and smiled sweetly up at Mr. Wright. Then my eyes narrowed and, in that low, throaty voice, said, "Get rid of me? Just try, Mr. Wright, just try."

"Two can play this game, Francis." Mr. Wright put his feet up on the desk and refilled his pipe, slowly, taking his time. I felt irritated. I had the feeling I was losing control. I said nothing. I felt a growing agitation within.

Finally, after a long pause, unable to stand it any longer, I went deeper. "I've been around a long time, you know. For a while, you confused me with Sister Anne. Remember? Ugh! I assure you, I didn't enjoy that cover! Shit!" I straightened myself in the chair and, with all the seductiveness I could master, said, "You really love *me*, don't you, Mr. Wright?" Then, getting up slowly, I walked around the desk toward Joseph. My body moved differently from Anne's, much more sensually. Joseph put his feet down, his pipe back on his desk. *I have him on the defensive. Good!* I could feel Joseph's body grow rigid as I sat down on his lap. Putting my face close to his, I breathed. "Hmmm, this is getting interesting! You talk too much, Mr. Wright. You know that?" Joseph was remembering, I'm sure, that night in his office and my cold grip on his neck. He roughly took my arms, pinning them to my sides.

"What do you want, Francis? Love you? Love you? That's an obscenity! There's nothing lovable about you, Francis! It's *Anne* who is lovable!" He was afire with the energy of his convictions.

I must stop him! My eyes flashed hate. My body grew rigid. *"An obscenity" . . . how dare he.*

"Why don't you just give up, Francis. You're losing, you know. You're weak—weak!"

"I hate you, Mr. Wright, hate you!" I tried pulling my arms away. I wanted to kill him. His hold became tighter. I challenged his strength in trying to free myself, but Joseph held on. I continued to struggle.

"Go ahead, Francis, struggle—struggle with all you've got! You won't win, Francis—never—*never!* You're a liar . . . a phantom . . . a no-thing . . . a vacuum . . . a no thing . . . Nothing . . . NOTHING!"

Nothing . . . Nothing . . . No! Wrapped in an ice-cold shroud, my strength was ebbing; I could no longer struggle. *The cold.* I became quiet, my body limp, lifeless in Joseph's arms. I could feel myself being put back in the chair, arms holding me there. I would not fall. I was safe. My body relaxed in his embrace. "Anne," he said. "Anne!"

Anne . . . Anne. I opened my eyes. I was in the unfamiliar small office with the swirling smoke. Joseph was holding me. "Joseph . . . Joseph."

"Yes, Anne, this is Joseph. You're OK. Do you know what is happening?" His eyes searched my face for I knew not what.

"I'm not sure. Did I fall asleep? I drifted off—somewhere. I'm so tired!" I covered my eyes with trembling hands.

"Stay with me, Anne. I need to know—are you aware of Francis?" A key question.

I took a deep breath and shivered with the cold. Reaching deep within, I knew the answer. "Yes. I know about her. I'm afraid of her. I'm nothing like her, you know."

"That's sure true!" Joseph had been quick to agree with me and I was encouraged to go on.

"Actually, I feel inferior to her. I can't compete with her! She's more attractive—smarter—more self-assured. It embarrasses me to say this, Joseph, but she is sensual—sexy! She likes men!" I felt color coming into my cheeks, and my body grew warmer.

"That's not all bad, Anne. Personality is a coalescence of many attributes. You need to break this Francis entity up into pieces! In time, you can incorporate qualities of hers that you want to be part of yourself, of Anne. The important thing is that you are the one in control—not Francis! You have no reason to be afraid of her, Anne. She doesn't have any power except what you give her." His fist jabbed the air for emphasis.

"I know when that is." I stopped, fearful of going on.

"When is that, Anne?" *He never lets up!*

"When I'm just trying to be myself . . . to feel free . . . simply being what I want to be! In the midst of something . . . I'll just feel her begin to take over . . . stopping me. It's very subtle."

"She'll certainly try to do that, Anne. She's fighting for her life too, you know. The enemy is within you. She is the one you must kill without any hesitation or qualms. She'll find your holes, your weak spots, and will be ruthless!"

"Why do you think, Joseph, that Francis is showing herself right now—and to you?" I looked up at him, questioning; I was truly puzzled by this.

"Because you're stronger, Anne. It's just her last stand. It's not that she is getting stronger. All these moves you're making to create a new life for yourself, she can't stand that!"

"What can I do!" I felt overwhelmed, my voice a plaintive wail.

"Right off, the last thing you do is play helpless! Like now—stop the wailing! Tell her off! Call her a liar! She is, you know. Bottom line is that you don't let her intimidate you, Anne. And when she *does* get the best of you, just acknowledge it, and pick up and start over." Joseph stood up and held me to him. "You can do it, Anne, I know you can. You've more strength than you know. Much more."

I wanted to believe that. Joseph seemed to know the depths of my struggles, yet he believed I could make it. *Lord, help thou my unbelief!* I did attend Mass at the nearby Catholic church. Joseph knelt at my side and watched me go through the struggle to overcome the death set and find life. The Mass did become a celebration of life for me. Francis had no part in it.

Chapter 41

TRYING THE WORLD

F-R-A-N-C-I-S. With a flourish I signed my name to the letter written in large bold script and then studied it in admiration.

> Dear Mr. Wright,
>
> It seems we have mutual respect. I am intelligent—as you said, Anne would lose on the grounds of wit alone. You're brilliant, I say—brilliant, again and again. I'd like to get the upper hand with you! We are a good match, really. Why don't you love me rather than Anne? Are you sure she is a good match? Am I giving you doubts, Mr. Wright? She couldn't have done it without me, you know. Does she draw too much strength from you? Think about it.

Rereading the letter, I smirked, knowing my carefully selected words would put Mr. Wright on the defensive. *I really enjoy sparring with that man! Finally met his match, I'd say.* Folding the letter, I slipped it into the envelope addressed to Joseph Wright. My irreverence, as he called it, was obviously disturbing to him. I mused on our rather extraordinary relationship as I walked to the nurses' station. I dropped the envelope into the in-house communications box, visualizing Mr. Wright's reaction when he read my letter. I laughed to myself. It felt so good to stir things up this morning!

I knew the battleground was laid out for the day. *Shopping at the mall! Mass was one thing—after all, that's holy! But the mall! Has Anne forgotten about the "den of thieves" and all that! Well, she's on her own—forget me! Of course, she's too weak to go—I must remind her of that.*

Suddenly, I felt the blood rush to my head, a swelling sensation, causing pressure and disorientation. The hallway spun in circles and I gripped the handrails to steady myself. My chest felt in a vise, making it hard to breathe. Paula was passing by, saw my distress, and took my arm, leading me back to my room.

"What happened, Anne? You look so flushed!"

"I feel so hot, like my head's about to burst, and I'm dizzy! I thought I was going to collapse." These were not the symptoms I was accustomed to, unfamiliar and disturbing.

"I think you better lie down now, Anne, and rest for a while. Dr. Thompson is making his rounds this morning—he should be here in a few moments." She drew the blanket over me and quietly left.

I had barely closed my eyes when Dr. Thompson entered the room. "Good morning, Anne. Paula tells me you aren't feeling too well."

"Just had a dizzy spell, that's all, and I'm so hot. The blood rushed to my head—felt like it was about to burst! It frightened me, Doctor! It's the opposite of what usually happens to me!" I didn't think I could handle anything like this today of all days!

Dr. Thompson put the blood pressure cuff on my arm and pumped the small rubber ball. "Seems you've had a hypertensive episode. Your blood pressure is elevated. Is this happening much?"

"Yes, daily, sometimes several times a day."

"Well, we'll keep an eye on it. Perhaps we need to review your medications. You're facing a lot of new things—incredible changes, Anne. Change is stress—even when it's positive! I understand Joseph is taking you to the mall this afternoon. Your first shopping spree! Quite a step for you, isn't it?"

"Yes! Can you believe I've never been to a mall! They didn't exist in my day. I'm afraid—but I'll do it, of course." I hesitated, reluctant to express my reservation. "But . . . but what if I collapse?"

"It's a risk, isn't it? We'll see what you do!" He smiled reassuringly, touched my shoulder. "I'm betting on you, Anne!" On that note, he left me with my worries. I was anything but confident.

Betting on me . . . on me . . . Anne . . . Anne.

My discharge was projected for the end of the month, and I would be facing the world alone. What was an everyday, casual event in the lives of most people was for me a Mount Everest. And so many of them! The mall was just one. All were of equal importance, links in a chain leading me to independent living—and my freedom. It was breaking out of the cloister of invalidism as much as that of the convent.

At one o'clock that afternoon, I was at the door of Joseph's office, overwhelmed by a feeling of panic. "I can't do it, Joseph, I can't! I'll collapse! I know I will!" My breathing was shallow, my eyes hooded with fear.

"Going to play helpless, Anne? 'Can't do it!' Who's telling you that, Anne? Who is it?" Joseph's voice was raised and had more than a sharp edge.

"I don't know who!" I murmured.

"Yes, you do, Anne. Is it Francis? She's been around today, hasn't she! Telling you how weak you are! She's a liar, remember?"

Joseph's voice grew faint and I felt myself fading, coldness gripping my bones, the coldness of fear.

"OH, NO, YOU DON'T!" Joseph grabbed me by the shoulders, believing one battle was as important as the next. "Open your eyes, Anne! Who are you?" He shook me vigorously, and I felt the fierceness of his touch.

I responded, opening my eyes, and looking past Joseph to the little window in the door, knowing full well its potential to incite fear. *No! I can't look!* Joseph, deciding to face the issue head-on, pushed me toward the door. "Open your eyes, Anne! Open your eyes!" I knew I was at a choice point and I could not turn back. Cautiously, I opened my eyes. I looked, seeing a vague form in the little window, a reflection. I felt the silent screams deep within, tried to move away, tried to release Joseph's hold on me.

"What do you see, Anne? *Whom* do you see?" Joseph held me there, pressed to the door with the little window.

I looked again and the form took shape, and I could see quite simply my own reflection. "That's Anne—Anne! I can be Anne! Francis can't stop me. I won't let her." I spoke with vehemence. I was now mobilized.

Joseph released me, and his words were once again gentle, encouraging. "She'll pull out all the stops, Anne. Dr. Thompson told me what happened this morning."

"You mean the hypertensive episode?" I hadn't intended to bring that up.

"Yes." Joseph waited.

"Why do you think that is happening now, Joseph? It's really upsetting to me. It's so extreme—quite the opposite of what usually happens." I felt at my wit's end.

"I think it is a reaction to so much good and freedom all at once. You've lived in darkness for so long you can't tolerate the light! It's a reaching to life, I believe. I see it as a positive sign—in spite of its discomfort."

Joseph's interpretation appealed to me. I agreed with him. "What you are saying makes sense. I do feel overwhelmed right now with all the opportunities coming my way. In all these new experiences, I feel such a disparity at times with my life as a nun. Neither in one world or the other." I was beginning to wonder if this would ever change.

"You expect too much too fast, Anne. You get depressed over your limitations, go helpless and weak! You've got to learn to be more realistic in your expectations! All this is going to take time—time, Anne! OK, now, are you ready to go?" Joseph sounded very matter-of-fact.

"Yes!" My choice was made. I would not be ruled by fear. This steadfast position was my only hope of recovery.

In the vise of fear and foreboding, I had nothing to say on the way to the mall; Joseph, at the wheel, was also silent, praying that it would be an uneventful, normal shopping experience. Actually, I think he was more nervous than I at this point. We both realized the risk we had set up for ourselves this November afternoon. We also realized that whenever I came through a confrontation, I was stronger for the next situation. I struggled with my fears and doubts, however, trying to change the old tapes, to silence the Francis voice that said I was weak, too weak to live, no right to live. Well, I knew what to do! Quite simply, choose the voice I would listen to and *put one foot on front of the other.*

Joseph parked the GTO, and we walked across the parking lot, hand in hand, my grip like ice. You'd think he was leading me into the lion's den! He had no intention of supporting me beyond the main entrance, and I left him on a bench to smoke a cigarette. "Enjoy yourself," he called out casually, as I was swallowed up in the holiday shopping crowd.

I was quickly overwhelmed. So many people! So many *things*! *Yes, a den of thieves. Anne! No! I will not listen!* I walked through J. C. Penney's, seeing racks and racks of clothing. I had decided to buy a blouse and, by some miracle, found my way to the right section. Pushing the hangers across the rack, I was easily confused by the wide selection. Size? What size did I wear! I had no idea, certainly not the size I wore before entering the convent twenty years ago! I had told Joseph I'd only be about fifteen minutes, so I didn't want to take the time to try anything on. Or was it I didn't have the courage to stand in front of a three-way mirror! I'd just have to make an estimate, better too large than too small. And the styles and the colors! *I really should choose something conservative, black, and tailored . . . though I do love this bright coral . . .*

The blouses blurred on the rack, and the floor moved under my feet. I felt the blood rush to my head, my face flush. *No! No! I will not die, but live! Anne . . . Anne.* My cold, wet hands gripped the blouse rack; and I waited, concentrating on breathing deeply, regularly. Slowly, the sensations subsided. I had not collapsed! But it was difficult to think. I wished I could sit down. *One foot in front of the other, Anne!* I continued to look at the blouses, barely able to distinguish one from the other. Finally, I pulled one out—a stripe of black, gold, and beige, with long sleeves and a mandarin collar. I thought the colors were becoming, but I wasn't sure. Well, it was a beginning. The price tag was meaningless. I had yet to learn the value of a dollar. There was certainly nothing in the price range I had remembered from 1951! I paid for my purchase and quickly left Penney's as one fleeing the battlefield, satisfied with some minor victory.

As I approached the mall entrance, I could see Joseph, cigarette in hand, pacing the back and forth and looking at his watch. "You weren't worried, were you, Joseph?" I smiled broadly, trying to act nonchalant.

He let out a great sigh, his features relaxed. "Well, I *am* relieved! To be honest, I was beginning to listen for ambulance sirens and expecting the worst. Fifteen minutes?" Pointing at his watch for emphasis, he let me know that nearly an hour had slipped by. "I was about to go in and look for you, Anne." Seeing the look of on my face, a mixture of satisfaction and exhaustion, he let go of his concerns and hugged me right there amidst the holiday shoppers, my plastic bag crushed between us.

Chapter 42

GUILT

"Lenny, Lenny, I really didn't mean to do that." I drew back from him, upset with my own unreasonable responses. We had been dancing. It was late in the evening, so we had the recreation room to ourselves. Lenny was his usual, caring self. His attentions were not lost on me, yet I was naive. I kept taking and taking, and Lenny, giving and giving. When I needed to arrange for my classes at the nearby college, he was there, offering me a ride. He even chauffeured me around town, apartment hunting.

My budget had narrowed my choices down to a one-room studio apartment with a pull-down bed and small kitchen. The landlord had a doubtful look on his face when I claimed there would be only one occupant. He glanced suspiciously at Lenny standing there next to me, shifting his weight from one foot to the other, staring at the floor, looking most uncomfortable. I had never given poor Lenny a thought, oblivious to the awkward position I had put him in. I used Lenny without even knowing it. He was a tool helping me to bridge with the outside world. And I enjoyed being with him—but my heart was elsewhere.

It was not inappropriate that Lenny should ask me to dance in the empty rec room as he turned on the stereo. The music was slow and enticing, stirring an urge in me to accept, but my reaction was "*No, no, of course not.*" Then, I checked myself; I always had to be the observer of my own behavior. *Why not dance? I love to dance!* It was *reaching for life,* as I had come to think of any choice breaking those barriers that had restricted me for so many years.

"Why not, Lenny? Just don't expect too much. It's been a while!" I felt slightly uncomfortable in his arms, my hand on his shoulder. Lenny had always kept a respectful distance—after all, he had come to know me as Sister Anne. I relaxed to the music as we moved across the floor in silence. Then, I felt a pressure on my back as he pressed me closer, and before I realized what was happening, he was kissing me. Something dark surged within me. Without hesitation, I fiercely pulled my hand away from his, reached up, and slapped him. It was hard to say which one of us was more shocked. Lenny's kiss was certainly not out of line; my response to it was. I had the good sense to recognize this right away. "Lenny. Lenny. I didn't mean to do that." *Dear, good, kindhearted Lenny.* He stood there staring at me as though he were seeing a stranger and then, without a word, quietly left the rec room, leaving me alone with my feelings of social inadequacy and guilt.

This was one of those times I needed to hear the voice of Dr. Thompson. I walked down the hall to the medical director's office, where he would often be at work late into the evening. As I approached his office door, he was locking up, briefcase in hand, obviously through for the day. "Anne! How are you?" I hesitated to delay him, but as always, he made me feel like he had all the time in the world. These impromptu visits were not too unusual.

"Do you have just a moment, Dr. Thompson?" He knew it would be more than a moment, but he drew me into his office with a smile and gestured to one of the two big chairs by the window. The drapes had been drawn for the night and the lamp on the small table between us cast a subtle glow over the room. For a few moments, we talked about generalities, and then I plunged in—avoiding, however, any mention of Lenny.

"I'm struggling with so many new experiences, Doctor. I just need to hear another voice at times other than Joseph's." Dr. Thompson nodded knowingly, not needing any further explanation. He well knew Joseph encouraged his involvement in my therapy for his own protection. "I find myself still questioning so much of what is happening, not even trusting Joseph completely. And the guilt . . . it overwhelms me. I can't shake the feeling that much of what I'm doing is wrong." I had a hard time admitting to the *burns* on my skin, feeling they were incriminating in some way. Overcoming my reticence, however, I talked to him as a friend as much as a doctor.

"Sounds like a pretty bad rash of some kind. I'll check it out on my rounds in the morning. You're doing so well, Anne—remarkable really."

You're bound to have guilt—not that I'm pointing to that as the cause—but changing values that are so deep-seated can have consequences. But you can't let guilt—any more than fear—decide your life. In time, your guilt will diminish. The kind of changes you are making requires reeducation of the whole person."

"You know, Doctor, deep down I have always had this fear that if I should lose my vocation, I would lose my faith." I dared to express this fear to Dr. Thompson because I knew he could relate to the issue. He was a thinker and a seeker, unafraid of new experiences in matters of faith. While standing on solid ground of his Catholicism, he was always on the cusp of new ideas and directions in his spiritual life.

"There's no reason to believe that, Anne. I realize everything must seem very unsettling to you right now—like standing on shifting sand! Your faith can be an anchor, a thread of continuity with your past. I believe we should not destroy the past, but build on it. Give yourself time to find your way." In his subtle way, I knew he was trying to support my own, deep Catholicism.

"Yes, I know you are right. Through all of this I feel a rootedness in something that never changes. Perhaps that *is* my faith." The idea of building on my twenty years as a nun rather than wiping them out was a new perspective and gave me great comfort. I thought of the elm tree outside my window in the convent, its roots reaching down into the earth.

We talked for some time, and then I got up to leave. The weariness on my physician's his face from a long day had not escaped me. It had been a long day for me too. I went directly to my room and to bed, but sleep eluded me. Perhaps, writing would help; it usually did. As I pulled my notebook off the nightstand, a sheet of paper fell to the floor. *What's this?* I picked it up and read it.

> Dear Anne,
> Anne, you're a good egg. I'd sure like to tell that Mr. Wright what I think of him! Do you know what he is doing to you? Oh, that guy is so sure of himself. But how about you? Haven't you everything to lose and nothing to gain? What is there to gain? Shame, guilt, pleasure—is it pleasure at all? Sin, sin, more sin. Sores, sores, and more sores. So you don't deserve it, Anne! Well, I think you do. You are a degenerate, sinful woman. You will not be free of me . . . or will you?

The signature spread across the page defiantly, FRANCIS.

Chapter 43

SURRENDER

*M*r. *Wright sure walks at a fast clip! Well, so can I!* My head thrown back, I took long strides, enjoying the sensuous sway of my hips. Within moments, Joseph and I were abreast of each other and walking toward his office for our morning session. I had considered skipping it today. *Sure can't take much more of this crap!* My head ached and I felt tired, unusual for me. I waited for Joseph to acknowledge me, but he did not, just kept clipping along! *That son of a bitch!* I nudged his arm playfully and winked. "Hello there, Mr. Wright! I bit the *T* more than usual.

"Oh, so *you're* here today, Francis!" It pleased me that he never failed to recognize my presence.

"Anne's feeling lousy! But we sure don't need her, do we, Mr. Wright?" I put my face close to his and showed my teeth.

Joseph unlocked the door to his office and stepped back, waiting for me to enter first. I smiled knowingly. "You're not afraid to turn your back on me now, are you?" I snickered loud enough to be heard. Joseph didn't even smile. *God, what a wet blanket!* I could see he was all business and knew I'd better shape up, especially if I was going to call the shots. *No shin kicking today, Francis!*

I handed Joseph a letter I had written the night before, the reason I wanted to look good today. "Please, Mr. Wright, please don't read this until *after* our session."

"Oh, another letter, Francis? Busy, aren't you!" He threw the letter down on his desk without even glancing at it. "Well, let's get one thing straight right off. You're not in control here—I am! I'll set the terms." My eyes flashing in anger, I was just about to fling back a contemptuous retort when I caught myself, remembering I wanted to be on my best behavior today. *My best isn't much, I realize that!*

"Oh, of course, you're in control, Mr. Wright. This is your pad, isn't it?" And I smiled sweetly, somewhat like Anne. This did not come easily.

Joseph obviously felt this was not worthy of a comment, so he got on with the session. "What's on your mind, Francis?"

"Anne's really upset today. You should see her! I really let Lenny have it last night." I leaned forward, smirking. "Men are *evil,* you know—*you* should know, Mr. Wright!" *I love innuendoes!* Leaning back in my chair, crossing my legs seductively, I laughed my hard and raucous laugh. "You are not laughing with me, Mr. Wright!"

"No, I'm not, Francis. I think *you're* the one who is evil. Is it really Anne who is upset? Or is it you, Francis?" He looked me straight in the eye, and I could see he was taken aback by the hatred he saw there. *Wouldn't you think he'd get used to me!*

"Clever, aren't you!" My voice rose in pitch as I warmed to my subject. "Of course, I'm upset. Anne running around making all these plans! College! Apartment! Shopping! Do you know she's even got a driver's license now? She really thinks she's going to make it in the world. Well, not if I can help it!" And I laughed again, leaning forward, narrowing my eyes to slits for the effect. "And you, Mr. Wright, you know what else—"

"What *else,* Francis? Are you afraid of the word? Is it sex, Francis, *sex?*" Joseph's voice was rising too.

Very sweetly, like Anne, I replied, "You should know the answer to that one, Joseph." My voice dripped with sarcasm. This was the first time I had called Mr. Wright Joseph, mimicking Anne. "Have you seen Anne lately? I know how to handle all this. She's a mess! If I didn't hate her so, I'd really feel sorry for her. I've made her quite untouchable, you know." Again the sweet voice, the sweet smile.

"You know more about how to be untouchable than Anne, Francis."

My *head . . . the pain . . . this weakness.* "You, Francis, not Anne, are untouchable! Here, let me touch you, Francis!" Joseph's voice was reaching a screaming pitch as he bounded out of his swivel chair and reached out to grab me. I saw it coming. *NO! You've gone too far!* I felt things slipping away from me. *I'm losing control!* My body slumped forward and I started falling, falling, into some bottomless black pit until there was nothing but frigid darkness—Nothing. And then silence. *Cast into outer darkness.*

"Anne! Anne!" I heard Joseph's voice full of tenderness and concern and felt his arms around me, supporting me. *It's so cold.*

"Joseph, I want to come back."

"You can, Anne, you can." He took my cold hands in his and rubbed them. I began to feel warmth and was able to open my eyes and get my bearings. Gradually, breathing came more easily.

As always, Joseph reassured me, "It's OK, Anne—you're OK. How are you this morning?" It was a new session with a different client. Anne was back.

"Look at me, Joseph! This is terrible!" My voice revealed the distress I was in. I stretched out my arms for him to see. "My whole body, Joseph—like this!"

Joseph looked at my arms and shook his head. It looked like someone had taken a lit cigarette and very precisely, repeatedly, pressed it into my skin. My arms were covered with sores that appeared like burns and felt like burns. From Dr. Thompson's entry on my chart that morning, Joseph was aware the sores indeed covered my entire body. Only my face was clear, untouched. The condition was not only painful to me but also loathsome.

"You see, I'm not touchable, Joseph! I remember reading in a religious book once how a woman was covered with sores as a punishment for her sins against purity."

"Is that what you're trying to do to yourself, Anne—punish yourself? For *what?* For simply being touchable! My god, Anne, you're still a virgin! *A virgin!* You've done nothing wrong! Your guilt is pseudoguilt—without substance. So you want to make yourself untouchable! Remain *pure*! Well, it's not going to work—not unless you want it to!" Joseph reached over and put his hands on my arms, touching the repulsive sores. "This is not all you are, Anne. These sores are not *you.*"

I drew back my arms, tried to hide them. "No, Joseph, no!" I could see how I was going away from him, could not accept unconditional love. Then rejecting my initial reaction, I threw my arms around Joseph's neck. "I do want you, Joseph! I do want to be touched . . . to be loved!"

"Then you'll have me, Anne—sores or not." We held each other, as we often did. Holding, touching, was a source of strength and healing for me and an integral part of what had become a very unorthodox but effective therapy. We both recognized the uniqueness of the situation for many reasons. I was getting well, and the physical ground I had covered attested to that. March Air Force Base had been notified that there was no longer a need for the G suit. In less than a week, I was to be discharged.

"There's a letter here, Anne—addressed to me from Francis." He picked up an envelope from his desk and held it out to me.

Startled, I drew back. "What do you mean, a letter from Francis!"

"Well, she gave it to me at the beginning of the session. Wanted me to wait until after she was gone to read it. I think you should hear what she has to say—whatever it is!" Joseph opened the envelope and began reading aloud.

November 18, 1971

Dear Mr. Wright,

Anne wants to be separate. So be it then! I want to be rid of you too with your search for truth, your adherence to integrity! You think integrity is so important! You sure can't live on it—Anne will learn that! I could have given her security. Now it is too late. Anne has made all these plans. I have to admit she's doing very well. Perhaps I should take pride in her. I can't seem to prevent her from going on with life. I'll miss her. May she be dull without me—ha-ha! I better leave now. I'm tired. Total surrender! I give up, Mr. Wright. It is difficult for even death to die.

"And she signs it in her large bold script: FRANCIS."

A heavy silence hung in the air when Joseph finished reading. It was hard for me not to say, "Yes, Francis, you're right," and I felt a sadness along with relief. *Total surrender.* "Is it possible, Joseph, I am free of Francis?"

"Probably not. What's important is that you, *Anne*, are in control! That is your freedom. Don't let yourself be intimidated by her, Anne! As long as you nourish feelings of inferiority, of helplessness, she has the upper hand! Just keep on making your choices to live—that's what it's all about. Life or death! Remember, we've said it before; Francis is a phantom that occupies the darkness, fills the vacuum left by your denial of what's happened to you. Even she refers to herself as death!"

I unabashedly stretched out my arms, saying, "Like these sores—not letting them stop me from going on and living. It becomes so practical!"

"Right. Based on what you've been telling me, Anne, they're possibly a physical manifestation of your groundless guilt and self-inflicted punishment. Your guilt is a *lie*! You've done nothing wrong! You're not a sinner! Francis, remember, is a liar!"

"Well, now I know how to heal these sores—get rid of the guilt! If only it was that easy. Last night, Dr. Thompson and I were talking about this—how guilt cannot direct our lives. He warned me reeducation takes time. And the body has a long memory!" I sighed, wishing I could hurry along the process.

"Anne, I feel this letter has substance and is significant in regard to your recovery. Francis is losing her power—or I should say, you're claiming your power. Even though this letter is a form of capitulation, I also know Francis! I think she's angling for a compromise, some recognition from me."

Joseph picked up his pen and began writing on the bottom of Francis's letter. When he finished, he handed it to me to read but made no further comment.

> Francis, I Accept. No malice or vengeance. I like good and honorable losers as well as courageous and honorable winners.

The note was signed Mr. Wright.

I folded the letter and put it in my pocket. Looking up at my therapist, I said, "Joseph, when I am no longer afraid of Francis, I'll know she is truly dead—that will be the final victory."

Without another word, I rose from my chair and walked out of the office. I was not yet feeling an "honorable winner." My entire body burned with sores.

Chapter 44

SOUL CHAMBERS

Can't stop . . . can't stop . . . running . . . running . . . running madly through the soul chambers, spaces wherein the soul moves . . . rambles . . . when some inner sense is lost about the self, not quite sure just who it is. Can't stop . . . running . . . running . . . heart beating wildly, trying to keep pace with my feet . . . chest heaving, crushed by some unknown weight, making it impossible to breathe. Can't breathe . . . can't breathe . . . can't stop . . . can't stop . . . running . . . running . . . rambling through the shadowed ghostlike spaces of the soul chambers. So hot . . . so hot . . . blood pulsing . . . beating in my head, fullness . . . pressure . . . the heat . . . can't stop . . . running . . . because there are others there!

Faintly, I see them in the shadowed corners, watching my running frenzy . . . watching . . . waiting . . . biding their time for the cultured moment to assert themselves. I think there are four, four entities, latent powers to be, wholly dependent for life. NOTHING OF THEMSELVES!

As I run through the soul chambers, I can barely distinguish their forms, phantomlike in the semidarkness. A small child in a high chair, squirming and pointing at the door . . . running . . . running . . . a young nun in a narrow hospital bed, clutching a wood-and-brass crucifix . . . running . . . running . . . an older woman, preening herself at a vanity table . . . running . . . running . . . the fourth I could not quite make out, an embryo form huddled on the floor, quite still. When I turned my gaze on them, running by, they looked away, pretending not to care, as though I held little interest for them.

I keep running . . . running . . . can't stop . . . can't stop . . . They keep watching like vultures watching the dying from some distant place . . . watching . . . waiting . . . for the final great weakness when all movement stops, *a death space, a vacuum, which they can fill. The tension for me is unbearable! I can't relax . . . can't let down . . . always on guard. So I keep running . . . running . . . never stopping.*

The heat . . . the heat . . . can't breathe . . . can't breathe . . . I must not allow them to take over . . . must keep saying empty things . . . doing empty things . . . running . . . running . . . never stopping. The problem was my empty running was creating the vacuum, just the condition for which they waited . . . watched . . . The heat . . . heat . . . just the condition for a corpse to rot, inviting smaller, dependent creatures, worms, maggots, to move in. But I keep running! They can wait forever, these entities, but how long can I keep running! No matter the distance I cover, they come nearer . . . nearer . . . as the vacuum sucks them in . . . closer . . . closer . . . Overwhelming heat! Can't breathe . . . growing weak . . . weak . . . words slur . . . steps drag. A sluggish vacuous being! Just right for the takeover! And I collapse . . . panting for air . . . clutching my chest . . . knowing the vultures are aware the running—all movement—*has stopped!*

There is nothing to do but give them their time. "COME! I INVITE YOU! I AM NOT AFRAID NOW!" *Now* I *am the one who waits . . . watches. There is a moment of strained silence, and then quite suddenly, all bedlam breaks out! A great din rocks the soul chambers! Loud, raucous laughter, piercing child screams, shouted prayers, Miserere—all clashing dissonantly, a welter of discordant sounds, filling every recess of the soul chambers. The silent one remained silent. There was nothing else . . .* Nothing.

My strength returning, I pulled myself upright and faced the four. My voice rang forth, sweeping through all the chambers of my soul, "STOP! STOP! IT IS YOU WHO MUST STOP!" *They began moving . . . moving toward me . . . their fearsome figures like dark shadows lengthening . . . now looming over me . . . vultures swooping down on their prey.*

This time I claimed my power . . . JESUS! Stretching forth my arms, I cried fearlessly, "PEACE! BE STILL! STOP! IT IS I WHO AM IN COMMAND! I WHO AM IN CONTROL!" *Immediately, the clamorous sound receded into silence and the entities slithered back into their dark corners of impotence.*

My forehead felt cool, my breathing regular, as I began walking . . . walking . . . through the soul chambers, my eyes scanning every recess to ferret out the entities. The faint cry of the child drew me to the farthest chamber. Though the light was dim, I could see a golden-haired baby girl, sitting in a highchair, with enormous blue eyes that brimmed with silent tears. She kept reaching out to me in a trusting manner, as though wanting to be loved. "Anne! Anne!" *I did not hesitate to lift her chubby form out of the high chair and hold her in my arms. She seemed to know me and snuggled her head into my shoulder, content. When I looked down, I was startled to see the baby changing—growing. I'd judge her now to be at least a year old. "You do live here, little one. Don't worry about that. And this house has no little panes of glass. Nothing is going to frighten you! You're safe with me." Cuddling her in my arms . . . drying her silent tears . . . feeling the radiance of her smile . . . I carry her with me on my journey. I HAD RECOGNIZED HER AS THE LOST CHILD! Her needs gave me the courage to go on.*

Miserere . . . out of the depths I cry unto thee, O Lord! I followed the sound of prayer to the next chamber. There, on the narrow hospital bed, lay a young nun, very pale, very thin. IN EXTREMIS! Her eyes are shut and her mouth is moving in prayer. The crucifix is held tightly in her blue-veined hands, and the expression on her sunken face tells me she is rapt in God.

"Sister Anne! Sister Anne! We must go our separate ways! Perhaps you will find perfection in some other soul." Sorrow oppressed my spirit. "All is not lost. Leave with me your love of God, your faith, your spirit of prayer."

Sister Anne fixed her large eyes with their deep black wells on me and said, "Don't grieve for me, Anne. Here, I give you this crucifix, symbol of life and love, the one I received on my reception day. Go now and live!" As she spoke, her visage faded into some kind of ethereal light until she was no more. And I wept for her passage. Only the light remained, clinging to me, and the soul chamber was less dark.

The lost child was weighing me down. I could hold her no longer. I put her on the floor and then realized how she had grown—ten years old, I would say. She clutched my hand and we walked on, going in the direction of the loud, raucous laugh. It led us to the darkest of chambers. There at the vanity table sat the older woman, putting on her face. I was struck at how much she looked like the mother of deception with her bright-red mouth and hair in waves about her ears quite becomingly. The woman stopped when she saw me and spun around, laughing. "Well, what have we here! A couple of sorry survivors, I'd say!" I didn't feel equal to her wit and sarcasm and said so. She laughed all the more, making me feel even more inferior.

The lost child hung back and I shared her fear, wanting to get away! I held my ground, however, and found my voice. Looking the woman right in the eye, I said, "There's something redeeming even about you, Francis! You can handle anything! You've no inhibitions. You're fearless. So self-confident! You have gifts that could be helpful to me in the world. Leave me with these. For you must go, you know. NOW!" Even as I spoke, her body began to decompose. But she responded. "Here, take this pocket watch of silver with my name on it. It was a gift for my profession day. See the engraving? 'March 19, 1954—To Sister Francis—From Mother and Dad.' I've always treasured it. Now I want to give it to you, Anne. It will be useful in the world, a symbol of adaptation and . . ."

Francis stopped abruptly, parts of her now falling off, or rather vaporizing, becoming vapor as though there were no substance, a phantom form, which she truly was. Vaporization, incense *of the lower world!*

The lost child's tug on my hand took me away from the distasteful scene. The lost child, however, was a child no longer. She turned and faced me, and we were equal in height, even in age. Before my eyes she had changed . . . grown . . . matured into adulthood like pictures on a fast-frame film!

"What shall I give you?" She reached in her pocket and placed an olive-seed rosary in my hand. "I've had this since I was six years old. It is very precious to me. I want you to have it now, Anne, a symbol of trust and joy. May it remind you that the beads of life experiences are linked together, each one important in leading to the next. The mysteries of the rosary are the mysteries of life!" She kissed me lovingly, a long, tender kiss that melded into a deep, quiet feeling of joy, of expansive light encompassing us both until we became one.

I was alone. The soul chambers, now full of light . . . empty. But no! There had been four. *What of the last? I had almost forgotten! When running . . . running . . . not stopping . . . I had seen her each time I passed the deepest . . . darkest recess . . . quite out of the way. The silent figure huddled on the floor—she was dead. A corpse! I never wanted to look at her but out of the corner of my eye could see that she was fully clothed and curled up in a fetal position, her head turned down, face hidden. I could not give her a name.* Nameless. *So I kept running past. However, at times I noticed she moved.* MOVED! *Or did I imagine it? But no, the next time I was* sure. *She moved, but slightly every now and then. It sent chills up my spine. I never lingered for a better look . . . kept running . . . running . . . never stopping.*

Now I stood alone in the depths of the soul-chambers . . . watching . . . waiting . . . There had been four entities. I missed Sister Anne, would always love her. I was relieved Francis was gone. The lost child, now grown, was internalized. I fingered the mementoes in my pocket—the brass-and-wood crucifix, the silver engraved pocket watch, the olive-seed rosary—remembering the symbolism of each.

Suddenly, I felt a presence behind me. Slowly, fearfully, I turned around, afraid for what I might see. OPEN YOUR EYES, ANNE! LOOK! *"God, no! The corpse!" She had entered the soul chamber! There she was, standing, obviously alive. Alive! Still, I was frightened by her visage. Her dark hair, long and stringy, fell in tangled curls . . . her scaly skin sallow, mottled gray. It looked like she had already started to decompose and the process was now reversing itself. She was tall, thin, with eyes large and luminous. Under more normal circumstances, she probably was rather attractive.*

The revived corpse smiled at me, a wan smile, and reached out her mottled-gray arms, as if wanting to embrace me. She acted like she knew me well, as though she were seeing a long-lost friend. I drew back, repulsed! She started to move toward me . . . slowly moving toward me . . . coming closer . . . closer . . . NO! She would not be stopped! There was no escape.

The mottled-gray arms wrapped themselves around me and I trembled . . . cringed . . . grew still . . . stopped. My raspy voice of fear whispered, "Who are you?"

"I am . . ."

"Who? I didn't quite get your name."

The voice was tomb-like, low, faint, gentle as a feather in the wind barely brushing the air. "I am . . . I am . . . I am . . ."

Chapter 45

THEREFORE, CHOOSE LIFE

Sunday. My last Sunday in the hospital. I was hurrying down the hallway on my way to meet Joseph in the parking lot, dressed in my new blouse of stripes—black, gold, and beige. We were going out to celebrate the discharge that was now imminent, less than a week away. As I passed the patient cafeteria, out came Lenny, carrying a tray. Always, his face would light up whenever he saw me. But not this time. He stopped and looked at me. I saw the hurt and angered expression. "Why didn't you tell me you were involved with Joseph Wright?" It was an accusation more than a question. Before I could respond, Lenny was gone, walking down the hall to deliver the tray. I too kept walking. I had not wanted to hurt Lenny, but by the time I had reached the parking lot, I had forgotten all about him. Joseph was waiting for me.

The sports car climbed the mountain, leaving the city with its congestion and pollution—and cares—behind. The rarefied atmosphere was symbolic of our high spirits. We felt light and carefree and deeply happy. Quite simply, we were in love. We both realized it had been unimaginable and that neither one of us could have planned it.

Joseph began to sing, "Amazing grace, how sweet the sound." Surprisingly, I did not know this historic hymn, so as we drove the winding mountain road, he taught me the words. *Blind, but now I see.* I reached over and took Joseph's hand. I was aware how warm mine was in his.

Within an hour, we had reached our destination, the Mountain Lodge Restaurant, nestled in the pines. Parking the car, we decided on a trail walk through the forest before dinner while there was still light. And it would give us some time alone. We were meeting friends of Joseph's for dinner, the Hartmans. Another first for me and one I did not take casually. For all my lightheartedness, I had a deep fear of being socially with another couple. I felt so inadequate, so ignorant of the world. But as with all hurdles, none of this mattered. I would simply do it.

I felt utterly alone, totally without a social support system. This had become a real therapeutic issue for me in going out into the world. I had no friends beyond the convent walls, and this was terribly threatening to me. I had always been surrounded by my community and enjoyed very solid, good relationships in the order. Yes, the nuns would still be my friends, but we moved now in separate worlds. Joseph and I also recognized we could not be a world unto ourselves—exist in a vacuum. He brought to the relationship a circle of friends, and he wanted to share that dimension with me—as tonight. I knew it was essential for me to be open to this new experience and not allow fear to determine my course.

The richness of the forest made it easy for me to set my fears aside as I walked hand in hand with Joseph. The path was easy to follow and not too steep as it wound its way through the forest. My eyes were no longer *in custody* but looking right and left, as far as one could see, into the green density of the pines.

"Isn't it beautiful, Joseph?" My arms swept the sea of green. "My father always said the trees cleared the cobwebs from his mind!"

"I'd agree with him! My dream is to live midst the trees one day. Guess that was part of Cambria's attraction. I had planned to relocate there, you know." Joseph spoke in wistful tones.

"Have you given up on that?" Secretly, I hoped that he had.

"No, not completely. Let's say it's on hold. So much has changed for me in the past few months—our relationship, of course, which was wholly unexpected, and then the hospital has changed too. There's a new administrator, new direction. I see a broader scope of opportunities for Curt and me, as partners, to work together in the holistic model of patient care. The signs are that this is simply not the time for me to leave Mountain View."

"To be honest, I'm glad you're going to be around. I'll be attending classes at Cal Poly to get my California teaching credentials. I should finish by next summer. You know, I still believe I was born to teach." I kicked a pinecone down the path—and then another, enjoying what I had done as a child.

"I can see your enthusiasm! I'm glad you were able to separate your teaching career from religious vocation." Joseph pulled me toward the large boulder by the side of the path and we sat down, his arm around me. "The view of the valley is lovely from here." For a few moments we remained silent, absorbing the beauty before us.

My mind was leaping ahead into the future, realizing how busy—and separate—our lives would be. An unknown future was sobering. Joseph and I had no permanent plans beyond the present in regard to our relationship. I turned my face to him, addressing the subtle fears. "We're going to be awfully busy, Joseph! You with your practice and me back in school—"

"Oh, I think we'll find time for each other," he was quick to say with a sly smile. We laughed together, knowing it could be no other way. "And don't forget our plans for the long holiday weekend coming up!"

I looked at him. *"Forget?" How shall we be as lovers when we move beyond the reaching, the innocent touch—beyond the confines of therapy when "the two shall become one"? How shall we be?*

We continued our trek through the forest. The path narrowed and I walked ahead of Joseph, freely swinging my arms. I remembered what it was like to walk with my hands held together beneath the black cape of a nun, out of sight. Breathing deeply, I enjoyed the pine-scented fragrance of the mountain air. My feet felt solid under me as I stepped over the twigs and stones that littered the pine-needle-cushioned path. *I AM ALIVE! ALIVE! I AM ANNE!* The joy was almost more than I could tolerate. I had been cold for so long in my own gray, dead world—and alone. The sense of life was so overwhelming that it was too much. I felt it start to ebb away, that old feeling so familiar to me. I turned to reach to Joseph and felt his arms around me and his voice in the far-off distance, "Anne! Open your eyes, Anne!" And then Nothing. The cold, gray, dead world had closed in and I was lost, though not beyond reach.

Within minutes I was aware of the hard ground under me, the pine needles, Joseph's arm around my shoulders. "Talk to me, Anne. What's going on in you? You fainted."

It was a few moments before I could speak, and my eyes were brimming with tears when I said, "I still draw back, Joseph, from having all this, as if I've no right, no right to even live."

"You've got to claim it, Anne." We sat on the forest floor, saying the words we had said so often before.

"Will this struggle ever be over?" I felt such frustration that this had occurred, just when I was feeling the fullness of life.

"Probably never, to one degree or another. But you have a strong base from which to fight. You know *how* to fight now. Every day you'll have your choices—like this dinner tonight with people you've never met before. It may never be easy—probably won't for you. But you can do it, Anne!"

As he talked, my panic subsided and I felt myself getting a hold, again, of the principles by which I had come to live. *Therefore, choose life, loving the Lord thy god with thy whole heart and whole mind.* Life, not death. I felt the warmth coming back into my body and turned my face up to Joseph's, wanting, waiting to be kissed. *I will never stop fighting!* Embracing, we sank down onto the earth, and the golden light of the setting sun streamed through the pine-needled branches overhead in what I wanted to think was in blessing.

The waterwheel just inside the restaurant door was turning slowly, the sloshing, dripping sound of falling water creating a mood compatible with the rustic surroundings. Joseph and I were shown to a table in the far corner where his friends were waiting. My knees were still a bit shaky, and the fear of the evening ahead, no doubt, was just as much a factor as the fainting spell. *FEAR IS A SYMPTOM OF LIFE!*

Joseph put everyone at ease. "Anne, I want you to meet my dearest and oldest friends, Neil and Naomi." They reached out their hands to me, and I felt the warmth of their hearts. We all sat down, and I was one of them, made to feel so by their graciousness. My knees stopped shaking as my fears subsided. *Anne . . . you're OK . . . Anne . . . OK.*

Joseph had told me earlier that he and Dr. Hartman had been partners in private practice for many years and that he had consulted with him on my case these past months. Naomi was studying for her master's degree in early childhood education while teaching at a local college. Common interests among the four of us served as a strong base for meaningful sharing. By the time the bread was served, conversation flowed, as did the Chardonnay. Seeing Joseph with his friends of many years made him more *real*, gave his life apart from the hospital, apart from me, more substance. It was like watching a play and the main character walks off stage but continues to be seen by the audience, who is made privy to his private life. The hospital walls dissolved to be no more.

Throughout dinner I learned much about Neil and Naomi and found myself able to talk about *me*. I too was becoming more real. *Why had I been so afraid! Groundless fears.* I looked across the table and knew this was the beginning of enduring friendships. *I am not alone!* The soft-spoken, gentle Naomi with her beautiful white hair and elegant dress helped me to be myself. I felt accepted. Neil's straightforward manner and even brusqueness of speech, ironically, put me at ease. "I didn't expect you to be so . . . so damn attractive, Anne! Well, you certainly don't look like a nun." He recognized and reached to the strength within *me*, and I responded. He too allowed me to be Anne.

"Strangers in the night . . ." The band music got underway just as chocolate mousse and coffee were being served. Neil asked Naomi to dance. I waited, looked at Joseph, fully expecting to be asked as well. But no! "Joseph, aren't you going to ask me to dance?"

"I don't dance—never could." It was said with great finality.

"Well, you do now!" I stood up and reached for Joseph's hand. He obliged though reluctantly. The roles had been reversed, and I had my own kind of *scalpel*.

We moved clumsily at first to the music, but before the dance was over, we were in step, moving together rhythmically. Joseph was dancing for the first time in his life and, in spite of himself, enjoying it.

"There, you see, Joseph?" It felt good to have taken the initiative.

"With you, Anne, maybe I *can* dance." We walked back to our table, beaming.

As we settled down in the leather armchairs, I said to Neil, "Don't you agree with me that Joseph needs to loosen up a bit?"

"Well, he always has been a serious kind of guy. But go for it, Anne!" Then, turning to his friend, he added, "A little loosening up wouldn't hurt you, Joseph."

"It's my background," Joseph readily agreed. The Brethren were a serious lot. Dancing—even music—was frowned upon."

Naomi chimed in, "Neil and I are also members of the Church of the Brethren. It's true, Anne—we've changed much through the years. So many things were frowned upon." She held up her glass. "Even white wine! It's only lately that I've been able to give myself permission to enjoy it." Naomi shook her head, truly bothered by the conflict and guilt spawned by such restrictions.

Conversation wound down and it was time to leave. We walked to the parking lot together under starlit skies and said our good-byes. Neil and Naomi hugged me and said they looked forward to sharing another evening soon.

Joseph and I climbed in the GTO, and he maneuvered the car down the winding mountain road. Strains of "Strangers in the Night" went through my head. I looked at Joseph's strong profile in the semi-darkness intent on his driving. *Stranger . . . stranger no longer.* Many words had been spoken between us, but it was not the words—not the words, but the spaces between wherein we recognized a communion of souls. *In the night . . . night no longer.* I put my head on Joseph's shoulder. *Yes, Joseph, you are the one!*

Chapter 46

SEASON OF THE SUN

My last day in Mountain View Hospital, November 24, 1971. In the early morning, Dr. Thompson and Joseph stood at the foot of my bed. They both were smiling, as was I. Today I was being discharged. The *two or three gathered in my name* Jesus had referred to came to my mind. It, indeed, had taken three—Dr. Thompson, my physician and confidant, managing my rehabilitation, monitoring my course of psychotherapy, risking a great deal in terms of himself as well as the hospital; Joseph, my therapist and friend, putting himself on the line every day with everything at risk, professionally as well as personally; Anne, the dedicated nun and patient, always believing and making her choices as the *solitary individual,* risking life itself. A point in time, a convergence of energy and courage . . . *There I am in your midst.*

The three of us had little to say this last day. What does one say in the face of mystery, of inexplicable healing? We only knew that I had been *raised* and that there was no viable medical explanation.

The religious order, as well, gave recognition to the workings of the spirit in my transformation, as expressed by its president in a letter to me.

> I am so happy to learn that you are in so peaceful a state of soul and mind. That is a sure sign of the workings of the Holy Spirit and should give you great consolation.

Yes, my consolation *is* great, I thought, as I packed my small bag, all that I owned in the world. Tucked in among articles of clothing were the gold-and-brass crucifix, the silver pocket watch, and the olive-seed rosary. I said good-bye to so many friends and walked out the front door, into the sunlight. Had I really been carried in on a stretcher only five short months ago? I breathed now what was truly my freedom, the beginning of a new life in the world, a world that I knew so little about and had to face alone. But I would learn.

My joy superseded my fear, and I lifted my face to the sun. I thought of the elm tree and its seasons and that wintry day so long ago when I stood under its barren branches, feeling the weight of impending disaster. *The premonition.* It was gone. This was the season of the sun, when branches are green and laden with fruit. *By their fruit, you shall know them.* I am well. And tomorrow, tomorrow, Thanksgiving Day, I am going to Cambria with Joseph. Joseph and Anne. The hymn of Thanksgiving for redemption, which I had chanted in choir as a nun, rose from my heart: *BENEDICTUS!*

> *Blessed be the Lord,*
> *the God of Israel;*
> *He has visited his people,*
> *He has come to their rescue . . .*
> *Such is the merciful*
> *kindness of our God,*
> *To give light to those*
> *who live in darkness,*
> *in the shadow of death,*
> *and to guide our feet*
> *into the way of peace.*
>
> —Luke 1:68-79

Epilogue

THE LOVERS

1972

Black angular forms, shadow nuns, taking life on the walls of my small apartment this late December afternoon. *They are with me still. Jesus, Light of all the World.* The familiar Christmas hymn of convent years coming from shadow lips, thin, distant—yet sweet and touching some place within of what had been. The pain of missing, of remembering, but going the way of shadows to disappear into the night. *O Light Divine . . .* My voice swelled the mystic choir as I reached for the black crucifix with the brass figure, the one that had hung on the ebony rosary at my side those twenty years. It was dusted with face powder and set among my lipsticks and cologne there on my dressing table. It was cold to the warm touch of my hand. *Bless this day, O God. Bless Joseph and me.* It was our wedding day, one year after my discharge from Mountain View Hospital.

I stood in front of the mirror, gazing at my reflection. I was a teacher once again, and the fatigue of a Friday night showed in my eyes. There was color in my cheeks, however, and a dab of powder was all the makeup I needed. Carefully, I lined my lips with a shade of pink that blended with my dress—soft, pale. I stepped back from the dressing table and let my eyes take in my full image. As I did so, the Christmas tree lights in the next room sparkled brilliantly on the mirror, creating a surreal reflection. I smiled with satisfaction at what I saw. The pink wedding dress was of a filmy crepe, the bodice hugging my slender figure and showing the full curve of my breasts. The low-cut neckline was edged with delicate lace and the skirt full and falling to just below my knees. I smoothed my blond hair piled high on my head in an upsweep and pulled a few curls forward. Now, my mother's pearl earrings, the matching pearl necklace—the set was her wedding gift to me. I was now forty years of age but knew at least ten of those years were not visible, the gray years of that place of *Nothing*, suspending me in time.

I did see in the mirror an expression of strength and independence hard-won. My first year back in *the world* had been especially tumultuous and difficult, constant challenges forcing me to make constant choices of the person I would be. Now I was going to be Mrs. Joseph Wright. It seemed fitting that Dr. Thompson and Paula were to be the witnesses to our marriage vows at the candlelit evening ceremony.

The ringing of the doorbell broke into my looking-glass reverie. *That must be Joseph!* A final glance in the mirror and then I quickly went to answer the door. Joseph stood on the threshold, his arms held out to me. "Anne," he said, his dark eyes shining, "beautiful Anne." I felt his arms around me and, for a long moment, rested in his embrace. I had come home. "Anne," he kept saying repeatedly. "Anne."

Yes, my God . . . yes, I would be Anne.

A Word From The Author

PERSPECTIVE OF TIME

*B*enedictus has had a life of its own, moving from hand to hand among interested readers over the years. With few exceptions, the reaction was, invariably, "*Publish it!*" The manuscript set on a shelf, ripening, I like to think, and waiting for its time while patiently enduring rewrites. The typewriter, referred to in the introduction, was replaced by a computer, and I kept returning to what had become *my child*. I felt I was working on shifting sands as life has a way of clarifying and even changing perceptions as it moves along and dips into deeper waters. I've come to the literary point of letting go and setting the *child* free, no matter what her destiny. I will do so with the following few words as to what was to come and how the future opened up the past:

Joseph and Anne, defying the odds, according to many, were married for nearly forty years. Each anniversary had been a celebration of life and an occasion to once again give thanks for the crossing of their paths, which they believed was beyond human calculation. It was an undulating road Anne traveled upon of hilltops and deep valleys. There were long stretches when her recovery, to all appearances, had been complete. She was intent on learning the ways of the world and determined to maintain the independence she had gained at such high cost. The voice of the heart, however, grew louder and stronger as the years progressed; and the time came when she could no longer navigate in the world she had chosen. The medical system now had the technical resources to make the diagnosis of dilated cardiomyopathy, a terminal disease of the heart muscle, which exacerbated the condition of postural hypotension so pivotal to the course of her journey as described in this book. Once again, however, she *chose life*—and all that that would involve—and escaped a *death sentence*, to the amazement of her cardiologist, who proclaimed that medically he could not explain it—"but maybe Jesus Christ could." Perhaps he was closer to the truth than he realized. Rather than answers coming to Anne, however, the mystery only deepened with this revelation, possibly throwing a whole new light on the story you have just read.

Perhaps there never is a time when we can say "This is it. I now understand." Perhaps the mystery is always with us and we are meant to live it rather than unravel it. The condition of postural hypotension continues to be a challenge to Anne with the limitations it imposes, but what is important is that it no longer determines the course of her life. Joseph remained at her side with his unconditional love, infinite patience, and support.

Just as this book was nearing completion, the veil between the worlds parted for Joseph, and he made the final transition from this world to life everlasting. Anne had the consolation of being at his side, holding him as he drew his last breaths. *Lovers* to the end.

Joseph Has the Last Word

I am feeling overwhelmed to realize it is now forty years since I walked into Anne's hospital room at Mountain View and saw her for the first time. I had no idea what she would come to mean in my life. Looking back, it is obvious that spirit had set the stage for a cataclysmic transformation of our lives—if we had the courage to accept it. My role was to offer a hand to lift her out of her dilemma; hers was to grasp my hand and not let go. We both were at a choice point in our lives that demanded extraordinary choices. Amazingly, the time and place were perfect for such risk-taking decisions, and to our credit, we accepted the challenge *to choose life*.

I honestly can say, even in the most-trying moments, I have not ever regretted my choice to love Anne—if, in fact, it was a choice. I prefer to acknowledge it as a phenomenon that occurred spontaneously out of the depths of our being. If I, or Anne, had seriously rejected that love, I am convinced it would have been to our unforgivable regret.

Acknowledgments

The story of Sister Anne spans a significant period of time, so there are many individuals to whom I owe a thank-you: among the numerous medical doctors are Dr. George Griffith, Dr. Paul Hoagland, Dr. Paul LaBissoniere, and Dr. Herbert Johnson. Dr. Johnson was a key figure in bringing Joseph and Anne together, and he will never be forgotten. Always in my heart are my fellow religious of those convent years, whose loving support enabled me to stay the course in my search for truth. Important to the ongoing life of this book were the literary agents who believed in its merit and sent me back to the drawing board to plumb the issues more deeply. Allan Elias, my representative with Xlibris Publishing, who was relentless in a positive way of seeing to it that I did not give up. The many readers over the years who kept the book alive—their comments fed my soul and kept me at the keyboard. To my sister, Peggy, who always encouraged me as a writer. To Pam Hyman, who saved many a day with her expert technical support. To Dr. Alberto Villoldo, shaman and mentor, who brought further light to the pages of this story. And lastly but foremost, I give thanks for Laban (aka Joseph), my husband and soul mate. Without him, there would not be a *story of Sister Anne*.

Copyedited by Kimberly Joyce Veloso.

Reference Notes

All biblical references throughout the book *Benedictus* are from the Jerusalem Bible (1966, New York: Doubleday & Company Inc.).

The biblical references throughout the account of the first solemn High Mass are from the Song of Songs. There are various interpretations of the allegorical relationship of the bride and bridegroom, one being the soul's mystical union with God.

To share your thoughts on *Benedictus,* and for information on books that continue the story of Joseph and Anne:

annebook3@charter.net

Made in the USA
Middletown, DE
20 December 2021